SIEGE & SEDUCTION

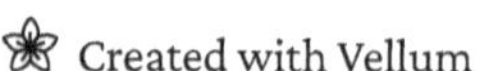 Created with Vellum

SIEGE & SEDUCTION

JILL RAMSOWER

CHAPTER

ONE

MORGAN

It's said that hatred can consume a person. In my experience, hate was the fuel that strengthened the fire already burning inside.

Hatred didn't consume me; I consumed it.

Not a generalized hatred for the world—I wasn't quite so far gone. My wrath was focused on a few select individuals, the Seelie Queen occupying the top of that list. Her name was written in all caps, underlined, and etched in permanent ink so that it would never fade. No matter how much time passed, I wouldn't allow myself to forget. Not ever.

She was the source of it all. The other names on my list were merely a byproduct of association.

At the moment, my most hated of her minions was the powerful Fae sorcerer who had recently imprisoned me. My adoptive father, Merlin.

Our past was already complicated, but the lengths he'd gone to lock me away gouged the knife in my back that much deeper. I didn't care that his intentions were purportedly benevolent or that my prison looked more like a posh mountain resort than Guantanamo Bay. I was equally as trapped and almost entirely alone, all because he believed the very worst of me. Always had and always would.

He stopped in on occasion to attempt conversation in his efforts to rehabilitate me, but the exchanges rarely went well. Otherwise, I was left to my own devices—or at least, what little I could do without my magic. The iron cuffs he'd banded onto each of my wrists ensured that I was as helpless as a child. Escape was seemingly impossible between the cuffs and the impenetrable walls surrounding my luxury prison.

The one consolation to my imprisonment was the vast acreage of forest where I was being kept. It wasn't just any ordinary forest. When I gazed out the window at the bantiff trees and flowering canips, there was no question about where I was. It had been centuries since I had seen a wooded Seelie forest, but its beauty could not be mistaken.

These were Seelie Lands.

Despite the extensive wards Queen Guin had used to keep me out of her Seelie kingdom, Merlin had managed to smuggle me in—a feat I had not managed after centuries of attempts. I was *finally* back on Seelie Lands, closer than ever to my objective.

I wasn't sure if I wanted to strangle Merlin or send him a thank-you card.

How he'd managed to get me past wards specifically designed to keep me out, I had no idea. But that was Merlin. He appeared in places he could not be and knew things no one else did. He'd managed the impossible, and I was doing everything I could to use this new turn of events to my advantage. If I could find a way to escape, I could move about Faery freely. Everything I'd fought to achieve was finally within my grasp—the only thing stopping me now was a ten-foot wall and its protective ward bordering the property.

Within my grasp might have been a slight exaggeration.

I'd been holed up in my makeshift prison for over a month, and despite my relentless pursuit of a way past the wall, I'd come up empty. Day and night, I walked the winding trails through the woods, searching for weaknesses. While my walks weren't particularly productive, I had to begrudgingly admit that they were enjoyable nonetheless. The Wilds where I had been living was similar to Seelie Lands but not as densely vegetated. It had been so long since I'd seen the vast variety of plants and creatures in the Seelie kingdom that I often found myself distracted by the wonders around me. Lush green plants in every shape and size filled the landscape peppered with gnarled tree trunks that branched into a leafy canopy that veiled the sky overhead. If it wasn't for the nearly full moon, I wouldn't have been able to see a thing wandering around in the middle of the night.

The shadows didn't scare me. Maybe it was presumptive, but I doubted Merlin wouldn't have kept me alive just to let me be eaten by forest creatures. He'd likely ensured the property was relatively free of threats, which gave me the confidence to take one of my frequent nighttime strolls.

Captivity wasn't conducive to maintaining a standard schedule.

I slept at odd hours and roamed when I had energy, which was how I found myself yet again wandering the forest paths in the cool night air. I had wrapped myself in a long red cloak to keep out the chill and immersed myself in the Faery nightlife, hoping a solution to my problems would soon present itself.

Quieting my thoughts, I opened my senses to the world around me. Escape would likely require creativity, so I couldn't afford to limit myself.

The air chittered with insects and nocturnal creatures while a light breeze rustled the leaves and vining under-growth. The night was peaceful until a cloying sense of awareness began to claw at my skin. It was a sensation I was familiar with, though I hadn't experienced it in some time.

The feeling of being watched.

Hunted.

My magic never would have allowed someone to sneak up on me, but in my powerless state, I was vulnerable.

A twinge of fear—something I had not experienced in centuries—uncoiled in my belly.

My steps faltered, and I slowly turned to see what form of creature stalked me in the night. My eyes darted around at first, unable to find the source of my unease. The moonlight was enough to guide me along the path but also cast gaping shadows in the thick foliage. It wasn't until my ears caught a rumbling growl that I was able to hone in on the location of my pursuer.

From the depths of an impenetrable shadow, golden eyes glared out at me. Head lowered and ears back, an enormous white wolf slowly emerged from the darkness. The moonlight shone off its stark white fur, and for a moment, I was too mesmerized to think.

The creature was magnificent—snow white fur shimmering in the moonlight disguised the brutal build of a deadly hunter.

I shook myself from my musings when its lips lifted in a vicious snarl. I couldn't get enough air, and my feet stumbled backward of their own accord. I knew not to run from a predator, but my vulnerable state seemed to create a disconnect between my thoughts and my actions.

Logic no longer ruled my body.

Primal fear had taken over.

The monstrous wolf stepped directly onto the path some thirty feet in front of me, its hackles raised aggressively. This wolf was far larger than any I'd ever seen. When standing on all fours, its head was as high as my chest. This beast didn't just stare at me like I was its next meal; its eyes bore into me like it wanted to rip me to shreds.

I took several deep breaths and chided myself to remember who I was and all I'd accomplished. I was a sorceress trained by Merlin Ambrosius himself. I was known throughout Earth as the merciless Morgan Le Fay and feared throughout Faery as Morgan, Lady of the Lake.

I planted my feet firmly and straightened my spine.

"Leave this place," I growled back at the wolf, infusing my voice with as much aggression as possible. "*Go on*, get out of here! I'll slice your hide straight from your back and wear your fur as a cloak," I snarled as I lifted the small blade I'd brought with me.

Undaunted, the wolf continued to stalk ever closer to where I stood. Each step it took was a steady, calculated advancement on its prey.

The irony of the situation hit me, and a bubble of laughter burst from my lips.

I was one of the most powerful Fae alive. I had waged war against the Erlking Arthur, first leader of the Wild Hunt. I'd mastered a way to circumvent the wards between worlds and traveled at my own discretion. Just a month prior, I'd been moments from leading an army of Unseelie against the Seelie Queen. Yet I now sat powerless as a simple human, about to be disemboweled by a wolf.

I threw my head back and unleashed a howl of laughter.

For a moment, the wolf stalled. The growling stopped, and it appeared to assess me for the first time as a possible threat.

My peels of hysterical cackling subsided, and I wrapped myself with ferocity. "*That's right!*" I raged. "You want me? Come and get me, but I won't go down without a fight," I bellowed at the overgrown dog.

Unfortunately, my threats were deemed unworthy of retreat.

The great white beast launched its attack.

It lunged forward with a vicious roar, and I softened my stance to prepare for the force of its attack. Just when it was mere feet from reaching me, the air between us shimmered, and Merlin materialized. The wolf locked its legs and halted inches from the Fae man.

Merlin bore down on the wolf with his arms held wide and spoke sternly. "You are confused, my friend. She is not one of them."

My friend? Was this Merlin's rumored canine companion? I'd heard a handful of stories over the years about a dog but paid them little mind. It appeared I should have been more vigilant.

The animal looked from the man back to me in an assessing manner, but as soon as its eyes landed on my form, its snarl returned, and it began to stalk in my direction yet again.

"Merlin, *do* something! What was the point in bringing me here if you're just going to stand there and let me be eaten alive?" I spat.

Merlin seemed to ignore my insolence, swinging out his hand to cast a magical strike at the beast. "Morgan, take off your cloak, *now*," he commanded sternly.

I narrowed my eyes with confusion but did as he ordered. I removed the garment and cast it some feet away into the leafy shadows, leaving me in nothing but a thin nightgown. The wolf quickly recovered from Merlin's assault and sprang into action. It dove at the lifeless cloak, snatching the red fabric into its clenched jaw and disappearing into the darkness.

"What in the seven hells was *that?*" I asked on an exasperated breath.

Merlin closed the distance between us, his features drawn with remorse and concern. "I apologize. My friend had come to check in on you, but I had not anticipated your wardrobe choice. I'm afraid he has a sordid history with the Red Caps, and your cloak seemed to dredge up memories of that dark past."

"I should have known he was sent here by you. First, you bind my magic, then you send a crazed wolf to attack me."

"Had I wanted you dead, you would be," Merlin pointed out. "While you're here, there should be no reason for the use of magic. As long as you don't wear the cloak, Knight will not be a threat. No other dangerous creatures exist on the grounds, so nothing here will harm you."

I'd suspected as much, but my racing heart begged to differ.

"That's terribly reassuring, just a deranged wolf and me," I muttered.

"My friendship with Knight, as he's being called these days, goes back centuries." Merlin began to walk toward the house, and I begrudgingly fell into step beside him. "When I first found him, he was being held captive by a particularly nasty band of Red Caps."

His mention of the vile race of Unseelie brought to mind images of the creatures. They looked like withered old men, but their appearance was deceptive. They were inconceivably strong and had the ability to trace, something not many Unseelie possessed. Atop their large bald heads, they wore caps used to soak up the blood of their slain enemies—trophies of their violent exploits.

The Red Caps were absolutely ruthless, known for their bloodlust and occasional bouts of cannibalism. I had formed a tentative alliance with some during my rebellion, but I never made the mistake of trusting them. The thought of being held prisoner by such soulless beings made me unbearably cold.

Merlin continued as I shook the image. "I was able to secure Knight's freedom and spent a good deal of time with him while he recovered from their mistreatment. It became clear to me that he was highly intelligent, and I wondered if he had truly been a wolf. I searched in vain for years to find a spell or counter curse that might turn him back to his rightful form. If magic was used on my dear friend, I have not been able to reverse it. He has remained my trusted companion all these years, and I assure you that you are not in danger by his presence."

"Are you implying he's staying *here* with *me*?" I scoffed.

"I think some companionship would do you wonders."

"If it's companionship I need, locking me away from the world will hardly do the job."

"There are many worse places you could be. I'm sure Knight would have happily traded places with you rather than enduring his stay with the Red Caps," he mused with a touch of reproach.

"You're never going to free me, are you? You'll keep me prisoner here, just like you've done with my mother." The words were more a statement of my own frustration than an actual question, but Merlin answered anyway.

"Have you let go of your hatred, Morgan?" he asked, sounding tired. "Or are you still plotting ways to get your revenge on Guin?" The ancient man rarely sounded his age, but in this instance, weariness pulled at his words. "I know how deeply you cared for Lancelot, but his affair with Guin and her sentencing him to exile was ages ago. You must let it go."

My teeth ground together at hearing the name of the wretched woman who had caused me to lose everything I had loved in the world, or at least everything I'd had left after my mother's death. For that, she held the distinction of being the person I hated most in the world.

Her mindless minions worshiped her, but they had no idea how malicious she was on the inside and the atrocities she was capable of. I was no saint, but at least I owned up to my nature.

Guin was the rotten core inside a shiny red apple.

Swallowing the comment I wanted to make, I instead offered sweetly, "You're right. After having weeks to reflect, I realize that I need to move on with my life."

Merlin's eyes cut to me, and his lips spread into an amused grin. "Liar," he chided.

"You can't keep me here forever," I sulked.

"It's better than the alternative."

I instantly stopped and narrowed a hard glare in his direction. "You would kill me?"

His responding look was unexpectedly dark. "You are a danger to others, and I will not allow that. Had you not been family, you would have been dead after that rebellion you tried to orchestrate. Please believe that I want your freedom just as much as you, but it cannot be at the cost of other people's lives, whether human or Fae. Until you let go of your need for revenge, you will be a danger to everyone around you. I hope that during your time here, you will see reason and can one day be freed."

"And what reason is there to forgive those who have so egregiously harmed me?"

Merlin's lips lifted in a sad smile. "That is something only you will be able to answer. Just remember that the only thing any of us can dictate with any certainty is our own happiness. Life exists in a chaos of variables that we can only pretend to control. There is often no rhyme or reason to life, and pointing blame can be as futile as using a net to capture the wind. Focusing on the who and why of a tragedy will only foster bitterness and keep you from seeing the good in the world. You will not be able to move forward with your life until you release the hatred in your heart."

"Well, then, I fear I may be here for a very long time."

"Perhaps," he said with a small smirk before vanishing.

My shoulders slumped under a wave of sudden exhaustion. Doubts and fears that I fought so hard to contain seized the opportunity to wriggle free and pummel my confidence. I had trained as Merlin's apprentice for years and had pursued my own learning for centuries, but I still possessed only a fraction of his knowledge. The disparity in our abilities kept him one step ahead of me. It was the reason he'd been able to capture me when I'd been mere minutes away from long-awaited success. He'd chosen to protect Guin over me, the same as he'd done before.

I couldn't help but hate him.

What had she ever done to instill such loyalty? His power far surpassed hers, so he had no reason to fear her. What should the lives of monarchs matter to a man who had achieved an almost godly status? They shouldn't matter.

Guin shouldn't have mattered to him, yet she did, and I hated him for it.

He could try to assuage his guilt by making my prison as fancy as he liked, but it changed nothing. He was still my captor, and I would stop at nothing to escape.

CHAPTER

TWO

MORGAN

THE HOME WHERE MERLIN HAD IMPRISONED ME WAS TYPICAL OF Faery nobility. Not nearly as ostentatious as human royalty, but a far cry from the standard wooden cottages most Fae lived in. Secreted away in a dense forest, it was a single-story home constructed entirely of wood, save for the enormous windows. Floor-to-ceiling glass panes made the house feel like a part of the wilderness. No draperies—privacy wasn't an issue—and no ornate carvings or cluttered details. The home was a statement on simplicity, and it suited me more than I cared to admit.

Tension melted from my shoulders the second I stepped inside. Whenever I walked, especially at night, returning to the quiet house was a shocking contrast to the chorus of sounds in the forest. As usual, the empty house was silent.

My night had been eventful, but now I was alone again. As always.

I grabbed a glass of water from the kitchen, then headed back to my bedroom. When I flicked on the light, I nearly dropped the glass at the sight of the white wolf lounging on my bed.

"Jesus *Christ*!" My hand slapped over my heart in a futile attempt to keep it from bursting from my chest.

Unlike our last encounter, the wolf was entirely indifferent to my presence—he didn't even lift his head from where it rested on the pale-blue quilt. His eyes glanced up, and his ears swiveled in my direction, but he stayed otherwise unmoved.

"What do you think you're doing here? Get *out*." I crossed my arms over my chest and glared down at the unwelcome intruder. "This is my room—my *house*, for that matter—you can't just let yourself in like you own the place!" My arms started waving about, water splashing onto the ivory rug.

Clearly unimpressed, he yawned, then flopped his furry chin onto his front paws.

I set the glass of water on the dresser and crossed to the side of the bed opposite where he lay. "Shoo, get down." I waved my hands at him but got no response, so I slowly climbed onto the bed and approached his backside. "I don't care who you're friends with. You're filthy, and you need to get. Off. My. Bed." I accentuated each word with a shove to his back, but my efforts were futile.

The two-hundred-pound behemoth refused to budge.

I flopped back against the headboard with a loud exhale. "I'm not sleeping on that wretched sofa, and I'm too cold and tired to fight you. I suppose there's enough room for both of us although you seem to take up more than your fair share. Just know that if you get bugs in my bed, I will gut you while you sleep."

The furry mutt let out a huff, and I made for the bathroom to tidy up before slipping under the covers. I couldn't remember the last time I'd slept with someone in my bed, man or beast. As much as I liked my solitude, I was surprised to find myself comforted by the presence of another. I was probably just going crazy after weeks of solitude. Whatever the reason, a sense of calm settled over me in the darkened room.

The wolf spun around in a circle to resituate himself and plopped back down just inches from where my hand lay. I watched my fingers in the soft moonlight as they reached for his thick white fur. He didn't move as I ran my hand across his coat. It was softer than I would have expected, and I slipped my fingers into the warmth of his fur.

"Your coat is really very lovely. And I'm not sure I've ever seen eyes with such an amber glow," I said with a yawn. "Beautiful, really. Even those nasty teeth of yours were impressive. I can't imagine being stuck in the body of a dog. Of course, maybe you're just a dog. I would think that if magic had turned you into a wolf-dog, Merlin would have been able to find a way to turn you back. If anyone could undo a spell, it's Merlin. But more than likely, you're just a dog, and I'm the only one who's stuck. You're probably not even awake, and I'm lying here rambling to myself like a madwoman. It would be fitting.

That's what everyone thinks, that I've lost my sanity. Fortunately, I don't care what *they* think."

I pulled my hand back to tuck beneath the covers, but my bedmate rolled closer as if asking for more.

"You want me to keep petting you? Aside from fussy and stinky, you're needy too—just *lovely*," I groused before lazily stroking his fur. "I don't know what Merlin expects you to accomplish here, but it's not going to happen. I can guarantee he's got something up his sleeve. That man is always scheming. I've tried to get a step ahead of him all my life, and not once have I succeeded."

The rhythm of his steady breaths lulled me deeper into the murky waters of sleep.

"So many times I've debated telling him my reasons for everything. They all think it's just my hatred for Guin that motivates me—that I'm some kind of monster. They don't know," I murmured. "No one does. I would tell Merlin and ask for his help, but I know what his answer would be, and I can't accept that. He would stop me. The uprising, the attacks, none of it was truly about Guin. Don't get me wrong, I would gladly see the bitch dead, but..." My heavy eyelids dropped shut. "The cauldron is the real reason for it all. I must ... get my hands ... on the cauldron."

I snuggled closer to the warmth beside me and fell into a peaceful sleep where my mind drifted from one pleasant dream to the next. When I found myself in strong masculine arms, I held firmly to the comforting sensation. I lay strewn across a broad chest, encircled in protective warmth. The man's breath ghosted on my forehead, and I lifted my face so that my lips could seek out the firm lips of the man beneath me.

The fog of sleep slowly dissipated as our lips touched, and I became aware that the man in my bed was not a dream.

I jerked back with a gasp and scuttled off the bed, arms and legs flailing animatedly. When no pursuer followed, I halted my retreat. Stopping at the bedroom door, I flipped on the light to reveal a primitive-looking man in my bed. He sat upright, long hair and beard covering most of his face, but I could see his rounded eyes clearly.

Amber eyes.

"It can't be," I whispered. "Was this some kind of joke between you and Merlin?" The tirade forming on my lips fell short as I took in his stunned expression. Through his unguarded, vibrant eyes, I could clearly read his astonished disbelief.

He was just as shocked at his transformation as I was, probably more so.

He ignored me completely as his eyes darted around the room before scanning his own shaking hands held out before him. His skin was youthful—smooth and taut over rippling muscle. Yet his dark hair bore streaks of white, something normally foreign to the ageless Fae. He had retained a touch of his wolf. The white strands of hair through his dark mane were striking.

A single barked laugh burst from his chest, and our eyes were drawn together again.

He bound from the bed in my direction, and I held out my hands to keep him away, but my effort was futile. He lifted me up against his chest, swinging me around in circles with a delighted rumble of masculine laughter.

It occurred to me I could fight him. After all, I was well trained in many forms of combat. However, his boyish exuberance was disarming, and I allowed myself to be swept up in his arms.

"Too tight, I can't breathe," I groaned as the room spun around me.

He instantly stopped and set me back on my feet. "Sorry," he coughed, clearing the gravel from his neglected vocal cords. "I got a little carried away." His golden eyes shone down with a joyous excitement that was foreign to me.

The reality of his truth struck me.

"It wasn't a trick. You really have been stuck as a wolf—only now you've been freed. How? Why now?" I asked breathlessly.

His eyes flashed at the reminder of his suffering, and guilt settled over me for mentioning his torment in the long-awaited moment of his freedom.

"The Red Caps," his raspy voice offered. He cleared his throat again, his voice nearly gone from lack of use. "They placed a curse upon me. I thought there was no undoing it. I had given up hope of ever being a man again." His mouth lifted in a smirk, which was somewhat hard to see under the heavy beard. "But I'm free now." He lowered his face, and before I could stop him, he licked the length of my right cheek.

"*Ugh!* Stop that!" I wiped at my wet cheek and stepped back out of his reach.

The man looked at me with a sheepish grin. "Sorry,

again—I'm just so excited. I've been a wolf for so long. It's going to take time to adjust."

I nodded, my thoughts coming back to me enough to realize that the man standing next to me was naked—breathtakingly, magnificently naked.

As a Fae woman who needed sex to charge her magic, nudity and intercourse were everyday facets of life. Sexuality didn't embarrass me, which was why it was so surprising that my cheeks flushed at the sight of him. Agitated at myself more than uncomfortable with his appearance, I spun around to face the window, but his naked form reflected back at me off the glass.

"You need to put some clothes on. Surely, you haven't forgotten that much. Then you need to leave."

With soundless steps, he closed the distance between us until I could feel the heat from his body against my back. He leaned down until his lips were near my ear. "You're just upset I know your secret."

My entire body went rigid.

When I slowly turned around, my eyes were shards of cut glass. "How *dare* you? You filthy *mutt*, I'll kill you." My verbal attack would have brought most men to their knees, but the bearded Neanderthal wasn't affected in the slightest.

A wide grin spread across his face. "And how will you do that? With your impressive magic, or perhaps that tiny knife you wielded in the forest?"

I couldn't remember the last time I'd been treated with such insolence. Rage and indignation bubbled to a boiling fury in my veins as my hands gripped into fists so tight my nails sliced into the soft skin of my palms. "*Get out.* Go tell your master everything you've learned and leave me alone."

My treacherous companion stepped closer until he was a breath away from me and lowered his face toward mine. "The name is Knight, and I'm not going anywhere."

CHAPTER
THREE

MORGAN

THIS HAD TO BE THE UNIVERSE TESTING ME. WHAT OTHER explanation could there be? One extraordinary event after another, and now I was being harnessed to an insufferable jailor who held my life in his hands. It really wasn't fair. That, or I'd been a real bitch in a past life.

"Fine!" I hissed. "Stay if you like, but I'm out of here." I whipped around and stormed from the house, slamming the door behind me. Childish, I know, but I was pissed with little other means for expressing my bubbling anger. "Freaking mutt thinks he can waltz into my prison and just claim the upper bunk," I muttered to myself as I stomped down one of the forest paths. "I've got news for Scooby-Doo. I'm getting off this Alcatraz whether he's here or not."

The one and only time I ever told my plans to another living soul, and the furry mongrel sprouts vocal cords.

That wasn't the only thing he'd sprouted.

Fido had transformed into a red-blooded man—from his gloriously sculpted shoulders to his rippling abdominals and down to his powerfully built legs—one-hundred-percent man and one-hundred-percent naked. Every square inch had been on display, and he was just as comfortable in his skin as he had been in fur.

The consummate predator. Confident. Aggressive. Unpredictable.

My mouth had gone dry at the sight of him.

As if stealing my secrets wasn't enough, his miraculous metamorphosis was also a painful reminder of just how long it had been since I'd enjoyed a taste of the opposite sex. Hell, even the men I *had* been with seemed like boys compared to the raw masculinity that wafted off him in waves.

He was two-hundred pounds of panty-melting, drool-inducing, jaw-dropping man.

At least on the outside. His salt-and-pepper hair and glowing amber eyes were signs that the wolf wasn't entirely gone. I figured that was to be expected after hundreds of years in another form. There had hardly been any precedent for this type of thing. I wasn't even aware such magic existed, but I had lived long enough to know that nothing was impossible.

I should have known there was more to the beast, considering his master.

What was his story? How had he ended up as a wolf? Why did he have so many gruesome scars?

While his facial features had been obscured beneath

the heavy growth of a full beard, the rest of his body had been unabashedly on display. Someone had permanently marred his skin at some point in his life, disfiguring his perfection. Not just once or twice, but hundreds of times. His god-like physique was marked with innumerable scars where the skin was shiny and texturized. His arms, legs, and torso were all covered with a multitude of slash marks. As a wolf, his fur had hidden the evidence of his wounds, but the scars were plain to see as a man.

The Fae healed quickly, so I couldn't imagine what brutalities he'd endured to receive such everlasting reminders. Merlin said the wolf had been held prisoner by Red Caps—a vicious caste of Unseelie, wicked to their marrow and capable of unthinkable atrocities. How long did his captivity last to earn such a roadmap of pain?

It was almost enough to garner my pity, but that would have done him a disservice. If anything, he had my begrudging respect.

He had survived.

Those marks spoke to his worthiness as an adversary. They didn't mar his perfection—they added to his appeal because they were evidence of his inner strength.

It would serve me well not to underestimate him.

Like you did when you opened your big mouth and ratted yourself out.

I had known better than to give away my secrets. But how was I supposed to know Merlin's lapdog for the past century would miraculously transform into a man? Unlike the stories in human books and movies, animals didn't just transform into people and vice versa, even in Faery.

It didn't matter how slim the chances. You never should have spoken the words aloud, whether to a dog or a potted cactus.

I blamed temporary insanity for my lack of discretion. I liked alone time as much as the next girl, but after a month by myself, I'd been minutes away from talking to the birds like some kind of fucked-up Disney Princess.

Prisoners were punished with solitary confinement for a reason. It sucked.

When my furry friend came along, I gave in to the weakness—the need for companionship. I said more than I should have, and Merlin's lackey would undoubtedly blab what he'd learned directly to the almighty Fae sorcerer. It would complicate my life immeasurably. My chances of succeeding with my plans hadn't been great before, but now, they were downright abysmal.

Weighed down by my foolhardy mistake, I sighed and slowed my punishing pace. No matter how harshly I chastised myself, it wouldn't change my situation.

I had screwed up.

My heart ached in a way I hadn't experienced in ages. The piercing pain in my chest helped dull the frozen throbbing in my fingers and toes from the crisp morning air. I had burst from the house in nothing but a satin nightgown. While my agitation had initially sent ample fire through my veins to keep me warm, the cold wrapped its icy tendrils around me as my temper settled.

When I neared the stone wall that stood guard around my lush prison, crushing desperation was a heavy boulder on my chest. I had sworn I would escape but had no idea how. Merlin had been careful to ensure no tools were available in the house that might aid me in getting the cuffs off my wrists. The iron wasn't terribly thick, less than a quarter inch, but the cuffs were well-fitted, solid bands about an inch wide. Unlike a jewelry cuff that might have a break where the wearer could slide the cuff on and off, these were solid all the way around as though they'd been forged on my body. I had no idea how to remove them.

Dropping my gaze to the rocky ground, I picked up a large stone and launched it with all my might at the deplorable wall. I put all my hate and frustration, my longing and pain into my throw and pummeled the wall with rock after rock.

"I doubt that's going to help," a gravelly voice said from behind me.

I had lost myself in my frustrations so thoroughly that I failed to hear him approach.

Yet another mistake.

Oversights and missteps had become my new MO.

"There's little that *will* help unless you'd like to remove these cuffs from my wrists." I paused just long enough to aim a murderous look his direction.

He shook his head. "No way in hell." He had managed to locate clothing but still had his bare feet exposed.

Even his damn feet are sexy.

I launched another rock, this time envisioning his ruggedly handsome face as my target. The stone shattered against the wall, and I enjoyed a small sense of satisfaction.

Undaunted by my boiling temper, the man took another step closer.

"You and I got off on the wrong foot. Let's start over.

My name is Knight," he offered graciously with an exaggerated bow.

My first thought was, *who the fuck cares?* However, I reminded myself not to let my anger blind me to the possibilities of escape. It wouldn't hurt me to talk to the man. He might be of help or at least a good source of information.

Continuing my target practice, I threw another rock. "And who exactly are you, Knight?"

His head cocked to the side precisely like a dog, and I snickered under my breath as he spoke.

"I'm not entirely sure who I *was*, but for as long as I can remember, I've been Merlin's eyes and ears."

I paused and turned back in surprise. "You don't know who you are?"

"No, I don't know who I *was*. I don't remember anything before my time with the Red Caps." His voice lowered a fraction on the last words as he forced them out with palpable distaste.

"You were a wolf the whole time you were with the Red Caps?"

"Yes."

"So maybe you've always been a wolf. Maybe that's who you were."

He arched a brow. "I may not remember who I was, but I recall other things. I wasn't originally a wolf; I just can't remember the details."

"Well then, do you know who *I* am?"

Beneath the heavy beard, his lips pulled back in a lazy smile.

"You're Morgan Le Fay, Morgana, Lady of the Lake—enchantress and sorceress extraordinaire."

I lifted my chin in approval. If he'd heard the stories about me, it might give him a healthy dose of respect. Respect was power. I was happy to garner any power I could in the situation.

"And what did you plan to do here before your miraculous metamorphosis? Spy on me? Track my every movement and report back to Merlin?"

"You make it sound criminal. I was just going to make sure you didn't need anything and be here to keep you company." He peered up at me innocently from under his thick lashes. It was the very look that coined the term "puppy-dog eyes." No doubt he had become well-versed in using the look to get what he wanted as a dog.

I crossed my arms over my chest. "So you were here to keep me from escaping."

"Yes, if that was your plan. This place isn't exactly an eyesore. Is it so terrible to be here?"

"You know why I need to leave," I ground out.

"There's no way you can find the cauldron. It hasn't been seen by anyone in our lifetime or long before. The Hunt and countless others have spent centuries looking without success. Why waste your time?"

"And that's the exact reason I've never told anyone my plans." My anger ignited. "If it's so impossible, I suggest you forget what you heard," I warned, stepping closer.

Knight slowly began to walk a circle around me, and I pivoted to keep him in my sights.

"Why do you want the cauldron?" he asked, his amber

eyes narrowed. "I hear you have a monumental grudge against Queen Guin, but my understanding is that the cauldron brings life and doesn't take it."

Wanting to show Benji that his posturing didn't faze me, I held my ground as he continued to edge around behind me.

"I'm not telling you why I want the cauldron, and now that I know who you are, you're not going to trick the information out of me. If the cauldron is only capable of life and healing, why would it matter to you and Merlin if I found it?"

"Because we know you, know what you're capable of. There's no way your reasons are purely benevolent."

I glanced at him behind me. "You know me, do you? Aside from my grudge against Guin, what else have you heard about me?"

As expected, he spouted an exhaustive list of my exploits.

"You were Merlin's apprentice as a teen after your mother was killed by Merlin's twin sister, Mab. At Court, you were known to trick men into sleeping with you and even got yourself banished for your role in the death of your half brother, Arthur. You have attempted to kill Queen Guin on more than one occasion. Most recently, you led a rebellion of Unseelie against the Seelie Court and caused the deaths of dozens of humans in the process. In order to achieve your rebellion, you sent a young man by the name of Ronan to infiltrate the Wild Hunt and provide you with information. And as your coup de gras, you killed the Erlking Alberich with your bare hands. Have I left anything out?" His voice was cold and clinical while he recited each of my transgressions. He paused his pacing and stilled at my back, making me feel like the target of a firing squad as my final verdict was being read.

I was surprised at the stir of feeling his words provoked. I had thought myself past that kind of weakness. Doing what I had done on so many occasions before, I squashed each of the treacherous emotions.

"I see you've been paying attention all these years, despite your inability to talk. I suppose you know all there is to know about me, which likely means you won't be helping me out of here. I don't need your help, anyway. I've spent lifetimes managing on my own. Working with someone else would only be an added aggravation." With a ghost of a glance in his direction, just long enough for my defiant gaze to touch his, I walked away from Knight and all he represented.

The rumors. The manipulation. The lies.

Nothing he said should have surprised me. My descent into villainy had begun early on, long before I'd even met Guin. I'd been only ten when the world began to chip away at my softness and paint me in shades of corruption and depravity. I could recall it well—the first steps of my fall from grace.

It was the year Merlin's twin sister, Mab, came to our home to unleash her wrath upon my unsuspecting mother. Regardless of the centuries that had unfolded since, I remembered that day as if it had just happened.

I'd been forced to forget once, and I would never allow it to happen again.

My mother had fallen deeply in love with Merlin almost as soon as they'd met. From that moment on, he was a regular part of our lives for years. He stayed with us whenever his work allowed, and he became like a father to me.

I had met his sister, Mab, at a couple of social gatherings but never knew her well. Just like Merlin, Mab had white-blond hair and glacial blue eyes. However, where his eyes crinkled in the corners and spoke to his unerring compassion, hers bore evidence of a frozen heart.

She was striking, regal even. Ruling over the Unseelie Wilds, she had made herself queen of what few others had the power to control. Even as a child, I could sense that the woman was not to be trifled with. When she appeared on the doorstep of my home, fear formed a leaden pit in my stomach.

"Morgan," she'd cooed in a seductive tone. "Is your mother home, child? I need to speak with her."

Rendered mute with intimidation, I merely nodded and stepped back to allow her in.

She wore a full-length ivory gown with glints of gold brocade sewn throughout. The pale fabric on top of her porcelain skin gave her a ghostly appearance, making her blue eyes shine that much brighter. Her platinum hair was wound in intricate braids atop her head, and all together, the look was mesmerizing.

It was an eerie beauty that bespoke her terrible power.

I ran for my mother.

Our home wasn't big, just a cottage by a serene lake on the outskirts of Seelie Lands. My mother was a water

Nymph, the Lady of the Lake she was called. We lived a quiet life surrounded by nature.

It had been the perfect childhood until that day.

"Mamma, Queen Mab is here. She wants to speak with you." The words flew out in a rush as I hurried out back to where my mother kneeled in the garden, tending to her flowers.

Her features hinted at surprise, but she didn't appear worried, and that confidence settled my child's mind. She shook off the soil and leaves from her morning gown and led the way back inside. "Mab, what a pleasure." My mother dipped her head in a respectful bow and smiled warmly at our guest. "Please, sit down. May I offer you a drink?"

Mab didn't return the bow. Instead, her chin lifted, and her eyes narrowed. "My brother seems to have taken a liking to you. I hardly see him anymore." She held her hands clasped behind her back and began to slowly pace farther into the room.

"I care for him a great deal," my mother offered softly.

Mab turned her face back to my mother, and a deviously wicked grin spread across her pale lips. "You care for him a great deal? Do you have any idea how *pathetic* that sounds? Merlin is the other half of my *soul*." Mab's voice grew louder and more irate with each word.

My heart sped to a pounding rhythm, and the pit in my stomach expanded until I was sure I would be sick. Something was very wrong—we were in grave danger.

Before my mother could respond, Mab launched into a rant.

"Merlin and I are two pieces of the same whole. I do not simply *care* for him; he is my *world!* You think you can weasel your way between us and lure him away from me, but you will never succeed." Her face twisted with grotesque rage, and she flung her hand out to cast a powerful blast of magic toward my mother.

With barely time to raise a shield, my mother was blown backward against the cottage wall but was able to protect herself from the full extent of the blast.

I cried out in horror and ran for my mother.

Without a glance in my direction, Mab used her magic to fling me into one of our wingback chairs and immobilize me with invisible bindings. With my mouth fixed shut, I was unable to do anything but watch helplessly as Mab brutalized my weeping mother.

A Nymph's water magic was ill-equipped to combat Mab's powerful abilities.

Tears streaked down my cheeks as Mab rained down blow after blow on my defenseless mother. Her blond hair, so like mine, fell from where it had been pinned atop her head, and blood trickled down from a gash in her temple.

I felt my heart being ripped in two as I screamed relentlessly through a mouth that would not open.

When my mother was no longer conscious, Mab lifted her with arms so thin they did not look capable of such strength. The evil queen approached where I sat, numb from the horrors I'd been forced to witness.

"Dear Morgan," she cooed. "Your mother was the victim of a horrible tragedy today."

My eyes shot up to hers, the first spark of hatred

igniting inside me. But just as the flame took hold, it was quickly doused by a supernatural calm.

Mab continued speaking in a melodic tone, and I felt my mind twist and warp with her words. "While she tended to her garden, your mother was spotted by a wayward Grindylow. The evil water demon attacked her, and her cries woke you from your sleep just in time to see the beast carry her off into the Wilds. There was nothing you could do but wait for help to arrive."

Her words unburdened my mind.

I sat in a haze as she turned and strode out of the cottage, my mother still motionless in her arms.

Even after I emerged from my stupor, I stayed in the house practically motionless for days. I considered going for help but felt an inexplicable resistance to leave every time I tried. I needed to stay and wait for help to arrive.

My body grew weak without sustenance, an outward reflection of my broken heart within. The entire episode felt like a horrible nightmare, but I never woke, and my mother never came home.

Tearless cries wrenched from my dehydrated body when I finally conceded that I was alone.

My mother was gone.

I scraped myself together and began to perform the tasks I'd watched my mother carry out on a daily basis. Each day, I grew stronger and more hardened to my new reality.

When Merlin came to visit almost a month later, I explained calmly how the Grindylow had taken my mother while he was away. He told me how very sorry he was and promised he would never stop searching for her.

Still more traumatized than I knew at the time, I was cocooned in numbness—not angry with his absence or relieved upon his return. I was in survival mode and incapable of anything more.

Merlin insisted I come with him, explaining that he would become my guardian. He took me to Avalon where he lived, and over time, I began to heal. Just when I began to settle into my new life, everything unraveled. Merlin figured out the truth behind my mother's abduction—that his sister had been to blame. When he killed her in an attempt to save my mother, the spell binding my memories dissolved, and I was assaulted by a flood of images from the day my mother was attacked.

I remembered every brutal detail. The fear. The helplessness.

And on top of it all, Merlin informed me that my mother had not survived.

Believing a Grindylow had taken her, I'd held out hope that she might still be alive. When Merlin informed me that my mother was dead, I relived her loss all over again. But this time, I knew that I had been witness to her abduction and unknowingly held information that might have saved her. I had contributed to her death, no matter how unwittingly.

I might have only been twelve years old, but I lost what was left of my innocence that day.

I spent the following years learning everything I could because knowledge was power, and I never wanted to be weak again. As Merlin's apprentice, I had access to his vast knowledge of sorcery and gleaned every morsel I could get. My memories of my mother kept me focused. They reminded me that no one was to be trusted, and only the strong survived—a lesson I would never forget.

But that was the past.

A time when every sneer and whisper, every snub and attack, felt like a blade slicing into tender flesh. Death by a thousand cuts, but not a physical death. Morgan of the Lake had been reborn as the sorceress Morgan Le Fay, stronger and more resilient than ever. She didn't give a fuck what anyone thought. All that mattered was getting the cauldron, and I was closer than I had ever been. I had to keep myself focused on the present. On my mission.

For centuries, I had worked tirelessly to get back onto Seelie Lands, seeking out archaic spells and barbaric runes in the hopes one might get me past Guin's wards. I had come to the conclusion that the only way to get past her wards was to kill her. Upon her death, all her magic would cease to exist. The wards would fall, and I would be free to go after the cauldron.

As the saying went, easier said than done.

Guin hadn't become the Seelie Queen based on her winning personality.

Upon the death of the previous queen, Guin had been chosen by the magic of Faery as the most powerful Fae woman and ruler of the Seelie. Not to mention, she had over a thousand years of practice keeping her crown.

In order to orchestrate a rebellion that had a chance to overthrow her, I had forged alliances with the deadliest Shadow Fae and rallied hordes of Unseelie. Years of research and strategizing culminated on the sacred night of Beltane when the veil between the worlds was the thinnest, and there was a swell of magic in the air. While not everything had gone exactly to plan, overall, the rebellion had unfolded according to my design. On the night my revolution was to occur, I was drunk with the knowledge my struggles would soon be at an end.

Until *she* showed up—the human-turned-Fae woman Merlin had plucked from obscurity and ordained the savior of her people.

Rebecca.

In a matter of minutes, she used the unique powers Merlin had bestowed upon her to crush everything I had worked toward.

Yet again, he had won.

I gazed up at the bantiff tree that towered over me. It stood tall and proud, each full-grown tree nearly as wide as they were tall. Their brilliant green leaves spread out in clusters at the end of each branch, creating a multilayered canopy over the forest floor. Had it not been for the wards, the branches would have made a perfect ladder to help me over the cursed wall. I had attempted to scale the wall on the first day I arrived. One touch of Merlin's ward, and I was blasted backward as if I had grabbed hold of a live powerline.

I had no need to repeat the experience.

Without my magic, I was a bird without wings. The wall was secure, and my powers were bound. At present, there was no way to change either of those situations.

The only unknown variable was Knight.

He had entered my prison of his own volition and could likely leave in the same fashion. Whether he used his magic to take me with him or removed my iron cuffs, he had the ability to help me. He claimed he wouldn't, but stranger things had been known to happen. What kind of negotiator was I if I walked away the first time I was told no?

The direct approach hadn't worked. Fine. Maybe I could find another way to win him over ... perhaps appeal to his more ... elemental nature.

Two people might find common ground in a lot of ways.

FEELING MORE CENTERED, I walked back to the simple one-story house tucked beneath the canopy of trees like a child hiding under their blanket. The house was not a standard Fae dwelling, much too modern to appeal to the traditional Seelie tastes. Considering only a handful of Seelie had been exposed to the progress of modern human culture, I could only imagine the house had been designed by Merlin himself. While I was not a fan of the man personally, I had to give him credit for the clean lines of the transitional design.

Floor-to-ceiling windows throughout the space gave the feel of outdoor living with the finest of indoor comforts available. Knight hadn't been wrong—the house was far from unpleasant. The electromagnetic pulses common in Faery didn't allow for the use of electronics, but Merlin had found a way to duplicate the use of modern human amenities in his home. Not only was the place temperature controlled but there was also a refrigerator and modern plumbing. On my first day at the house, I had been immensely relieved to discover he had fashioned a shower with hot running water.

A long, hot shower was exactly what I needed to eradicate the chill that had seeped beneath the surface and deep into my bones. Once I had thawed myself inside and out, I would attempt to warm Knight to my cause. I could be rather persuasive when I wanted to be.

CHAPTER
FOUR

KNIGHT

I didn't return to the house immediately. I was too taken with the sights around me and my stunning change of circumstances to race after Morgan. As a wolf, my impeccable hearing had been undeniably helpful; however, I was limited to seeing life through the greyscale lens of a wolf's eyes. While I couldn't recall my life before I was turned, I had an innate sense of the rainbow of colors that existed just outside my reach. Walking through the rich forest and seeing the vibrant colors around me with the crisp clarity of my Fae eyes was like being reborn.

The bite of brisk air against my bare skin and the rocky forest floor beneath the soft arches of my feet—neither were particularly comfortable, but both were welcome as they evidenced all I had regained. Hell, just having opposable thumbs was worth a celebration. Now that I could see color again, speak to those around me, and bathe instead of using my tongue—things were definitely looking up for me. I would even have the full use of my powers once I was able to recharge my magic.

The one thing I would miss about being a wolf was the ability to go unnoticed. I hadn't been literally been invisible, but as a dog, I might as well have been. It never ceased to amaze me what people would say and do in my presence.

Morgan had been a perfect example.

Lazily drifting her hand through my thick fur—which felt fucking phenomenal—she had been lulled into unburdening one of her deepest secrets. When she dashed from my arms the next morning and flipped on the light, her revelation had been broadcasted in her expressive eyes. She knew instantly what she'd done and had been livid.

Those vibrant blue eyes had sparked with fury, and her porcelain skin pinked with the rush of blood. Her short, platinum-blond hair waved in all directions as she stood in her satin gown that exposed the full length of her shapely legs. Only something so engrossing as my own shock at my transformation had been enough to pull my attention from the mesmerizing beauty before me.

And even then, just momentarily.

When I spun her in my arms, lost in my exciting revelation, the wolf that still resided inside me surged with possessiveness. Morgan was relatively short for a Seelie woman, and next to my large frame, she was delicate in comparison. Her scent was an intense aphrodisiac, and her womanly curves fit perfectly against my newly transformed body. And to top it off, her fighting spirit had called to my wolfish side.

She was a riled wildcat, and I couldn't help but test her limits. Her insults and death threats had the opposite effect than she'd intended. I was more intrigued than ever. When she finally shot her parting blow and left the house, I couldn't take my eyes from her curvy backside as it swayed with each furious step.

While she had attacked me verbally with unfettered rage, she never once lifted a hand against me. Knowing who she was, I had no doubt she was a skilled fighter and could have done damage had she desired. Her exercise of restraint was a baffling curiosity to me. The woman was renowned for her selfish nature and ruthless pursuit of her desires. If I had information that she didn't want me to have, killing me would have been an easy solution. Perhaps it was as simple as Morgan seeing me as her best chance at escaping her confinement. All I could do was guess her motivations. I got the feeling Morgan was an exceptionally complicated woman, one who could only be understood if she chose to allow such insight.

When I returned to the house, I could see her through the large windows, stretching from one position to another.

Yoga. The great Morgan Le Fay, sorceress and supervillain, was doing yoga.

She was the very definition of a mystery, and I found myself compelled to seek out answers. She would challenge me in every way, but I had nothing better to do with my time. No family that I could recall, save for my new friends back in Belfast. A part of me wanted to race off to share the news of my transformation with them. However, another highly vocal part of me insisted I stay. Not just the part of me that wanted to keep my word to Merlin. This was a deeper, more primal part of me—a side that viewed life in absolutes and acted on basic instincts. He saw something he wanted and threatened to pulverize me if I even entertained the thought of leaving.

I wasn't sure where the inner barbarian had come from. It could very well have been a part of every man, but since I didn't know who I had been before, it was hard to interpret my urges and reactions. If I was drawn to swimming, did that mean I had been a swimmer? If I hated heights, did that mean I had fallen in my earlier life? If I was drawn to a willful woman, was that my preference or the wolf's?

The darkness of uncertainty cast an ugly shadow over everything else in my life. Long ago, I had chosen to turn my back on that darkness and focus on the light, but regaining my body had brought that uncertainty back to the forefront of my mind. Outwardly, I had perfected a laid-back approach to life, but inside, it was a struggle to ignore the mystery of my past.

Shoving those thoughts aside, I entered the house and leaned against a wall as I watched Morgan's lithe body bend and twist to a silent rhythm. She had clearly spent a good amount of time on Earth. Her interests, mannerisms, and wardrobe were heavily influenced by human culture. I wondered where she had been hiding out and what she had been doing during those years.

After a few minutes, she stood and met my hooded eyes, slowly sashaying into the kitchen to pour herself a glass of water.

"You came back," she said in a breathy voice between

sips, eyes peering up at me through her lashes. Her cheeks were flushed from the exercise, and I imagined how the rest of her body would color with the proper stimulation.

"There's no place I'd rather be."

"That makes one of us."

"Come on, it's not so bad."

Her eyes leisurely strolled down my torso. "Not so bad today as it was yesterday."

"It's good to see your attitude has changed." My lips spread wide in an amused grin. "A couple of hours ago, you were ready to slit my throat." I knew what she was doing with her sultry flirting, and I was more than happy to play along.

"After I had time to cool down, I realized what you said was true. We did get off on the wrong foot. If you're going to stay here with me, there's no reason we can't be ... pleasant." She inched around the counter, closer to where I leaned against the wall, her eyes never leaving mine.

"Your change in outlook wouldn't happen to have anything to do with me getting you out of here, would it?" My voice was a low rumble as her hand reached up and gently ghosted down the planes of my chest.

"Of course, it does," she admitted. "I know you're not an idiot, but I also know being ugly to you isn't going to improve my chances. Believe it or not, I can be rather reasonable."

I lifted my hand to a strand of her hair that had fallen across her eyes and placed it back where it belonged, intentionally swiping my fingers across her forehead. I wanted to touch her. Needed to feel the silky softness of her skin.

"I hope you understand. It's hard to believe someone who is well known for their tricks and manipulation."

For a split second, hurt flashed in her unguarded expression before her confident façade was back in place. It had been so seemingly genuine, I *almost* believed it.

The woman was good.

Very good.

"I doubt there's anything I can say to change your opinion of me, and I understand that. What I'm asking of you is to consider that it might be possible for us to work together toward a common goal." This time, her hands traced the width of my shoulders as if straightening nonexistent wrinkles, then slid along the contours of my arms.

The sensation of her touch aroused a surprisingly strong urge to flip our positions and press my body against hers. I wanted to cage her against the wall where I could taste and savor her. I shook away the image, knowing better than to get caught up in someone like Morgan.

"And what, pray tell, could we possibly have in common?" I asked wryly. She had my attention—I would give her that. I couldn't fathom what might align me with her cause.

Her teeth grazed across her full bottom lip as she peered up at me.

"The cauldron not only restores life, it restores health, heals the sick and injured—it could give you back your memories," she whispered.

I stiffened with surprise.

"What makes you think I want those memories? I've

lived a lifetime without them, created new memories, moved on." It was bluster and bluff, but she didn't know that. She had managed to zero in on the one and only thing that might give her leverage over me, and I didn't want her to know it.

"Who wouldn't want to know their past?" she purred. "What about your family? You don't know if you even have one. That uncertainty would eat any man alive."

"I'm not just *any* man. I've had plenty of time to get over the loss of any family I might have had." My reply was more clipped than I would have liked.

"Keep telling yourself that, and perhaps you'll believe it one day."

"Merlin is my family now, and he wants you to remain here. Why would I betray him like that?" I pulled myself off the wall and began casually pacing by the large living room windows, hoping I came across as indifferent rather than how I truly felt, which was overwhelmed.

"If he's your family, he would want this for you. He would want what's best for you."

"Maybe having my memories isn't what's best for me. Betraying his trust is surely not best for *him*."

"He told you to stay with me, which you would be doing. That's not a betrayal. I'm not planning to go on a killing spree, nor do I have any other secret agenda. I. Just. Want. The. Cauldron. If you would benefit from its magic as well, what would be the harm in helping me?" Her words were an alluring honeycomb, dripping with sweet temptation and loaded with hidden dangers.

"If your purpose is so pure, why haven't you asked Merlin yourself for his help to acquire the cauldron?" I glanced at her, assessing every nuance of her posture and expression. Like an actor on stage, all kinds of activities were going on behind the scenes. I needed to understand more than just her performance to see the entire story, but she was too practiced to give anything away.

"Don't you think he would have retrieved something so powerful by now if he could have? As you mentioned, its location is secret. Merlin may be compassionate, but he's not perfect. Something so powerful as the cauldron would not have escaped his notice."

"Yet you still believe you'd be able to find it?"

She raised her chin defiantly but didn't answer.

My jaw began to ache, and I realized my teeth were tightly clenched. "I'm not going to help you escape from here. I wouldn't do that to my friend."

"Fine, live in darkness forever." Morgan's pink lips thinned, and those penetrating blue eyes narrowed. "But know this—I will obtain the cauldron, and when I do, don't come groveling to me for your precious memories." Her voice was as cold as steel and equally unyielding. She marched to the bedroom as soon as she finished, slamming the door behind her.

Normally, I would have found her childlike tantrum amusing. However, I was just as upset with myself for considering her proposal as she was upset with me for declining. I ate a quick meal, not tasting the food in my mouth, and returned to the forest to clear my thoughts.

I was ashamed I would even entertain the idea of releasing Morgan. Merlin had worked for decades to contain her—helping her escape would be unforgivable. Although she would hardly be free without the use of her magic. Allowing her to leave the premises would be more like taking a dog for a walk than leaving the gate open. My lips curled up deviously at the visual—Morgan collared and under my control. The alpha wolf inside found that concept extremely appealing.

As a wolf, when I encountered other wolves in the wild, I was all alpha. It was irrelevant that I had not started out as a wolf—the spirit of the animal found a home inside me. While I no longer wore the skin of the beast, many of its tendencies had become my own. My wolf rattled its cage at the sight of a powerful female, demanding to dominate and own her. The middle of the pack female rarely stirred his appetite.

Only an alpha female would suffice for an alpha male.

Morgan was the epitome of an alpha.

Thank the gods, I was more than just my wolf. I was a man capable of reason, logic, and loyalty. No matter the temptation of knowing my past or of Morgan's siren-like call, I would not do something thoughtless on a whim.

Was I tempted? Hell, yes.

Not just tempted by her soft curves and sharp wit—I was tempted by her suggestion. Getting my body back was a thrilling development but only half of who I'd been. My history was still lost. Finding the cauldron and getting my memories back would make me whole.

But I couldn't free Morgan, regardless of the appeal.

I walked for hours in the woods. I thought about what I would do next, where I would go, and what my new life would entail. Every course of action I envisioned led me to the same place—my past, the familiar black hole of nothingness that occupied the furthest recesses of my memory.

No matter where I began or what new adventures I pictured, I always ended up searching for answers.

My inability to see an alternative enraged me. I wanted to do what was right and not harm those I cared about, but I couldn't seem to reconcile where that would leave me. Didn't I have an obligation to do what was best for me as well? If I couldn't move forward without knowing where I'd been, was it not necessary to unveil that part of my story?

I was continually pulled in two directions, unable to make headway, one way or another. Only one person might be able to help me. Now that I had a voice and could explain my lack of memories, perhaps Merlin would have access to magic that would help. Before I did something irreversible, I owed it to him and to myself to see what other options might exist.

CHAPTER

FIVE

KNIGHT

AFTER MERLIN RESCUED ME FROM THE RED CAPS, IT TOOK months for him to draw me out of a feral state and almost two years until I didn't flinch around people. We spent a significant amount of time together during those years. He gave me the opportunity to heal on the inside and out. Not only would I be eternally grateful to him for saving me, I appreciated that he never treated me like a dog—not even when my erratic behavior warranted it.

Once I had reclaimed my sanity, Merlin placed an enchantment over me. I had no magic of my own as a wolf. To prevent me from being endangered again, the sorcerer gifted me with the ability to transport myself. Much the same as the Seelie could trace from place to place, the enchantment allowed me to take myself anywhere I could envision, so long as I had been there before. As a bonus, it also allowed me to walk through wards. Merlin had given me the security of knowing I would not be imprisoned again—or at least not easily.

I wasn't sure the enchantment would still work after my transformation—testing it would be the only way to find out. Closing my eyes, I imagined the small cabin by the lake I had seen on so many occasions. The customary tingling sensation engulfed my chest as the magic stirred to life.

When I opened my eyes, the first thing I did was peer down at my chest. It was something I had been unable to do as a wolf. I was stunned to see glowing, golden markings on my skin peeking out from beneath my shirt. I pulled down the collar to reveal an intricate swirling pattern of knotted lines extending down my left pectoral and onto my side. Even if I had been able to see that part of my chest as a wolf, the fur would have hidden the markings. While I couldn't see the glowing designs, I had always wondered about the strange burn that accompanied the use of the spell. I watched as the magic faded until the only markings on my skin were the crisscrossing remnants of my scars.

Looking around the rocky lakefront where I now stood, I spotted Merlin sitting on a wooden swing overlooking the water. His hair was almost as white as my fur had been, which made him easily identifiable. Adding to his unusual features, his eyes were exceptionally pale. I hadn't been able to tell their color before, but now I could see they were the same pale blue as the sky near the horizon. Those ageless eyes might have seemed cold and unapproachable if not for the hint of creases in the corners, evidencing his penchant for finding amusement in life.

For a man with such phenomenal power, he was surprisingly average in size and build. It was clear his pursuits were more academic than athletic. At a glance, he could easily have been mistaken for a human. Like Morgan, his time on Earth made him more apt to wear designer suits rather than the flashy attire of the Seelie Court. At home on his island, he wore loose linen pants and a silk, short-sleeve button-down, rippling gently in the sea breeze.

Viviene was not far from where he sat, standing motionless in waist-high water. Merlin had secured a remote Faery island where he and his ailing lover resided. He had erected a spell around the perimeter to make the place invisible to passing ships and repellant to all those who intended to pass through its location. Only someone who knew it existed and sought it specifically as a destination could find it. As far as I knew, I was the only person outside of Merlin and Viviene to ever step foot on the island.

One could walk its circumference in a matter of an hour. It was just large enough to contain a freshwater lake at the foot of a jungle-covered hillside. The property was rather ideal in every way, and I wouldn't have been surprised if Merlin had fashioned the island himself. He had needed somewhere secluded where Viviene could recuperate. She was a Water Nymph, so the freshwater lake was essential. There were no threats or distractions, just perpetual beauty and comfort.

From what I had seen of Viviene, Merlin's efforts had

been fruitless. I only knew the basics of her story and had not been able to ask questions, but her odd behaviors had been evidence enough that she had never fully recovered from whatever she had suffered.

I saw a part of myself in Viviene. When Merlin first rescued me, I hadn't been much more functional than she was now. Had I been held captive much longer, my fate might have been hers.

At first glance, a newcomer might not realize anything was wrong with her. She was a beautiful woman—strawberry-blond hair falling in waves down her back and delicate features that were the epitome of femininity—but I had seen enough to know her outward perfection was a stark contrast to how broken she was inside. Merlin's unwavering dedication to her was beyond admirable.

"My old friend." His eyes lit with instant recognition despite my outward changes. "This is truly cause to celebrate." He embraced me in a heartfelt hug, something unusual for the Fae, but I greatly appreciated the gesture. As a wolf, I had come to rely heavily on physical touch as a means for communication.

"I wondered if you would recognize me, but I should have known better," I said with a laugh as I pulled back to take in his smiling face.

"You, I would recognize anywhere. I'm just sorry it took as long as it did for this moment to come." As he spoke, we began to stroll along the rocky shore of the lake.

"You and me both. But if it hadn't been for you, I wouldn't be here at all—as a wolf or otherwise." I glanced beside me at the man I so respected. "Not only did you save me but you also helped me find myself. At least, who I was on the inside."

"I was glad for the company." He gave a half smile, not altogether comfortable with my praise.

"Is this your doing? Are you the one who reversed the spell?" While he had not been present for my transformation, a part of me assumed he had been behind the magic.

"I cannot take credit, I'm afraid. The dark magic responsible for your change was not something I was familiar with. I hunted for answers for many years without any luck. I'm delighted to see that the spell has been undone, regardless of the cause."

"I suppose it will have to remain a mystery if you weren't the one to remove the spell. I will be forever grateful all the same. However, some of us were not so delighted at my transformation back to manhood," I smirked, recalling Morgan's dash from the bed.

"Ah, yes. Tell me, how is my Morgan?"

"Prickly as ever," I confirmed what he undoubtedly already suspected.

He cast a dry glance at me, and we both chuckled.

"Do you still want me to keep an eye on her?" I asked. "She was far less ... receptive to my company when I no longer had fur and a tail."

"Please do. I feel it's important she not be alone during this time, and as you know, I cannot be gone from here for long. Morgan has known a great deal of loss in her life, and I can't help but think companionship might profoundly affect her outlook."

My lips drew down with doubt, but I nodded. "She's your family, and I'll do what I can to help, for your sake."

My eyes slid over to the haunting woman in the water. "And Viviene? How is she?" I asked softly.

The ancient man stared off toward his ailing love. "She's well enough. Each day is like every other—no real problems or progress. She's in there somewhere, but I cannot reach her," he said with a sadness that knew centuries of heartache.

"If your patience and kindness can't reach her, I don't know what else would. Not everyone can be fixed." I didn't want to hurt him with my words, but I hated seeing him trapped in a prison of his own making. At some point, he needed to accept that his lover wasn't coming back.

He gave me a sad smile, but there was a glint of amusement in his eyes. "We all have our share of irrational pursuits. She may not be the same as she was, but she's still my heart. Hope is not yet gone—look at what change a day has brought for you! Tell me, now that you are whole again, what are your plans?"

"Actually, I was hoping you could help me with that. I have no memories of my life before the Red Caps—who I was or anything about my history. I was hoping you might know of a way to restore those memories."

Merlin slowed to a stop, hands casually clasped behind him, and gazed out over the lake like its far shores held the answers to all his questions. "The mind is an exceedingly delicate matter. It is one thing to suggest a memory or an image that was not there to begin with—to trick the mind into believing something untrue—but it is entirely different to coax the mind into unveiling its own secrets. If I had the power to do that, I would have helped Viviene long ago. Unfortunately, I can't uncover the parts of the mind that have retreated into obscurity. In all my searches, I found only one possible source of such magic."

"The cauldron," I cut in wearily.

"Yes." Merlin's fathomless eyes peered back at me. "I can only speculate that its restorative powers would work on the mind. It has long been my belief, but I have no concrete proof."

"I take it you've tried to obtain it?"

"Oh, I have tried." His lips pulled back in a humorless smile. "The ornery thing has a mind of its own. It only reveals itself to those with the purest of intents. While my desire to heal Viviene would doubtless be considered pure, I cannot fully suppress my inquisitive nature that would desire the cauldron for other purposes. I am afraid my intentions are too complex to be considered pure—as is the case with most who would seek its powers."

I sighed deeply, nudging a stone with my foot as I absorbed the implication of Merlin's words. "If you couldn't obtain it, I can't imagine I would have any chance." The air in my lungs became heavy with the realization I might never know who I'd been. If one of the most compassionate men alive was not sufficiently "pure" of intent, Morgan and I certainly had no hope of acquiring the cauldron. If Merlin believed it was the only possible way, I wasn't about to doubt him.

That meant my past was lost.

Did I have a child out there? Parents? A lover? Had I been a part of the Court or a soldier? A farmer or a teacher? There was no way to know, and the realization was crushing. As a wolf, I had accepted over time that my life was no longer the same. Becoming Fae again reignited my need to know my past with a burning passion. Having that hope swiftly smothered was gut-wrenching.

Drawing my attention from my suffocating dismay, Viviene descended into the water, gracefully disappearing beneath. After only a brief silence, she breached the surface with her head back, eyes closed, and her lips parted sensually. It was the most vibrant and alive I had ever seen her.

"The water is the one place where she almost resembles the woman she once was," commented Merlin absently.

"Can you tell me about her—about what happened?" I asked hesitantly. She was such a large part of his life, and I wanted to understand that side of him. So many times in the past, I wished I could ask questions. Now that I had the ability, I wasn't missing an opportunity.

"To a good extent, Morgan's accusations are correct—Viviene's condition was my fault." His lips thinned. "I had sensed my sister, Mab, was upset about my relationship with Viviene. While I have a Seer ability and get glimpses of future events, my emotions cloud my sight where my life is concerned. My own future, and those of the people I am closest to, lie just outside my range of visibility. Perhaps I should have seen the true extent of Mab's hatred, but I didn't—not until it was too late. I never suspected my own sister would act in such a way that would hurt me so profoundly."

"How did you discover she was behind Viviene's disappearance?"

"I went for a visit one day, and young Morgan told me about the incident when I arrived. She said Viviene had been out gardening when she was attacked by a Grindylow and stolen off into the Wilds. Right away, I was struck by how odd it was for a Grindylow to harm a Water Nymph. While Grindylows can be nasty creatures, they are also relatively intelligent. The race relies on water as their home, and it's the Water Nymphs' magic that helps maintain the bodies of water in Faery. The Grindylow would only be harming himself if he had killed a Water Nymph. The niggling sense of doubt led me to examine the area. Inside the cottage, I found a single drop of blood by one wall. If the Grindylow had attacked Viviene in her garden, why had there been blood inside? It could have been unrelated, but my instincts told me to investigate further. However, I found little else to direct me. I hunted down all manner of water Fae and questioned Morgan innumerable times. No one had heard of a Water Nymph being taken, and Morgan described the scene in an eerily similar fashion every time she told the story. One day, many months later, I happened to notice Morgan flinch away from my sister. The motion had been a subconscious response, and I found it odd as Mab had never given Morgan reason to fear her. Instead of asking questions, I started to pay attention to what went unsaid. It didn't take long for me to realize something unnatural passed between Mab and Morgan every time they were together.

"Confronting Mab was the hardest thing I've ever had to do. I never intended to kill her, but it quickly became clear her death was unavoidable. Her mind had become so warped that I hardly recognized her. Once she was gone, I was able to get to Viviene, and my heart broke yet again. The truth can be a seductive mistress, but she is not always faithful. I was desperate to find Viviene, but learning the truth about her disappearance was shattering. Not only did I lose my lover, I lost a sister as well." His sorrowful eyes bore into mine as he continued. "Have an open mind when you seek the truth. There is no going back once you have found it."

I nodded gravely. "Seeking answers is always a gamble—one we hope will pay off in the long run. But you needn't worry. It sounds like my quest has ended before it ever began."

"I have found over the years, the things which are meant to be find a way of coming to pass. If you are meant to know your history, an opportunity to do so will present itself. Perhaps you will be recognized by an old acquaintance, or some obscure reference will jog your memories. If it is your wish to know, I truly hope you will find the answers you seek." Merlin spoke from the heart, not one to mince words.

We talked for over an hour, regaling times we'd spent together but had been unable to discuss previously. When it was time to go, I gave him a grateful hug goodbye. I had enjoyed my first official conversation with Merlin but was remorseful to return without any answers. Not only had he dashed my hopes of a magical memory cure but he had also put doubt in my mind about whether I even wanted to know my past. I had lived centuries since my imprisonment by the Red Caps. I knew the man I had become—did it matter who I had been before? On the other hand, if there was a chance to discover my past, was I unwilling to even try?

My logic circled itself round and round as I walked

back to Morgan's house in the woods. The only certainty I could discern was that there was no rush for a decision. I had lived without the knowledge of my past for centuries and managed to survive admirably. What was one more day or week in the life of an immortal?

As the Faery suns started to descend, I walked through the deepest parts of the forest. The foliage had thickened so noticeably that it was difficult to proceed, but I continued to push past the sharp leaves of holiander plants and sticky outcroppings of surry saplings. I wasn't sure why I didn't turn around. A part of me knew I should, but my burning desire to see what was on the other side of the dense forest overruled my caution.

When I stopped to catch my breath, I noticed an intricate red flower I had never seen before. Half a dozen crimson petals arched out from the center, each curling at the tip. A cluster of tiny stamens sprouted from the middle with bundles of golden pollen on each end. The flower and several others like it grew from a vining plant that had wrapped itself around most of the trees and other plants in sight.

I pushed my way toward one of the blossoms, kicking at something that had snagged my pant leg. As soon as I freed myself, I tried to step forward and found my other ankle anchored in place as if it had grown roots of its own. When I glanced down to see what gripped my foot so securely, a tendril of unease stirred across my skin.

The vining plant had wrapped itself around my leg.

I stomped at the vine, attempting to break off the offending portion of the plant, but the vine was impervious. Resorting to the use of magic, I attempted to send a blast of energy toward the vine, but nothing happened. I summoned my powers, only to come up empty—no telltale tingling in my palms or buzzing in my veins. I had no magic.

While my attention was distracted by my loss of power, a set of vines whipped out and seized each of my wrists faster than any typical plant should move, even in Faery. I yanked viciously as I cursed, but instead of the vine shredding to pieces, it snaked itself around my arms and legs. Once it secured its grip, it began to pull me in all four directions with astounding force.

I screamed out in blinding agony.

Without any leverage to fight back, I couldn't do anything to counter the vine's attack. My joints protested with unimaginable pain as they were pulled farther and farther apart. Even my skin grew taut with tension as the tissues inside me began to snap and tear.

Panic warred with pain to control my mind.

My body was being ripped apart, and there was nothing I could do. I had no magic, no one with me to help me, and no ability to defend myself.

I was helpless, and I was going to die.

All I could do was watch in horror as my left arm tore free from my body.

With a scream of desperation, I shot awake.

I was in the guest bed in Morgan's house, drenched in sweat and panting as if I'd been running for my life. I didn't think I had actually screamed, which was a relief. I had no interest in explaining myself to Morgan.

Taking a series of slow, deep breaths, I attempted to settle my racing heart. I lay back on the damp sheets to absorb the nighttime serenity like a soothing balm.

That was not the first time I'd had the dream.

There were only a few other instances over my long life, but the scene was too haunting not to stick with me. The dream was clearly meaningful, but I fumbled to grasp its significance. It was so profoundly disturbing and realistic that it had to be rooted in some memory of mine, but I couldn't access that part of my mind.

The impotence of being a prisoner of my own brain was maddening.

Had the dream been spurred on by my visit to Merlin and our discussion of my lost history? If so, what should I take from the dream? Was there something so dark and terrible in my past that it would be best left hidden? Or was the dream a reminder that my need to uncover my memories would haunt me forever if I didn't learn the truth? Were the red flowers just symbolic of the Red Caps and the vine a metaphoric representation of the torture that had broken me over the years? Or had it drawn from something else entirely?

I tried never to think about the monstrous Unseelie Red Caps. When I did, hatred permeated my being, causing rational thought to escape me. As much as I wanted to leave that part of my past behind me, it seemed hopeless when so many questions remained unanswered. Would it be worse to chase after an impossible dream—

such as finding the cauldron—or to live in the shadows of my prior life?

In the early years, I had tried every natural method available to recover my memories. I couldn't imagine that anything going forward was likely to do the trick if nothing in centuries had managed to trigger my memories.

Merlin had said the cauldron was the only possible source of magic that could force my mind to unveil its secrets. Chances of getting my hands on it were slim to none.

But a slim chance was still a chance.

It frustrated me to no end that I couldn't let it be, but I couldn't. I needed to know, and the uncertainty would eat at me for the rest of my life, which could be a very long fucking time.

CHAPTER

SIX

MORGAN

After arguing with Knight, I locked myself in the bedroom and didn't speak with him for the rest of the day. My one sighting of him had been from a distance. I caught a glimpse of his retreating form heading into the woods not long after I had stormed off. The front door had opened, and I peeked out the window to see what was going on, not lingering any longer than necessary. I didn't ogle the triangular shape of his torso where his broad shoulders tapered down to his narrow waist as he walked away. And I certainly didn't stay up well into the night, waiting to hear the door click open upon his return.

That would have been absurd.

Why did I care what the mongrel did? I wasn't his babysitter.

I never heard him come back to the house, but Knight was sprawled out in the bed when I walked by the second

63

bedroom the following morning. He had left the door open. Otherwise, I never would have noticed him. The only reason I ventured down the hallway was because I'd heard a strange noise.

A girl can never be too careful.

He lay on his stomach, arms encircling a pillow held to his chest beneath him, the sheet draped to cover everything below his waist. I lingered a moment to check for weapons or any possible threats. Once I was sure he didn't have a knife strapped to his bicep, or a gun secured to his bulging lats, I wiped the drool from my cheek and hurried to the kitchen.

Wanting to be as hospitable as possible, I decided to whip up a healthy breakfast. It was the most important meal of the day, and I hated to start the morning on an empty stomach. In my vigor to provide a healthy meal, I might have accidentally slammed a drawer or two and clanged a few pots together.

Not long after I got started, Knight prowled into the kitchen. He had pulled his long hair back with what appeared to be one of my hair ties and wore a loose pair of pajama bottoms slung low on his hips. I glanced his way in acknowledgment but otherwise ignored his presence as he came to stand next to where I worked at the stove.

"How thoughtful of you to make me breakfast," he rumbled in a voice so gravelly I could feel each syllable deep in my belly.

I forced myself to ignore the sensation and smiled up at him with saccharine sweetness. "I figured it was the least I could do before you head out."

"And where might I be headed, gorgeous?" A lazy grin softened his features, his eyes hooded.

"Anywhere but here. I can even pack food for you to take with you if that would help get you going sooner." My voice dripped with honey as I loaded up a plate and pressed it into his chest.

His hands overlapped with mine as he took the plate from me, lingering longer than necessary. He then lowered his head just a fraction and took in a deep breath. "Smells delicious," he rasped. "I look forward to savoring ... every ... bite."

He was toying with me for waking him, but that knowledge didn't dampen the effect he had over me. My nipples pebbled so hard, they ached with the need to be touched. As soon as I could pull air back into my lungs and wrestle my thoughts from their lust-filled haze, I yanked my hands out from beneath his and stepped back.

"I'm serious. You need to leave."

Hip propped against the counter, Knight picked up a morsel of food with his fingers and placed the bite into his mouth as if we were friends, chatting over tea. His eyes came back to mine as he began to chew, sucking the juice off his thumb and first two fingers.

"What if I told you I'd reconsidered helping you?" His question hung in the air between us, our eyes locked as we attempted to decipher one another's thoughts.

"You thought about it, or you've decided to do it?" I was cautious not to get my hopes up prematurely. He had already been teasing me, so perhaps this was still part of his game.

He continued to eat as if we were discussing the

weather or the appropriate method for cracking an egg rather than discussing the state of my imprisonment. "First, I want to know why you're so convinced you can find the cauldron when so many others have failed."

A legitimate question. *Interesting.*

I decided to take the bait and play along. Raising a brow, I leaned against the counter to mirror his casual stance. Two feet of space spanned between us, yet it was filled with miles of distrust.

"I know because I've been there before." There, let him chew on that for a while.

His jaw stopped moving mid-bite, and his eyes narrowed a fraction. The easygoing playboy had disappeared, and the wolf peeked out through Knight's eyes.

"Tell me more," he ordered.

"I'm not going to tell you how to get to it. You'd just go without me." Surely, he didn't think I was that big of an idiot.

"You tell me more, or I'm not agreeing to this." He set the plate down on the stove without breaking eye contact with me. "I want to know there's a legitimate chance we could find the cauldron before I betray the one man who has been my only family." His amber eyes flashed with an intensity that made goose bumps perch on the skin of my arms.

He was serious but still torn. Catching this fish was going to require just the right lure—too flashy and he'd see right through it, not tempting enough, and he'd move on to something better. I would have to give him just enough information to reel him in but not enough to find the cauldron on his own.

I forced down the knot in my throat and swallowed. "I spent my years in exile gathering information to make certain I could find it. That's why I've worked so hard to get onto Seelie Lands. The cauldron is here, but I couldn't get in."

"Why would you need clues if you've been there before?" he asked, skepticism clear in his voice.

"I was there as a child. I didn't want to leave it to chance that I could find it again, so I researched every aspect."

"Just because you've seen it before doesn't mean it'll appear for you again—especially considering all you've done since." He arched a brow at me.

Usually, I was excellent at keeping my emotions masked when needed. However, Knight had touched on my greatest fear. My lips pursed together in agitation, both at him and myself. "It's a chance I'm willing to take. Are you? As far as I can tell, I'm your best bet at getting those memories back. You have to decide if you're willing to take the risk of freeing me, or if you're willing to live knowing you never even tried."

My heart pounded at the walls of my chest as seconds ticked by in suffocating silence.

Knight edged closer until we were toe-to-toe. "If we do this, it's on my terms. Specifically, those cuffs stay put, and you will stick with me at all times."

Game, set, match.

My heart thrummed in my chest, making me light-headed with excitement. I didn't want to push my luck, but the use of my magic might be the difference between success and failure.

"What if you need my help?" I argued. "Wouldn't it be safer and give us the best chance of finding the cauldron if I have my magic?"

"I gave you my offer. Take it or leave it." He folded his arms across his chest, telegraphing an air of absolute finality. He was not going to budge, and I wasn't going to help my position by arguing further.

I gave him a single nod. "You figure out how to get me out of this place, and I'll take you to the cauldron."

"Not a problem. Gather your things, and we'll go."

We had entered a tentative truce.

I hadn't gotten everything I wanted, but that was the way of negotiation. Everyone walked away with just enough not to be pissed but not nearly enough to be totally satisfied. Technically, my end of the negotiation was still open. In less than a day, Knight had changed his mind about helping me find the cauldron. There was no reason he couldn't change his mind about the cuffs as well.

All I needed was a little time.

Lucky for me, we were about to spend every waking minute together.

CHAPTER
SEVEN

MORGAN

THERE WASN'T MUCH IN THE WAY OF TRAVEL GEAR AT THE HOUSE, but I collected what I could find and packed it into a backpack I had uncovered deep in a closet. As I prepared, my hands shook with the hint of a tremor—my body's response to the surge of emotions raging inside me. I was incredulous that I would be free on Seelie Lands in a matter of minutes. What felt like my entire life had been spent on this one task—all of my energy, my thoughts, and my hopes were tied up in one desire. Like a rabbit and that miserable carrot hanging just beyond its grasp, my dreams had always been outside of my reach, but I never gave up on the chase.

I might have been called many things, but "quitter" was not one of them.

Reminding myself there were never any guarantees in

life, I attempted to calm my racing heart. I knew better than anyone that nothing was ever as easy as it might seem. Getting onto Seelie Lands was progress, but it was just the beginning of the journey. There would still be a plethora of challenges before me.

Once I gathered everything I could find, I made my way to the living room. Knight lounged on the sofa, arms draped along the back cushions, ankles crossed like a man without a care in the world.

Must be nice to drift through life so leisurely.

He wore a snug white T-shirt with a pair of dark wash jeans and black boots. With his thick beard and his long hair pulled back in a knot, he looked like a spoiled celebrity on the cover of *Maxim*.

"Are you packed yet?" A quick glance around showed no evidence of any preparations on his part.

"Pack what? I have everything I need right here." He lifted his palms faceup to indicate himself.

I rolled my eyes. "I've got news for you, Toto. You aren't a dog anymore. Unless you can still sprout claws and fur, you might want to pack a knife and a blanket, at the very least."

He hefted his large frame off the sofa and stepped close enough that I had to crane my neck up at him as he spoke. "It warms my heart to hear you're worried about me, but I'll be just fine."

"*Ugh!* You wish." I narrowed my eyes at the overgrown buffoon. "I just don't want to end up carrying your dead weight. You want to travel unprepared, fine. Let's go." I whipped around, heading straight for the door, ignoring his thunderous laughter behind me.

I wasn't sure I'd ever met a man or creature who managed to agitate me to the degree Knight did on a regular basis. He was as thickheaded as a woodpecker on a metal lamppost. Even more infuriating, I got the feeling he dug his heels in deeper just for my benefit. Why be obliging when he could resist and revel in my irritation?

It was a power play. Each little move was his way of asserting power over me.

What he seemed to forget was just how easily those tables could turn. There was a delicate balance to power. The scales could tilt from one side to the other with a single misstep, and I was good at tipping scales. It would require subtlety and finesse; Knight wasn't the type to be bulldozed. Lucky for me, I could do finesse—as long as I didn't kill him first.

"You think Merlin won't know what we're up to?" he asked from a couple of steps behind me on our walk to the wall.

The Faery suns were warming the morning air on what promised to be a gorgeous day. I had hoped to enjoy the walk in silence, but it seemed that wasn't to be.

"You think he cares?" I mumbled back.

"He spent two decades plotting to capture you. I'd say that's some pretty substantial evidence the man cares."

"There's never any telling what goes on in that head of his."

"If there's anyone who would know, it's you. You should know him better than anyone, being his apprentice and all."

"At this point, you've spent more time with him than I ever did," I scoffed as I glanced back at him. "Regardless, I don't think anyone truly knows the man. Even during the height of his love affair with my mother, he only ever offered her scraps of himself. We never knew when he would visit us, how long he would stay, or what he was up to when he was away. When I asked my mother why he didn't just live with us, she said it was important for a man like Merlin to have a certain degree of freedom. While he was on one of his regular trips, enjoying his *freedom*, my mother was attacked and killed. Maybe if he had been willing to give up a little of his precious independence, he would have been there the day his sister came calling." My pace down the path quickened as my tirade built up steam. I hadn't meant to unload my baggage onto Knight —Merlin was a sensitive subject for me. Having a neutral discussion about him was a challenge.

Knight kept pace with his long-legged strides, catching up to walk beside me. "He's an important man with unique abilities. In my experience, Merlin is like those Buddhist monks who can make enormous sand murals. You and I see the individual grains of sand, but he sees the picture as a whole. Sometimes, he just gets lost in the task of ensuring the image turns out correctly."

"When I was younger, I used to feel the same," I explained. "But over time, I realized that it's not an excuse. Everyone feels their own life is particularly busy and complicated. That doesn't give us the right to abandon our responsibilities."

Knight was quiet for a long minute, forcing me to take a hesitant glance at him. His face was inscrutable as he walked, eyes down on the path before us.

"That's a rather surprising take for someone who instigates rebellions and murders anyone who gets in her way. You want him to take responsibility for the consequences of his actions, but what about you? What about the people who have died because of your choices?"

He thought I was a hypocrite—that I was too focused on my rebellion to see the casualties. Just because I made the difficult decision to proceed knowing there *would* be casualties didn't mean I was oblivious. It meant I had the guts to make the hard decisions few others could stomach. What greater good had been served when my mother was taken? None. Merlin had simply been too busy to bother with us.

"Who said I wasn't aware?" I bit back at him. "I never said I was perfect, but then again, I don't believe we were talking about me. I was merely explaining to you why Merlin is a crapshoot. You may think he's reliable, but *I* know better. It's entirely possible we make it back from this little jaunt and find him none the wiser."

"I'd say he does the best he can," Knight continued to argue.

I pulled up short, hands going to my hips as I glared at him. "Not long after Merlin made me his apprentice, he took me with him into the depths of the Shadow Lands— the place grown men fear to go. I was *thirteen*. He needed to negotiate with a Nuckalavee for something, so he left me outside the creature's cave to wait until he had finished. As if taking me to the doorstep of one of the most dangerous Shadow Fae alive wasn't enough, he left me alone. I was attacked by a group of Draugs and thought I was going to die. Any adult in their right mind would have known not to take a child on such an errand, but not Merlin. Was abandoning me in the Shadow Lands the *very best* he could do? Would it have been so difficult to find a proper caretaker for me while he went on his trip? Was the trip so crucial that he had to go at all? I'll agree his mind doesn't work the same as everyone else's, but I don't think that gives him a free pass. You and all the others think he's a saint. I, on the other hand, am painfully aware of his imperfections." My words were a harsh lashing, even surprising me at their fervor.

Knight never flinched or looked away as I said my peace. When I finished, he continued to stare in a way that made me feel like he could see down into the darkest parts of my soul.

I hated his scrutiny.

He was the same as all the others—they saw what they wanted to see—Morgan Le Fay, the woman with a blackened heart, evil to her core.

I jerked my eyes away and brushed past him to where I could see the wall just up ahead. Walking to the stone structure, I placed my hand against the porous gray stone. It retained a chill from the night air that seeped into my fingers like the cold touch of death.

"How will we get past the ward?" I asked Knight, never taking my eyes from the wall. He had come to stand directly behind me, and I could feel the buzz of energy in the air between us.

"Merlin gave me the power to pass through wards and even walls." His voice was a deep rumble, heavy with emotion. Unable to resist the lure, I glanced over my shoulder to see if I could discern his thoughts. His golden eyes had darkened to a deep amber, but his face was otherwise inscrutable.

"That's great for *you*,"—I cleared my throat and let my gaze fall to the ground—"but what about me?"

"I'm not sure," he replied thoughtfully.

My head shot back up. "Not sure? You said you could do it, '*not a problem.*' Now, you're not sure?"

Knight's lips quirked up at the corners. He was amused by my outrage—almost as if he had intentionally riled me up just to see my reaction.

My eyes narrowed to small slits, and I imagined rearranging his expression with my fist. Not that my animosity bothered him one bit. He glanced up and down the wall like a contractor eyeballing a new job, ignoring my presence entirely.

"I figure we'll just have to trick the ward into thinking you're me."

"That's it. That's your master plan?" I deadpanned.

He smiled wide, and his eyelids dropped to half-mast in a sleepy bedroom look. "It would be easier if my magic was fully charged."

Sex.

He was suggesting we have sex to charge his magic.

On a normal day, I wouldn't have batted an eye at the suggestion. When you grow up in a world where sex is a necessary, common part of Fae life, it holds none of the taboo as it did on Earth. If he needed his magic charged, we would have sex, and he would feed off the energy from my release—not a problem. However, this situation was different.

"I'm sure charging your magic would make things easier for us." I crossed my arms over my chest and glared at him. "It would also be easier if I didn't have these iron cuffs on my wrists."

If I didn't get to use my magic, he certainly wasn't getting to charge his.

Not even remotely fazed, he took a step forward, bringing us inches apart. "I told you that's not happening," he said in a sultry rumble. He was attempting to assert his control over the situation, but the rasp in his voice made it clear I still held a certain degree of power over him.

I leaned up to counter him. "Then I guess you'll just have to make do." As close as I was, his warm, earthy scent surrounded me. It flipped the switch on my arousal, and I could feel moisture flood my panties.

Shit. There went any power I had.

Knight's nostrils flared, and his golden eyes dilated until only a small ring of color surrounded his wide pupils. "Was it the arguing that got you or simply being near me?" he asked in a husky voice.

"Neither. I'm the outdoorsy type. Being out in all these trees revs my engine."

Way to recover, Morgan. He'd buy that one, no problem. I mentally slapped myself on the forehead.

"Outdoorsy ... right. Whatever helps you sleep at night." Eyes still dilated, his lips pulled back in a wolfish grin. "Now, take my hand."

With a shaky breath, I attempted to dowse my raging hormones.

Get a fucking grip. This man is not on the table. He's the enemy.

I reached out and placed my hand into his open palm, the heat of his touch blazing away the cold from the wall. A tingling warmth from where our hands met spread up my arm, down along my spine, and settled deep in my core.

So much for self-control.

Knight stepped up to the wall and pressed his free hand through the barrier as if the wall was nothing more than an optical illusion. The Fae could trace from one place to another, but I had never seen someone walk through an otherwise solid object. It was beautiful magic. I was stunned as his body disappeared, inch by inch, through the wall. When everything but his hand holding mine was through, he pulled me toward him, but my hand struck solid rock. He gave a couple of gentle tugs before walking back through to my side of the wall.

I pulled my hand free as my mind became overwhelmed with doubt and disappointment. If he couldn't get me through the wall, I would be trapped there at Merlin's mercy. I would never get out and be able to search for the cauldron.

Before my thoughts spiraled too far, Knight's hands cupped my cheeks and lifted my face to his. "Stop worrying. I've got this," he said in a quiet tone that brooked no argument.

I nodded in response and slammed the lid down on my emotions, letting his confident demeanor buoy me.

"We just have to get closer to one another. I'll need you to be as close to me as possible."

Without waiting for a response, Knight spun me around and pulled my back against his chest, wrapping his arms around me. Our fingers intertwined, and his cheek came down to rest gently against mine. His beard tickled my jawline in a way that was unsettlingly pleasant.

I cast away that thought like a week-old rotten egg.

"Ready?" he murmured so close, I could feel the vibrations from his chest reverberate into mine. "Right foot first, then left."

I followed his command, his hulking frame curved around mine possessively. As our toes reached the wall, a searing heat radiated from his chest, warming my back and filling my body. To my utter astonishment, our feet passed through the wall.

One small step at a time, we crossed through to the other side.

When we were clear of the wall, I pulled free and spun around to look back at the wretched wall that had kept me so thoroughly imprisoned. He had done it. I was finally on the other side, standing on Seelie Lands. With a whooping cry of glee, I threw myself into Knight's arms and squealed with exhilaration. It was a sound that hadn't left my lips since before my mother had been taken from me. He might not have known me long, but he had to realize how uncharacteristic my outburst was.

Instead of pushing me away or teasing me, he lifted me off the ground and spun me around with a hearty chuckle. When he stilled his twirling, his grip lessened just enough to allow my body to slide, inch by delicious inch, down his length. Even once my feet were firmly on the ground, he held me by the waist, pressed tightly against him.

I couldn't even be upset. I peered up at him with an idiotic grin plastered on my face. "I can't believe it. I can't believe I'm really here."

He stared down at me like I was an inscrutable puzzle, and he had been personally challenged to sort through the pieces. Reluctantly, he allowed me to pull away so I could examine the forest outside my prison. Everything looked more or less the same as inside the wall, but somehow, my outlook made everything brighter. The green leaves were the richest emerald I could ever recall seeing, and the small clusters of white moon flowers were an intricately woven layer of lace blanketing the forest floor.

"It's so beautiful," I whispered.

Knight came to stand beside me, still assessing me before looking back toward the trees. "Looks the same to me as it did on the other side."

"I suppose when you want something enough, it changes the way you see it," I surmised absently. When he didn't respond, I glanced over to find his features carefully blanked. I gave him a questioning look, but he turned his gaze away and stepped forward, silently refusing an explanation.

"I don't suppose this is the same forest where the mythical Castle Corbenic is located?" he asked with a hint of apprehension. Whatever he'd been thinking when I caught him staring at me had been locked away, which was just as well. I had no need for useless drama or anything that prolonged my search for the cauldron.

"That would be entirely too easy," I said wryly. "Castle Corbenic, where the cauldron is located, is in a forest across the Okeanos Sea. First, we have to find the gatekeeper."

"And how do we do that?"

"We head east as far as the land will take us."

"And what if we're as far west as we can get?"

"Then we'd better get walking."

CHAPTER
EIGHT

WE TRAIPSED THROUGH THE WOODS FOR A SOLID HALF HOUR before I gave in and started a conversation. It wasn't normally like me to fill the silence, but I was unnervingly curious about the man who walked beside me. So curious that a voice in my head warned me to shut my mouth for my own good.

I gave that bossy bitch a two-handed shove to the back of my mind.

"Tell me, why are you called Knight? And is that knight with a 'k' or night with an 'n'?" I asked as I pushed aside a branch and made sure it didn't fly back to whack him in the chest.

He flashed a devilish grin. "Knight with a 'k' for being a knight in shining armor."

I gave an exaggerated roll of my eyes. "I should have known."

"That I'm in the habit of saving damsels in distress?"

"That anything associated with you would be puerile."

"Careful, I believe you're included in those associations." Though I couldn't see him, I could hear the smirk in his voice.

"I am neither a damsel, nor am I in distress," I corrected.

"Right. A beautiful woman locked in a remote cottage in the woods—that doesn't sound like every fairy tale ever told."

"Damsel implies witless, and distress would indicate I was in need of help. I am neither. I would have found my own way out if you hadn't come along—it just might have taken a bit longer."

"Sure, princess, keep telling yourself that. As for my nickname, a number of months back, I helped protect a girl named Rebecca—"

"You have got to be kidding me," I exclaimed, cutting him off. "Rebecca, the wench who helped Merlin stop my uprising?"

He gripped my arm and whipped me around so fast I almost lost my footing.

"Watch who you're calling a wench," he growled. "She's a friend of mine, and she was almost killed when you sent Ronan after her."

"Ronan? I never sent him after her," I scoffed.

"So it was simply a coincidence he went after her on your behalf?" he snapped, eyes blazing.

I yanked my arm from his grip. "I don't know what you're implying. I never ordered him to kill Rebecca, although I wouldn't have mourned her loss. My war against Guin was none of her business—she's a sniveling child, drunk on heroics and blinded by rose-colored glasses," I hissed.

He made it sound like I had sent assassins to kill small children and burned babies for entertainment. Yes, some Unseelie made it to Earth as I attempted to perfect my ability to open portals. The Hunt would undoubtedly track down each of them. There were causalities, but that was the price of war. Some of the greatest generals in Fae and human history were responsible for massive body counts, but they were regarded as heroes.

It was all about perspective.

"Oh, that's rich," he grumbled under his breath as he resumed walking at a brisk pace. "You start the stone rolling down the hill but refuse to claim responsibility for the landslide—is that how it works? Ronan was psychotic, and you used him like a weapon."

Knight set a bruising pace that had me jogging to keep up.

"He was not psychotic! He might have been a little misguided, but that wasn't his fault. His father abandoned him as a child! You don't know half of what he went through before he came into my care."

Knight suddenly halted, sending me careening into his back. "Not psychotic?" he spat as he spun around. "He held a centuries-old grudge against Lochlan that was so consuming, he raped a woman and killed another just for vengeance—not exactly the pinnacle of stability. Although, maybe in your twisted mind, he was innocent as a choir boy. Not long ago, you were preaching about owning your actions. You were quick to point fingers at

Merlin for his shortcomings, but you sure as hell seem blind to your own."

His verbal assault stole my breath.

Ronan had raped a woman and killed another? For revenge against Lochlan? I couldn't reconcile Knight's words with the image of the young man I had helped raise. Granted, I rarely saw him after he had joined the Hunt centuries ago to gather information. It had been too dangerous. They couldn't find out he was connected to me, nor could he have any knowledge of the motivations behind my actions. The Huntsmen were linked by a bond with their leader, the Erlking. If Ronan had known anything about me, it might have been discovered.

Had Ronan changed so drastically in the years we were apart? Had he misinterpreted my aim and acted on my behalf? Would he have seen my actions as purely driven by vengeance and extrapolated my intent based on pain from his own past? What had gone on while I was busy recruiting the Unseelie?

I hadn't known Knight long, but he didn't seem the sort to make up such egregious allegations. The possible implications sent dread trickling down my spine like the first drops of a rainstorm crawling down a windowpane.

My stomach churned with uncertainty. "I didn't know," I offered weakly.

Knight released a long sigh before turning around and resuming our walk. This time, he maintained a more reasonable pace. I kept stride with him, but neither of us spoke for long minutes.

It was no wonder they all hated me if they believed I'd sent a monster into their midst. It pained me to think of Ronan in that way. He'd been troubled when I first met him, but after a while, he'd rarely showed me that side. I'd thought he'd matured beyond his past, but it appeared I'd been wrong.

Viewing myself from the perspective of Knight and his friends, I wondered at why he'd agreed to be near me at all, let alone voluntarily embark on an adventure with me. What did that say about him? Any number of assumptions came to mind—maybe he was that angelic sort who believed he could save everyone around him. Maybe he had a darker side to him that was drawn to my misdeeds. Maybe he was desperate for his memories, or maybe he was just bored. No one knew my motivations, so I wasn't about to guess at his.

Eventually, we entered a thicker part of the woods where the undergrowth was dense and vines hung heavily, crisscrossing our path. Some we were able to go around or under, others needed to be severed to clear a trail. Knight led the way, attempting to yank down vines and push past thick vegetation.

I pulled out the butcher knife I had absconded with and offered it to him. "Here, since you didn't deign it necessary to come prepared."

He took the knife into his wide grip. "Jesus, what else are you hiding in there? Should I be afraid to go to sleep tonight?"

I attempted to squash my ever-widening smile as I spoke. "I suggested you bring supplies."

How he managed to make me smile when I was annoyed with him, I would never know. It was his superpower—like he was Captain Chill, capable of lulling angry mobs into a false sense of serenity.

"Supplies are one thing; I'm worried you have an armory." He hacked at several vines blocking our path.

"Have no fear. The knife was the most dangerous item I could find in the house. If you'd taken the time to pack a few things, you might have noticed that Merlin was rather selective in what he made available to me."

"I suppose I can admit that the transition back to being Fae might have been more challenging than I initially suspected. I'm used to fending for myself and not relying on anyone or anything. I haven't had a home or any belongings in centuries. It's difficult to break the mindset."

He stretched up to grasp one of the vines, and his shirt lifted to reveal an inch of skin on his lower back. I'd never considered it a particularly erotic part of the body, but at that moment, that sliver of skin sucked every thought from my head. My eyes leisurely roved up his clothed back, over his bulging shoulders, and along the corded muscle of his raised arms. He had those thick forearms that made a girl think about how easily a man might be able to hold her against a wall as he pounded into her.

I might not have been thrilled about having a companion, but as companions went, he was definitely easy on the eyes. So easy that I completely lost track of what he'd been saying.

Ah yes, difficult transition, not a dog anymore.

"It's a long time to live as another species," I agreed. "You said you can't remember anything from your life before?"

"Nope. Nothing." He accented the words with swipes of the knife across dangling vines.

"What about your time … with the Red Caps?" My words hitched with uncertainty. He had been relatively open about discussing his past, but I understood some things were more sensitive than others.

"Lucky me, that's all clear as day."

"Did they turn you into a wolf?"

"I think it had been done before I fell into their hands, but since I don't remember that time period, I can't say for sure."

"So you don't remember who turned you?"

"No."

"Do you know how long you were captive?"

"I think around two years. It wasn't always easy to judge," he murmured.

"I'm surprised they kept you alive that long. Red Caps aren't exactly known for being merciful."

"If they had killed me, they would have lost their primary source of entertainment." He gave a sardonic laugh, void of any humor. "It was much more amusing to make me suffer."

I envisioned the multitude of silver lines decorating his body. "Your scars."

"That was just a fraction of what was done to me. Only those rare occurrences when they wanted to make certain I didn't heal." As he spoke, he violently ripped at a tree branch.

While I found his physique attractive, knowing what he'd survived was even more alluring. Those scars were more appealing to me than any bulging bicep or chiseled jawline, especially taking into account his cavalier personality. He was multidimensional. Intriguing. Torture that severe, even over a short time, could damage the mind irreparably. Two years of suffering? It was miraculous he didn't spend his days rocking in a corner.

My mind conjured images of my mother.

She had endured intense psychological torture for years. Merlin claimed she never recovered, but what did that mean? Had the emotional turmoil changed her physically? Would I even recognize her? Did she rave like a homeless person on a city street, or did she stare off into the distance with drool coming out the corner of her mouth?

I understood that she wasn't the same woman who raised me, but not knowing what had come of her was almost worse than thinking she had died.

Knight's determination to survive was definitely impressive.

"How did Merlin get you out?" I asked after a while.

He chuckled to himself. "My memories from those later months are still hazy. I was pretty far gone by then, but I don't think I'll ever forget seeing Merlin walk into the compound—not that I knew who he was at the time. As you probably know, Red Caps rarely live together for long before they start killing one another, but this group of fifteen had been banded together for years. Their encampment consisted of a couple of shanty structures in a cluster of trees deep in the woods. I was kept in a pit dug into the ground, but on that day, I was still above ground after my most recent ... entertainment session. Shackled to a tree, I watched as an elderly man cloaked in a long gray tunic hobbled into camp. He leaned heavily on a walking stick and wore a large, floppy hat, shielding his eyes. To all the world, he would seem an unassuming mouse wandering into the fox's den. Had I not been half mad, it would have been rather comical. My captors surrounded him as he gazed about with feigned blindness."

Knight continued to tell the story, lost in his memories.

"Hello? Is someone there?" the man asked feebly.

The leader of the group snickered to his brethren. "You're a long way from home, old man," he called out in a grating, nasally voice.

"Ah, yes. Excuse my intrusion." He bowed respectfully. "I noticed you happened to have a fine beast there in the shade. I was hoping you might be able to part with him for the sake of this old man. I have a great deal of trouble with my eyes lately and could use a helpful companion."

"The mutt is worthless and would be of no help to you," the leader responded.

"I have a way with animals, and he seems to need some medical attention. Perhaps there is something I might offer in the way of trade?"

For a moment, the Red Caps considered his offer, glancing at one another coolly.

"The beast is too valuable to trade, but that is a fine cap you wear. It would look lovely in red..." The clan of Red Caps lunged as one, descending on the old man with vicious ferocity.

Unfazed, the man held his ground. When the creatures were only a few feet away, they each slammed into an invisible barrier that surrounded him. All of them went crashing to the ground at his feet. His rounded back straightened, and he continued to rise, seeming to almost double in size. He towered over the Red Caps who scuttled backward in shock.

"Braeback Longclaw," the newcomer bellowed in a voice that echoed with power as an unnatural wind swirled around him. "You will release the beast unto me."

The leader scrambled to his feet and looked around frantically as if debating what he might do to fend off the sorcerer.

"NOW!" roared the man with so much force, the ground beneath us shook.

The leader hurried over to where I lay cowering. Grumbling under his breath, he unclasped my chain from the tree. By that time, I was conditioned to obey, so I scurried behind him as quickly as my broken body would allow.

The Red Cap thrust my iron leash at the sorcerer with a trembling hand. Not once in all my time with the clan had I ever seen one of them show signs of weakness. The open display of fear stirred to life a terror in me I had thought long dead. The intense fear I'd lived with early in my captivity had waned to a vacant numbness. I didn't need to fear pain—it was a guarantee. Pain was just a part of life—there was comfort in that certainty.

Now, I was being surrendered to an unknown master. Would he be worse than the Red Caps? I hadn't imagined my life could get worse, but what did I know? Maybe the devil I knew was better than the devil I didn't.

As soon as the ancient man gripped my chain, he began to wave his walking stick in circles as if he were stirring a giant cauldron. He murmured a series of words, and the winds whipped up to spiral in a violent storm before us. Each of the Red Caps was lifted up into the tempestuous vortex, screaming and pleading for their lives. With a flick of his wrist, the man commanded the storm to fling its swirling debris far off into the sky. The moment the Red Caps were gone, the winds settled, then dissipated as if nothing had ever happened.

The man was enormously powerful.

Dread for what I was about to face settled in my bones. When the man gazed down at me, eyes still glowing, my muscles coiled in preparation to fight for my life. I had been conditioned not to fight the Red Caps, but this enemy was new. My survival instincts made a resurgence.

All I had experienced was brutality and hatred, so I had no reason to think this man was any different.

He reached down his hand, and that's when I bit him.

"You bit Merlin?" I asked in stunned amazement.

He paused from clearing a path and glanced back at me, humor dancing in his eyes. "Thank the gods, he doesn't hold a grudge."

I coughed out a chuckle. "What I wouldn't have given to bite Merlin a time or two in the past."

"I get that losing your mother was rough, but has life seriously been that bad?" Knight appraised me with questioning eyes. He lowered himself to sit with his back to a large tree, clearly deciding it was time for a break.

I considered my answer as I sat down across from him. It wasn't something I practiced putting into words. In fact, I couldn't remember the last time I'd discussed my life with anyone. There was no one close to me to require a practiced explanation.

"I don't believe my life has been bad, although the early years got off to a rocky start."

"Then why so much hatred?" His head cocked to the side. Despite his assignment as my jailor, he seemed to have a genuine desire to understand my motivations. I would never explain myself fully to this stranger, but a part of me appreciated his interest and deemed him worthy of at least a partial explanation.

"Regardless of what everyone may think, my every thought is not ruled by hatred. I am highly motivated, and there is something I want. I also happen to be one of the few people willing to take the difficult stance of acknowledging the evil in this world and fighting against it."

He picked up a fallen leaf and traced the edges between his thumb and finger all the way around one curved edge before slowly gliding back up the other. My sex-deprived brain envisioned those long fingers skating across my skin in a similar fashion, and it made me light-headed.

He lifted his piercing eyes to gaze at me through his thick lashes. "Some would say *you* are evil."

His words made my chest ache, which only made me angry. There was no room in my world for sentimental weakness. "Sometimes it takes evil to fight evil."

"And what evil is it that you fight? Guin?"

I kept my eyes locked on his without an ounce of doubt or regret. "Yes."

"I'm going to need more than that, Morgan. Tell me why you think she's evil."

I absently picked up a small stone and tossed it toward a nearby tree. "That right there is precisely what makes her so terrifying—the fact none of you see it. If everyone knew what she was capable of, maybe they wouldn't follow her like mindless sheep," I spat with frustration.

"Like what? Tell me what she's capable of doing."

Where did I begin? Should I even bother? She had them all so fooled, I doubted telling him anything would change his opinion of her. None of the others I told in the past believed me, so why would he be any different? He'd probably just add 'liar' to my list of shining commendations.

Yet the words bubbled up inside me like a geyser. I gave up caring what anyone thought of me long ago, but for some godforsaken reason, I cared what Knight thought.

I didn't want him to see me as a monster.

Most likely, I was setting myself up for disappointment, but I took in a deep breath and let the words flow from deep within me. "Back when I still lived in Avalon, I fell in love with a man." No matter how softly I spoke the words, they boomed in my ears with a deafening force. It wasn't the actual sounds themselves but the brutal effect they had on my heart as they took shape and became real. "When Guin discovered our relationship, she exiled the man to Earth. She had been intimate with him before our relationship, and although their time together ended many months before, she was a jealous woman. Their tryst had not ended well, and she didn't want anyone else to capture the man's heart. The exile was particularly harsh on the man because he had already been cast out of the Hunt for his relationship with Guin, so her sentence was doubly painful. Now, he could not live in Faery, nor was he a part of his brotherhood. He was sent off alone."

"Is that Lancelot you're talking about?"

My lips lifted with the hint of a smile. "I see I'm not the only one you've heard rumors about over the years."

He angled his head back to rest against the tree, keeping his golden eyes trained on me. "Yeah, I've heard all types of rumors. One of which was the story of you tricking Lancelot into sleeping with you to lure him away from Guin."

My shoulders curved in to ease the ache in my chest caused by the ugly accusation. It wasn't the first time I'd heard it, and doubtless, it would not be the last. I wished his words had not affected me, but it had been too painful a memory not to trigger the emotions. Knowing how keenly observant Knight was, I had no doubt he had noticed my change in posture.

"I'm familiar with that rumor as well," I conceded, my eyes landing anywhere but on his. "It wasn't true. I have no proof, so you'll just have to decide whether you believe me."

"If you loved him, why didn't you follow him to Earth?"

"I didn't learn about his sentence until weeks later. When I did, I confronted Guin. She exiled me to the Wilds. By the time I found a way onto Earth, it had been years. I used spells to help me locate him, and each time, the result was the same. He was dead." I paused with the remembered pain of losing yet another piece of my heart. At the time, the grief had been immeasurable—it was still there in the form of a hollow pit in my stomach.

So much loss in one lifetime.

Some days, I wondered if it would ever stop haunting me. Others, I relished the pain because it was all I had left of them.

"Anyway," I said as I stood and wiped the dirt from my

bottom and legs. "I know it's just one small example, but there's more to what she did to me than I can say. Plus, I know I'm not the sole victim of her cruelty. She has a habit of removing anyone who opposes her and destroying all evidence of her wrongdoings. Guin is wholly self-serving and without empathy. She is calculating, devious, and utterly heartless. She doesn't deserve to live, let alone rule over the lives of others."

"I thought your goal was to get the cauldron. How does killing Guin play into that?"

"My primary goal *is* the cauldron. Until now, I believed the only way to get on Seelie Lands and acquire the cauldron was to kill Guin so her wards would fall. The two goals were entwined."

"And now that you're here without having to kill Guin, does that mean you will no longer attempt to kill her?" I could hear it in his voice. He would still defend her.

I gave him an icy glare. "I will do what's best for the Seelie people."

After a tense silence, Knight rose and resumed leading the way through the dense undergrowth. "So you still want to kill the queen over the death of a man that happened centuries ago?"

"What? No! Did you even listen to anything I said?"

"I heard you," he said as he stepped into a small clearing. "You hate Guin for stealing the love of your life."

I bellowed a groan of frustration and shoved at Knight's back, barely budging the hulking male. "I can't help it if you're too dense to understand."

He turned around, eyes narrowed.

"You're just like all the other pea-brained idiots out

there." I shoved his chest, and he took a step back as I continued. "You believe every little bird that whispers in your ear." *Shove.* "And you never think to question authority because it's just easier." *Shove.* "But I see the truth." *Shove.* "Guin is rotten to the core, and I. Will. Take. Her. Throne." *Shove, shove, shove, shove.*

With my last shove, I whipped around and began to pace, needing an escape for my furious energy. I didn't care that Knight gaped at me like I'd gone mad. I was too angry that he was just the same as everyone else. My gut had told me to explain myself to him, but it had been pointless. He only saw the parts he wanted to see and discarded the rest.

Crazy, pathetic Morgan and her personal vendetta against the perfect Faery Queen.

"What the *fuck*?" called out Knight with an edge that instantly caught my attention.

I spun in his direction and stilled as I witnessed Knight slowly sinking into the ground. Pockets of air bubbled up from the quicksand-like dirt that was already rising to his knees. He attempted to lift a leg to step away, but the motion only sank him farther into the soil.

"Knight, stop playing around. Get out of there," I hissed anxiously.

He closed his eyes, and swirling golden designs began to glow through his shirt. They arced from his waist up around his chest to his neck, and I wondered what it would be like to touch them. One minute he was there in the dirt, and the next, he was back near the tree line.

I released the air I'd been holding in my burning lungs,

bending over to rest my hands on my knees. "Damn, that was close."

"Morgan, don't move!" Knight barked from across the clearing.

Instinctively, my eyes flew to him but then slowly fell to where my feet had been swallowed by the ground. In my concern for Knight, I hadn't even noticed the cool dirt rising up around my ankles.

"Knight, get me out of here!" I cried in a strangled whisper. My voice bore a note of hysteria as I sunk at an astonishing pace.

"I'm working on it." He rushed into the trees, scouring the area for something to use.

The urge to struggle was overwhelming. My arms and legs itched with the need to free myself, but I knew that would only cause me to sink faster. I took shaky breaths in through my nose and out through my mouth, attempting to calm my racing heart.

By the time he cautiously made his way over to me, the dirt had swallowed me up to my waist. Knight poked all around where I stood with a long branch, trying to gauge how close he could get. I had managed to center myself in a large pit of the sinking soil. He lifted the branch toward me, but I couldn't quite get my fingertips on the end.

"It's too short. Knight, I'm sinking. *Hurry!*" I was racing toward full-on panic, tears clouding my vision.

"*Dammit*, Morgan. I'll get you out. Just stand fuckin' still." He hurried back to the trees, careful to retrace his steps through solid ground.

Even though he was going to come back, watching his

retreating form was a terrifying feeling. Frustration at my situation had me lashing out.

"This is why you should have taken off my cuffs! I knew something like this would happen, but *noooo*, it was more important for you to keep me powerless." I raged at him because it was the only place to direct my helpless fury as the soil moved farther toward my chest. I knew he wasn't responsible, and I was a bitch for berating him while he was trying to help me, but I had to vent the frustration somewhere.

Knight ignored my venomous shots and rushed back to the edge of the pit, holding several layers of sheet bark that resembled thick roofing shingles. "Morgan, shut the fuck up and pay attention. I'm going to set these on the edge of the pit and use them to get me a couple of feet closer. I'll only have a matter of seconds to get the branch over to you and get back on solid ground. You have to grab it tightly and not let go. You got it?"

"Yes," I breathed with a quivering jaw.

"Ready? *Go.*" He dropped the bark and stepped on the pile, thrusting the branch toward me. I grabbed hold with both hands and clung to the wood as Knight stepped backward, dragging me through the dirt. As his feet stepped off the wooden planks, they disappeared beneath the grainy soil. With just my face and hands above ground, I held as still as possible as Knight towed me toward safety. Once I was in reach, he took my hands and hoisted me out of the dirt.

When I was free of the ground and could take in my first deep lungful of air, I clasped my hands around my rescuer and fought off an onslaught of tears. Knight wrapped his powerful arms around me and held me securely in his lap while my body shook from the rush of adrenaline. His hand pressed my head into the crook of his neck. It was the most protected and safe I could recall feeling since I was a child. Knight had kept me from being buried alive. Whether out of consideration for Merlin or another unspoken reason, he had saved me. I could almost feel the delicate threads of trust forming a tenuous bond between us.

This is bad, Morgan. Do not *form an attachment to this man.*

Not only was he working against me on my mission to take down Guin, but I had no more spare pieces of myself to hand out. He was the type to wrap his sexy self completely around a girl's heart and not let go. I couldn't afford to play such a dangerous game.

You shouldn't even be thinking about him at all.

I needed to focus on the upcoming challenges or how to avoid future sandpits from hell, not analyzing my feelings for a man I hardly knew.

I squirmed from his grasp and stood, taking my backpack off and batting at the moist dirt particles covering it.

"Thank you. Sorry I freaked out back there," I offered in a murmur, too upset to meet his eyes.

When he didn't respond, I peeked at his hard face. His brow was deeply furrowed, lips pressed in a thin line as he stared at me. Something was going on behind those amber eyes, but I couldn't make out the meaning, and he didn't offer an explanation.

Good. It's best for everyone if we pretend the incident never happened.

"I guess I'm a mess now. Maybe we'll find a creek soon, and I can wash off," I rambled in an attempt to fill the awkward silence. Two more days, and I'd be like every other simpering woman who jabbers every time there was a lull in the conversation.

"I doubt it'll be a problem," he indicated gruffly, eyes glancing up at the black clouds above.

Knight's mood had gone just as dark as the billowing clouds above us. Why had he withdrawn? Was he upset with himself for comforting me? He couldn't possibly be upset I had pulled away—could he?

I shook my head to myself. It didn't matter what bug had crawled up his ass. It wasn't my job to make him happy. Hell, he had my wrists in iron cuffs. I'm the one who should need cheering. We weren't lovers or even friends. I was his captive, and I needed to remember that.

"We're losing daylight. Let's keep going," he ordered before walking to the tree line and disappearing into its depths.

I followed gingerly in each of his footsteps, attempting to ignore my niggling unease at the tension between us.

CHAPTER

NINE

KNIGHT

WHAT THE HELL HAPPENED BACK THERE?

The sinking dirt pit hadn't been all that shocking—that kind of crazy shit happened all the time in Faery. It was my moment with Morgan that had taken me by surprise. When I pulled her from the ground, she had looked at me like I was her fucking savior. Like I had hung the stars in the sky just for her. It made the beast in me roar with pleasure, putting me even more at odds with myself.

Fuck.

If my wolf could have purred when I held Morgan in my arms, it would have. At that moment, with her head cradled against my chest and her shaking body wrapped in my arms, she gave me a glimpse of the vulnerable woman under the bravado. It was a good thing we were alone in the woods because had someone approached us, I

101

wasn't entirely sure I wouldn't have killed them. Like an injured animal, I had been reduced to my most basic nature—protect at all costs. My wolf had taken control and howled its claim of possession. My logical side knew Morgan was a hot mess, and I wanted no part of that. The trick was explaining that to my animalistic side. He had a mind of his own.

I did everything I could to shrug off the overwhelming urge to club Morgan over the head and drag her back to my cave. I had just met the woman, and what I had heard about her was less than flattering. So far, I hadn't personally witnessed any outrageous behavior, but her track record was proven.

Her claim that she hadn't sent Ronan after Rebecca was intriguing. I had detected an element of shock and dismay over what he had done. It had seemed sincere, but I wasn't about to believe her so easily. As for her claims about Guin, though they weren't complimentary, if true, they still weren't enough to make the Seelie monarch "evil." It was like Morgan had started with a seed of logic but watered it with pure emotion until it had morphed into a grotesque creation of her own imagination. She had spent her whole life demonizing Guin for the loss of her lover. How many people's sons, daughters, mothers, and brothers had lost their lives because of Morgan's vendetta? She talked about other people not owning their actions, but she didn't take responsibility for her behavior. Hypocrisy much?

At least she could admit she wasn't perfect, but nothing else she said made any sense. She was probably just as crazy as the stories implied, which meant I was a raving lunatic for following after her.

I had felt a magnetic pull to her since the moment I transformed, and she had scurried away from me. However, that wasn't enough to have me following her on a wild goose chase through the Seelie woods. The clincher was when she said she had been to Castle Corbenic. That was when she had me.

I had never heard of anyone else seeing the mythical castle. If she had been there once, would that help her chances of finding it again? How had she found it before? Had she seen the cauldron before? Was I a monumental fool for believing anything she said?

Probably.

She wasn't the only one with inner demons. Mine begged and pleaded with me to give her a chance, regardless of how absurd it seemed. I was angry with myself for volunteering to join in her foolhardy quest and for allowing her to slink her way under my skin. For miles, I berated myself and questioned how I had allowed myself to get sucked into her madness.

Neither of us said a word as we forged ahead, lost in our own tumultuous thoughts. Rain began to fall in sheets, soaking us through to the bone. The thick clouds brought darkness on early, so we made camp for the night when we came across a small cave. Not exactly a cave. A chunk of hillside carved out from erosion. There was enough of a hollow to protect us from the rain and a wall to our backs that would help keep us safe from the locals.

We wordlessly gathered the few bits of dry wood we could find and started a small fire. I took off my shirt, wrung it out, and laid the drenched fabric along the inner wall of our sanctuary in the hopes that the fire might help it dry. There was so much moisture in the air. It was a long shot but worth a try.

I hadn't expected Morgan to follow suit.

She pulled her heavy shirt over her head and situated it next to mine along the wall. I had to force my breathing to stay steady as my eyes drifted over to where she sat in a bright red bra, either unaware or uncaring of her effect on me. Her skin was so smooth and unblemished that it didn't seem real, like she was made of porcelain and should be kept on a shelf for display. Her softly rounded breasts were perfectly cupped in the lingerie, giving them a round firmness that begged to be squeezed. I could imagine the way my tongue would feel as it lapped a path from her graceful neck down to each of those rosy peaks.

What the fuck had I been thinking not getting laid before I went on this little adventure?

Not only would it have been ideal to recharge my magic, but I might have been able to think with my head instead of my dick.

Yeah, right. There was no way in hell I would have been able to sit across the fire from all that naked skin without wanting to taste it, whether I'd gotten off before the trip or not.

Oblivious to the rising tent in my pants, Morgan rifled through her bag until she pulled out a flask and took a swig of its contents. Head back, her neck contracted as she swallowed several gulps, then she licked the stray moisture from her lips. I wasn't sure she could have been any more tempting if she had tried.

"What do you have there?" I asked in a guttural baritone.

Way to keep that one under wraps.

She met my eyes, hers narrowing ever so slightly. "Faery wine, would you like some?" she offered, extending the flask toward me.

I took the cool metal and downed a generous portion of wine. The sweet drink was a welcome change, coating my throat and igniting an instant fire in my chest. Faery wine was potent. The Fae didn't dick around with their intoxicating drinks, and Morgan's wine had been especially well brewed. I could taste the swirl of several distinct fruit flavors along with the tang of picca fruit, which gave the wine its potency. I took one more swig before handing the flask back to her.

"You can't imagine what it's like seeing wine and other indulgences and not being able to enjoy them." I said a small prayer, thanking the gods my voice had returned to normal.

"You could have drunk wine, or whatever your drink of choice, while you were a wolf."

"Not having hands or the ability to talk made that somewhat difficult. I could have gotten my point across, but I guess it was never important enough to work at." I poked at our meager fire, hoping to keep it lit as long as possible.

Morgan handed me a protein bar from her bag and began to open one for herself. I knew Merlin had stocked the house with food for her, but seeing something as human as a protein bar in Faery was odd.

She took a bite of her bar, then fiddled with the foil wrapper. "What *was* important to you?"

"Enjoying each day I was given. Helping the man who had saved me. That was about it—life was pretty simple as a wolf." I smirked at her across the fire. "Eat, run, maybe an occasional fight over territory."

"You interacted with other wolves?" she gaped.

I took the flask for another drink, knowing where the conversation was headed. "Yeah, a part of me became my wolf. In particular, when I was around other wolves."

"Did you have wolf sex?"

And there it was—the question that had been inevitable. "Yeah … I did," I grumbled with a swig. "A wolf has urges, too."

She began to giggle uncontrollably, and it was obnoxiously cute. I smirked at the thought of telling Morgan just how *cute* she was. She would probably try to take my head off. She wasn't the type to appreciate being called cute, but that was precisely what made the look so appealing on her. Her smile softened her features and offered an unfettered glimpse at the woman she might have been had her mother not been taken from her at such an early age. The only reason I had been granted this exclusive peek at her mellow side was the wine. She was halfway drunk on just a few gulps from the canteen.

Good, maybe she won't remember the conversation.

I took one more swig and handed the flask back to her.

She calmed herself and took a drink, eyeing me sheepishly over the flask. "What kind of things do you do for Merlin, aside from guarding damsels in distress?"

"Whatever he needs, but I'm often on my own. We go long intervals without seeing one another."

"That sounds familiar. Being his apprentice was educational but it also involved a lot of self-study." Her words dripped with sarcasm. On some women, it made them bitchy; on Morgan, it made me want to kiss the sass out of her.

I lifted my shoulder in a small shrug. "I didn't mind so much. I like having time to myself. Plus, I couldn't complain. Merlin did so much for me, and I was fucking unbearable early on. He never gave up on me, even when it took me years to come back to myself."

When I glanced up at Morgan, her eyes were at half-mast. I wanted to ask her more about her relationship with Merlin. While I didn't want to upset our easy conversation, I figured catching her while she was tipsy was probably my best shot at getting answers.

"Tell me more about you and Merlin—why you hate him so much."

As I'd hoped, she didn't fly into an incensed rage this time. Her deep blue eyes stayed soft, and her head tilted softly to one side.

"He was the reason my mother was taken from me. It was his sister who took her and tortured her. All this time, he let me believe she was dead." Her voice faded, and for a second, I could see the terrified little girl she had been.

"You can't blame him for his sister's actions," I offered quietly.

"I know, but where was he when Mab showed at our door? Where was he when I was strapped in that chair and forced to watch as my mother was nearly beaten to death?

Why did it take him two long years to figure out who was behind her abduction? Why didn't he tell me she was alive?" Her voice broke on her last words, and the wolf raged inside me to pull her into my arms and protect her from all the pain.

"He's powerful, but he's not omniscient. Did you consider he may have been just as affected by her loss as you were? Maybe even more so as an adult because he carried the weight of his own blame."

I had pushed too far.

She sat tall, her blue eyes glinting with shards of ice. "I don't expect you to see it from my perspective. You think he can do no wrong, just like you think Guin walks on water."

"Actually, I can't say I have an opinion of her. I've never even met the woman."

Her rigid stance relaxed just a touch as she peered at me with confusion. "How? Don't you go to court with Merlin?"

I glanced down at my hand where I'd been toying with several pebbles. "I've always had a certain ... aversion to court. Merlin never forced the issue, so I never went. I've mostly called Earth home."

"Well, at least that's one thing we can agree on," she announced with a sigh.

I met her eyes with a grin. "Oh, yeah? You a fan of Earth?"

"Yeah." She nibbled on her bottom lip as her thoughts drifted to the place she called home. "I spent many years there when I wasn't working. I love it. I'd say you would fit in rather well on the streets of New York—very dog friendly, you know." She giggled as if she found herself enormously funny, and the sight of her laughter was almost more intoxicating than the wine. Her cheeks had flushed with color, and her childlike laughter was ridiculously endearing.

She lifted her hand to cover her mouth, and without thinking, I reached out to pull her hand away.

"Don't hide your smile. No reason to hide that beauty from the world." My fingers lingered on hers as though I was powerless to sever our connection.

I wasn't sure what had come over me. Was it her unexpected display of disarming innocence? Our proximity and varying degrees of undress? Perhaps it was my own acquired need for physical touch or the rapid change in my life's circumstances. Then again, it could have been the wine.

Dear God, let it simply be the wine.

CHAPTER

TEN

MORGAN

Knight's words created a vacuum that sucked every ounce of air from our small refuge. Only the fire continued to breathe as it popped and crackled beside us. My eyes stayed glued to his, transfixed by his bright amber irises, made even more dynamic as they reflected the dancing orange flames from the fire.

At that moment, there wasn't much I wouldn't have given to know what he was thinking, but as confident and accomplished as I was, I couldn't force the words past my lips to simply ask. Perhaps I didn't actually want to know, or perhaps, I was scared of the answer.

Ever so slowly, he pulled back, and his eyes broke our connection. As I took in a long, steadying breath, there was a flutter inside my chest I hadn't experienced in centuries, like a bottle of champagne had been uncorked in my stomach, and the little bubbles now coated my

110

insides. The sensation was exquisite and frightening all at once.

When I glanced up to see if Knight had been similarly affected, I froze as an icy chill skittered across my exposed skin. His eyes were ablaze with rapt intensity, muscles coiled at the ready, hand snaking out to take hold of my knife. As he lifted the long blade between us, I attempted to clear my intoxicated brain and summon a plan.

My reflexes sluggish, I never had the chance.

Knight stabbed out with lightning speed, the knife plunging into the dirt wall beside my head. I screeched and dove to the side, rounding to hunch in a defensive stance. The knife stuck straight out from the wall where it impaled a spider-like creature, body the size of a large potato, just inches from where my head had been.

I spun around toward the open air of the forest and took deep breaths to help keep my rebelling stomach from unloading its contents.

"It's a Kaché," said Knight from behind me. "Nasty buggers if they get their claws in you, but perfect for dinner. Hunting doesn't get any easier than that."

I whipped my head around and gaped at him. "You can't be serious."

He smiled up at me, eyes dancing. "Hell yeah, I am. Those things may be deadly, but once the pinchers are removed, that baby will be delicious."

I threw my hand over my mouth to battle against gagging. I should have known Snoopy's palate would be less than discerning. Hell, dogs ate their own shit. There was no way I would trust his opinion on food.

"Thanks, but I think I'll pass."

"Who said I was sharing?"

I rolled my eyes and huffed out a laugh.

Thirty minutes later, Knight had cooked off the fine hairs from the carcass, removed the legs and pinchers, then skewered the body to rotisserie over the fire. Once the creature had been reduced to a chunk of meat on a stick, I had to admit, it wasn't altogether unappealing. At least he was cooking the thing and not tearing into it raw.

I cringed at the mental image.

"You cold?" he asked in a deep rumble.

"No, just tired. I suppose I had more wine than I realized. Plus, it's been an eventful day."

He pulled the skewer off the fire and sliced into the Kaché fillet. "Perfect," he mused to himself. He pulled off a section of meat and sucked it into his mouth, huffing to keep from burning his tongue. The creature had been surprisingly fatty, dripping juices into the fire as it cooked. When he sucked the meat into his mouth, it left a glistening sheen of moisture on his lips that reflected the firelight.

I had a sudden overwhelming urge to lick the substance from his full lips. My own lips parted, and he must have misunderstood my look when he peered over at me. He took off a small sliver of meat and blew on it to cool it. Then he extended the morsel between his thumb and fingers until it was a breath away from touching my lips.

"Go ahead, try some. You'll never know if you like it unless you try it," he offered in a sultry murmur.

As if I was his to command, my jaw fell open. I accepted his offering, closing my lips to suck on his thick fingers as he slowly pulled them away. The intensity in his gaze brutalized my independence like a storm raging against a lighthouse. I could feel his unspoken need for me to bend to his will, and somewhere deep inside, I rejoiced at the prospect of turning over that control.

I was immensely proud that I was a strong, independent woman who could live her life without the help or involvement of a man. With that being said, having a break from endless responsibilities sounded enormously appealing—a time and place where I was safe to surrender those tightly held reins. It would be liberating, to say the least. My body seemed to recognize Knight as trustworthy hands in which to place those reins because I responded to him in ways I didn't with others.

The savory taste of the meat along with the pulsing arousal of having his fingers in my mouth ripped an unsolicited moan from my throat. With a responding growl, Knight dropped the skewer and was instantly on me, his lips colliding with mine as his hands angled my face up toward his. My head had already been spinning from the wine, but the kiss sent me into another universe. Our tongues met in a dance of discovery as my hands traced the heavenly planes of his chest and broad shoulders.

For countless minutes, we explored one another, lost in the haze of the wine and the thrill of the forbidden.

Knight pulled back and studied my slitted eyes. "You're drunk, aren't you?"

I found his words absurdly funny and broke into a fit of giggles. "Only as drunk as you are. We both drank the wine."

"Right, and that's why I'm the one laughing so hard, I

can't sit upright." He reached behind me to grab my shirt from the cave wall, and I leaned in to sniff along his body.

"Mmmm ... you smell so good—like man and rain," I murmured with my eyes closed. The hour must have been late because I found it increasingly hard to keep my eyes open.

"That's because I'm a man, and it's raining out."

"No, no. It's more than that—rich and earthly like pine needles in winter..." I trailed off, not sure where I had been going.

"All right, Shakespeare. Lift your arms."

I did as he told me, eyes still shut, and gasped as the cool fabric touched my skin.

"Sorry about that. It's not totally dry, but it's better than it was. You'll need to wear something tonight as it gets cooler and the fire dies." He carefully wove the shirt over my head, then directed my arms into the sleeves.

As soon as the shirt was in place, I rested my head down on my pack and curled into myself for warmth. The welcoming embrace of sleep wrapped itself around me, but just before I was swept into unconsciousness, I imagined the gentle sweep of a hand across my forehead and the warm press of lips against my flushed cheek.

The darkness sucked me under into a place I knew to be a dream but refused to acknowledge as such because I wished so desperately for it to be real. I was in a garden outside the city walls, one I knew well as it had been my favorite place to be after the loss of my mother. She had been gone for a number of years, and my life had moved on, even though it pained me to admit.

Every detail of the dream was crisp and clear because

it derived from a memory. The vibrant rows of herbs and flowers swayed gently in the warm summer breeze. The garden was a large shared project, tended by a number of us who lived inside the Seelie city of Avalon. When I had time, I would bring my basket and collect herbs while I trimmed dead buds and battled the incessant onslaught of weeds.

I loved the peacefulness of working in the garden. I felt alive with my hands in the cool, moist soil and the warm sunshine pressing against my back. The queen had scoffed at me any number of times for the dirt that stained the underside of my nails, but I didn't care what she thought. My mother had instilled in me at an early age how important the natural world was, and I wasn't about to forget the lesson now that she was gone. Gardening made me feel good, and that was all that mattered.

I had gone out that particular day to help assuage the ache that had resided in my chest ever since my half brother, Arthur, had been attacked a week earlier. We had shared a father, but Arthur was much older than me, and we hadn't met until I arrived at court. He had welcomed me graciously, and I had been happy to befriend him.

He was essentially the only family I had left.

I had Merlin, but my anger at him never subsided. As soon as I became an adult, I'd gone out on my own. I embraced that freedom and began to feel like a new woman, which was precisely when Arthur had been attacked by the traitor Mordred. He was alive but just barely.

I felt like the world had plotted against me to keep me on my knees, half broken. I walked through the routines of my daily life, entombed in a cocoon of numbness, unsure life was worth living.

When I ventured out to the garden where the sun could warm my bones, it was the first glimpse of hope I'd seen in a week. I found a particularly overgrown section, kneeled down, and began to devote all my attention to the plants.

I sat back to assess my progress after what felt like mere minutes to find the suns low in the evening sky. Shaking off the clippings and dirt from my skirt, I stood and stretched my cramped legs. When I turned, I discovered with a start that I wasn't alone. A man stood leaning against a large fruit tree, not far from where I had been working.

Not just any man—this man was familiar.

Lancelot du Lac.

He was Arthur's second in command of the Wild Hunt, which Arthur had formed after having a falling out with Guin and leaving the Seelie Court. When the men who served under Arthur pledged their continued allegiance to him, they formed an autonomous brotherhood and asserted their independence from the court. Since that time, Lancelot had been Arthur's emissary inside the palace. I had seen him a number of times with the queen, looking noticeably ... intimate.

They were rather striking together. Her red hair and ethereal beauty were the perfect complement to his thick, dark hair and deep brown eyes. He had always caught my eye even before I was of an age to notice such things. Now that I was grown, my gaze was drawn to him even more frequently. I didn't recall him ever noticing me, but all alone outside the city, there could be no mistaking his attention.

"Can I help you with something?" I asked awkwardly, unsure what to make of the situation.

"You're Morgan, Arthur's half sister, is that correct?" he inquired from his perch against the tree.

At my brother's mention, my head lowered, and my shoulders curved in a fraction as the gnawing ache made itself known again. "Yes," I offered softly.

He pushed off the tree and began to saunter toward me. "There are rumors you were responsible for Arthur's injuries. That you gave Mordred information on Arthur's whereabouts." His voice was hard as chiseled stone, his accusation unapologetic.

The combined effect of his words and merciless tone sent a flood of panic racing through my veins. "What are you talking about? Who would say such a thing?" My words rushed out as I dropped my basket at my feet.

He paused, eyes narrowing as he assessed every aspect of my being for deception. Eventually, his lips thinned, and he cast his gaze sideways toward the garden. "I was afraid of that," he mumbled under his breath.

"Afraid of what? What's going on here? You're frightening me," I called out anxiously as my hands waved about.

Lancelot's eyes slid back to mine. He prowled closer until he was standing directly before me. "The claims have come from the queen. Have you given her reason to harm you?"

My jaw dropped in disbelief, and my eyes flitted about, trying to discern a reasonable explanation for his words. "I don't ... why would she ... I don't even know..." I rambled incoherently, unable to finish a single thought.

Claiming my attention, Lancelot placed his warm hands against my dirty cheeks and lifted my gaze to his. "I believe you. It's why I severed ties with Guin. This is not the first deception she has committed, but I had to speak with you to determine for myself whether the words bore any truth."

"I swear to you, I had nothing to do with Arthur's attack. He's my brother. He's all the family I have left in the world. I've been terrified I might lose him." A tear slid down my cheek, and he gently swiped the moisture away with his thumb, then lowered his hands, filling me with an unsettling sense of loss. "He is the best of men. Seeing him so ravaged has pained me as well." His eyes then roved over my face and wandered lower, down the length of my body. "He spoke of you often—his baby sister. But you are not a child anymore, are you?"

I shook my head, unable to form a single word. I had no idea what was happening between us, but it felt like my world was shifting on its axis. Like that moment was in some way pivotal, but I didn't have the proper perspective to understand its importance.

When I thought I couldn't stand the heated tension another moment, Lancelot spoke.

"Come then, I'll walk you back to the gates. It grows dark, and a young woman should not be alone outside the city wall."

Thankful for the escort and the escape from his bewitching thrall, I obediently grabbed my basket and scurried after the man who had captivated me for so long.

Unbeknown to me, that day had been the first day of our love affair—one that was short-lived but burned brighter than any sun. Losing him had only added to the mountain of grief I had endured during my childhood. Arthur survived his attack, only to be killed months later, leaving me utterly alone.

My waking mind and active subconscious blurred as I roused from the dream. The comforting weight of a heavy arm draped over me, and I snuggled into the warmth at my back. A part of me desperately wanted to return to the dream and the happy months I spent with Lancelot. Another vocal part of me blared annoyingly that the man behind me was *not* Lancelot.

I was going to have to work on silencing my inner voices—some of them were salty bitches.

I blinked my eyes open to the dense blackness of night. The prior twenty-four hours came rushing back to me in a flood of memories. Not only was the man behind me not my Lancelot but he was also my jailor. He reported to a man who would see me fail if he knew my task.

Knight was a decent man. I had no qualms with him, but I couldn't allow our association to continue if there was a chance of escape. It was too risky. I squeezed myself out from beneath his arm, breathing a sigh of relief when he didn't stir. Not wanting to make any noise, I picked up my pack and crept from our makeshift campsite.

I knew the stars well and was able to direct myself eastward. Once I was a sufficient distance from the cave not to be heard, I dug a jacket out of my backpack and took a swig of water from my canteen. Just before I moved to return to the canteen, I heard a rustle of leaves not far from me.

Every muscle in my body was locked in anticipation. My ears scanned for any indication of what might be out there, and my eyes strained to see beyond the closest trees. For long minutes, I stood motionless, unsure if I was in danger or merely overreacting.

I had never in my life been afraid of the dark. My powers always provided ample protection. Now, I started to wonder what I'd been thinking, running headlong into the forest in the middle of the night without so much as a knife to protect me. The one I had brought with us was somewhere in the cave with Knight, discarded after he had disemboweled the Kaché. In my hurry to escape, I hadn't remembered to look for it. There was no time to go back. I had to put as much distance between us as possible.

One stealthy step at a time, I resumed walking. My imagination began to run wild, and even the slightest noise sounded like the most heinous creature. Soon, I picked up my pace to a steady jog, hoping to exhaust the fear from my system.

I went for miles in the seemingly endless forest.

The Faery suns crested over the horizon and gradually ascended into the sky. I took minimal breaks, hoping I could get far enough ahead of Knight to lose him. I had no doubt he would come after me. The question was whether I was skilled enough to evade him.

By afternoon, my energy levels had depleted dramatically. I had finished off the last of my water and hadn't located a single stream from which I could refill my canteen. Knowing I needed to take a break, I found a fallen tree to sit against and rested my head on the moist wood.

How did humans survive as a species?

Life was infinitely more difficult without the use of magic. In theory, I had known magic vastly affected daily life, but it hadn't been until my escape from Merlin's house that I had truly begun to understand the effects. Not even the month I had spent at the house before Knight arrived had been enough to demonstrate how substantially I relied on magic as a Fae.

Now that I was alone in a forest, without water and disturbingly low on energy, I finally grasped how advantageous magic was. Aside from Merlin's enchantment, Knight had been without magic his entire time as a wolf. I was amazed he was sane after his ordeal, but it was equally stunning that he had survived. As capable as I thought of myself, I was coming to realize my basic survival skills were abysmal. How did one find water without magic? How was I supposed to sleep without a protection spell around me? If the clouds obscured the stars, how would I know which direction to go at night?

I glared down at the garish iron cuffs around both my wrists. Who would have thought the mighty Morgan Le Fay could be rendered helpless as a child so easily? I began to cackle a humorless laugh. The sound resonated in the stillness of the woods, making me laugh even harder. Before long, the sound died in my throat as my eyes fell upon three tiny creatures watching me where I sat.

Spriggans.

Of all the bloody luck.

Spriggans were known for being savagely territorial. I

hoped it was a good sign I hadn't been instantly attacked, but my exposure to this solitary caste of Fae had been limited, so I wasn't confident in my assessment of the situation.

I inhaled deeply through my nose, hoping to oxygenate my blood in preparation for a fight. The creatures may have only been ten inches in height, but I knew better than to discount their threat. I held motionless, hoping to avoid a conflict.

"Hello," I offered with a cordial bow of my head. "Have I mistakenly intruded onto your territory? I'm more than happy to leave if that's the case."

The creature in the middle stepped forward, lip lifting in a vicious snarl to reveal jagged, razor-sharp teeth.

I was in terrible trouble.

"Calm down," I said soothingly, hands lifted in surrender. "I'll leave right now." Not knowing what else to do, I began to rise to my feet, never taking my eyes from the three angry men.

The man in the middle made a clicking sound, and within seconds, the creatures expanded from ten inches in height to a towering ten feet. They were gargantuan beasts with brown, pock-marked skin and two holes where a nose should have been.

I cried out and bolted for the trees. With an intense surge of adrenaline, my body pushed through its fatigue as I raced past shrubs and over fallen logs. From behind me, I could hear thunderous crashing and savage growls as the creatures closed the distance between us.

There was no way I could outrun them, but what other choice did I have than to try? I pushed my legs as hard as they could possibly go, pumping my arms and leaning into my momentum. One of the Spriggans closed in behind me, its claw snagging hold of my backpack. Just as I thought it had me, the canvas bag sprung free, catapulting me ahead. Already leaning forward precariously, the added momentum unbalanced me, and I dove into a forward roll to avoid face-planting on the forest floor.

I attempted to continue the roll and use evasive maneuvers to escape their grasp, but the Spriggans were on me in an instant. With a victorious roar, one of the creatures clamped its hand around my arm and yanked me back so hard, I thought my arm would dislocate.

Diplomacy had gotten me nowhere, and running had been a monumental failure.

It was time to fight.

With their numbers and size advantage and my inability to use magic, I had little hope of winning, but I wasn't going down without a struggle.

Momentarily surprising the creature who held me, I sprang to climb up his torso and thrust my fingers into his eyes until fluid oozed from the sockets. He bellowed in rage, flinging me off him with the force of an enraged dragon. I flew in the air until I cracked my back and head against the unforgiving trunk of a tree and fell in a heap to the ground.

Black spots dotted my vision, and the world dipped and swerved as I attempted to stand. Before I could regain my bearings, a second creature pummeled his fist into the side of my face, sending me careening back to the ground.

The world went dark for a second.

I cleared the cobwebs as quickly as I could and realized

my hand lay over a large stone the size of my fist. I clasped the rock tightly, my heart pounding a furious rhythm in my chest. When I was yanked back to my feet by another Spriggan, I used the momentum to swing the rock up and across its hideous face. He wailed out in anger but never eased his grip on my arm.

The third Spriggan approached, taking hold of my other arm, and the two stretched me wide until I was powerless. The one I had blinded was gone, but the two who remained were more than ready to avenge their friend.

I would not survive this.

The pain of realizing I had failed was a far greater agony than any blow I could have received from the Spriggans. My whole life, centuries spent getting onto Seelie Lands, and after only a day within its borders, my quest would end.

Please, forgive me. I tried so hard to get him back, but now, I've failed. At least if I die, there's still a chance we can be reunited.

The thoughts flashed through my mind erratically as I prepared for my death. It wouldn't take but a single well-placed blow for the Spriggans to shatter my skull. A sob tore from my chest as I was faced with a surprising revelation.

I didn't want to die.

So many times in my life I'd thought I was ready—that I would prefer death to the constant turmoil of life. It would be so much easier. No struggle, no pain. There was even the chance I would be reunited with those I had lost.

Sinking in the dirt had been terrifying, but I must have

had more faith than I realized that Knight would save me. Being held by the Spriggans was different. There was no rescuer. I was helpless and about to be beaten to death.

Never had I been faced with my own demise with such certainty.

When the moment was finally upon me, I had no doubt in my mind that I wanted to live. I kicked my legs frantically and yanked my arms against their hold.

"*Please*, no, let me go!" I cried with growing hysteria.

The Spriggan I had pummeled with the stone lifted his free arm to backhand me across the face. All I could do was lower my head and squeeze my eyes shut with a whimper as I prepared to receive the blow that might end me.

CHAPTER
ELEVEN

KNIGHT

It was a given Morgan would try to escape me, but I had hoped she wouldn't do anything stupid. So much for wishful thinking. Did she truly believe my presence was threatening enough to justify wandering off in the middle of the night? She hadn't even taken the knife with her.

She was defenseless, for fuck's sake.

I stomped through the woods with the knife tightly gripped in my fist, following her trail as I had done since I woke alone just before dawn. Thankfully, I had impeccable tracking skills. She maintained a breakneck pace with minimal stops, but that wasn't enough to shake me. Had she thought I would wake alone, shrug my shoulders, and simply saunter back home?

Who knew what the hell the crazy woman had been thinking.

I was livid at her for running and just as furious at

myself for worrying about her. I didn't want to have to tell Merlin his foster daughter had died on my watch, but it was more than that. I didn't want to see her hurt … or worse, and that fear bothered me. Morgan should be strictly business. An arrangement and nothing more.

I argued with myself relentlessly that it was only the cauldron I was after—if Morgan was killed, it would make my chances of finding the cauldron that much more difficult. That was the only reason I was upset. My racing heart had nothing to do with the way her soft lips had molded against mine or the way her body had fit perfectly pressed against me. If the wolf was acting possessive, it was irrelevant.

Morgan was a means to an end—that was it—and my means had made a run for it.

I came across a fallen tree with a butt-shaped area of compacted dirt evidencing her recent proximity. Instead of being relieved to see I was on the right track, a dark sense of foreboding wound its way into my gut. Next to where she had sat was a fresh, deep gouge in the soil along with an enormous footprint.

She wasn't alone.

Something had attacked her.

I tore off in the direction of the tracks, my blood rocketing through my veins, my mind consumed with the hunt. I hadn't run far when a pained cry reached my ears. Grounding to a halt, I peered through a smattering of trees and edged toward the sound.

Almost one hundred yards ahead, Morgan was held captive by two enormous Spriggans. Each of her arms was pulled wide by one of the beasts, and her head hung low in defeat as one of her captors lifted his hand back in what would doubtless be a devastating blow.

Without a second thought, I transported myself directly behind the creature. Leaping onto its back, I used the knife to slit its throat from ear to ear. Thick blue blood arced out from the gaping wound, spraying Morgan and the other creature.

The Spriggans both released her in their surprise, and she fell to the ground, scuttling away from the scene. I leaped off the bleeding Spriggan and lunged for its partner, wishing I could check on Morgan but knowing I could not afford to be distracted.

The creature hissed and swiped at me with its filthy black claws, stepping back in a defensive posture. We squared off, circling each other aggressively. Having no need to continue the fight any longer than necessary, I transported myself directly behind him with the expectation of disabling him as I had done his friend. The creature must have anticipated my move because as soon as I appeared, he whipped around and clenched my throat in his gnarled fingers.

Using skills I hadn't known I possessed, I dropped my body and spun backward to twist the Spriggan's arm. With his arm bent awkwardly, I slammed my arm down on his elbow with brutal force, causing him to roar in pain and release his grip on my neck. Not pausing a second, I took his hand and twisted it behind his back, then kicked the back of his legs to bring him crashing to his knees. Once he was reduced to my height, I slashed his throat as I had done to his brethren. With a gurgle of surprise, he clenched his hand over the spurting wound and hit the ground like a fallen tree.

For several breathless seconds, I stood towering over the creature in the eerie silence of the forest. As if aware danger was about, nothing but the wind dared make a sound.

As the adrenaline began to ebb in my system, I took a deep, cleansing breath and scanned the area for Morgan. She was nowhere in sight. Unease cooled my heated blood. I walked in the direction where I had seen her flee, scouring the area for signs of her.

"Morgan? Where are you?" Just when I started to wonder if she had continued to run from me, I caught sight of white-blond hair poking out from around a tree. As I rounded closer, Morgan's huddled form came into full view.

She sat with her back against the tree trunk, knees held tightly to her chest, cheeks wet from a barrage of tears. Her eyes stared blankly ahead, face battered and bloody. The sight of her made me wish I could kill those bastards again—this time, drawing out every possible second of pain until the end.

I clenched my jaw, tempering down my fury, and lifted Morgan into my arms. "I've got you," I murmured into her blond waves.

Walking to a nearby log, I sat down and held her close —both to comfort her and reassure myself of her safety. My anger toward her evaporated instantly at seeing her so broken. Morgan was the embodiment of female strength and power. She was confident, capable, and more courageous than any one person should be.

I doubted she had allowed herself many opportunities of weakness, let alone permitted anyone else to witness that fragility. This moment in the woods was costing her dearly.

"Why did you run from me?" I asked as gently as my gruff voice would allow.

"You're working with Merlin. You want to keep me caged. As soon as this is over, and you get your memories, you'll put me right back in that house and lock me away." Her voice was so small, I ached to assure her she was wrong, but I couldn't.

She was absolutely right. I had every intention of taking her back to Merlin when this was all done.

"Merlin won't keep you there forever," I offered as a weak consolation.

"It's not forever I'm worried about." She brought her hand up to trace her fingers along the edge of my shirt-sleeve. "There are things I have to do, places I have to go." She pulled her head back to peer up at me hesitantly. "I need the cauldron for a reason. There are reasons for everything I've done."

What was she trying to tell me?

From the day I met her, she hadn't explained, refuted, nor apologized for anything she had done in the past. She had seemed more than happy for me to believe her to be evil and ruthless as her image portrayed. Was she now claiming there was more to her plight?

"I don't suppose you're going to explain that any further?" I arched a brow at her, but of course, it did no good.

She peered up at me through her thick lashes. "I wish I could, but I can't."

"Here's what I propose. We have no idea how long this journey will last, and I can't keep worrying every five minutes that you're about to make a run for it. You're not safe out here unprotected. If you'll promise to stop running, I'll do my best to present your case to Merlin after we obtain the cauldron. I can't guarantee he'll release you, but maybe we can find some middle ground together."

She thought for a moment, then nodded, wiggling to sit upright but still on my lap—a fact which pleased me more than it should have.

"After we get the cauldron, there's someplace I have to go. You can ... come with me, but you have to promise me you won't stop me from going. I don't need to run if you'll grant me that one thing. I'm painfully aware of just how powerless I am. I have no desire to get myself killed before I ever reach the cauldron." Her eyes dropped to her fingers in her lap. "I've never felt so helpless in my life, except maybe when Mab attacked my mother." She glanced back up at me, and this time, I could see a hint of a sharp edge restored to her gaze. "I hate it. I hate being powerless."

I pulled her close and pressed my lips to her forehead. "I know." That was all I could offer her. What I didn't say was I hated it for her as well. Nothing I had been led to believe was accurate when it came to Morgan. Instead of being relieved she was helpless, I felt dirty as if I had helped to clip the wings of a majestic bird. A few days in her presence by no means undid her past track record, but I couldn't shake the feeling there was more to her. My animal instincts about people had been well-honed over the years, and my gut told me there was more to the beautiful blond in my lap than the rumors would have had me believe.

We cleaned up Morgan's wounds and wiped away as much of the Spriggan blood as we could before resuming our journey. I hadn't caught up to her until well into the day, and by the time we were ready to continue walking, it was late afternoon. I led us in the direction of a nearby stream where we both drank our share of water and filled the canteen.

After jogging most of the day and surviving our brush with the Spriggans, neither of us was all that eager to push ourselves, but we were both motivated to proceed. When we were sufficiently refreshed, we stretched our aching muscles and continued our journey.

"If I didn't know better, I'd say we were walking in circles. How big *is* this damn forest?" Morgan grumbled under her breath.

"You know how things change in Faery—walking in circles is not entirely out of the question," I smirked down at her beside me. "We don't have long now before we'll need to camp for the night, and we can both get some rest. In the meantime, why don't you tell me more about the cauldron? Aside from its powers to restore life, I don't know much about it."

"Its history goes way back to the origins of the Fae, to a people known as the Tuatha De Danann. When they first found their way to Earth, they were met with another race of magical beings known as the Formorians. The two peoples became instant enemies. In one of their constant skirmishes, the Formorians stole the Cauldron of Dagda and the Spear of Victory from the Tuatha De, who had come to Earth with four magical relics. After the theft, only the Sword of Light and the Stone of Destiny remained in the Tuatha De's possession.

"Over time, a man by the name of Lugh rose to become the champion of the Tuatha De. He had some help from his foster father, the sea god Mananaun, who gave him a number of magical tools, such as a horse that could carry him across land and sea and a set of impenetrable armor. When the Tuatha De confronted the Formorians in a final battle, Lugh came riding to the rescue in his golden armor and enabled the Tuatha De to defeat the Formorians. The king took back the cauldron and spear, then banished the Formorians from Earth. The Tuatha De Danann eventually became known as the Aos sí, then the Seelie, and the descendants of rogue Formorians who remained became the Unseelie. There's still animosity between the two groups, but a tentative peace has existed for centuries."

"A peace you sought to upend, if I recall correctly," I pointed out.

She glared at me and continued.

"Which brings us to the cauldron. Initially, it was believed that its sole power was to provide a never-ending supply of food or drink when needed; however, it was discovered that it also healed the sick and could raise the dead. Because of its unnatural and dangerous potential, the cauldron was put under an enchantment to keep it protected. Locked away in Castle Corbenic, the cauldron is guarded by the Fisher King and spelled to remain unseen except to those who would use its magic for the purest reasons. Needless to say, not many have proven worthy through the years."

The unspoken question was whether Morgan's intentions were pure enough to earn her the cauldron. If not hers, then perhaps mine? Was the desire to know who I'd been a sufficiently pure intention? What reasons did she have for the cauldron that had been so urgent to fuel her misguided efforts all these years?

One possibility was to heal her mother, but after hearing how she still mourned the loss of her lover, I wondered if that might be the true reason. The thought made me want to put my fist through a tree trunk. Would she bring her dead lover back to life? Would he be the same as he'd been? Would they instantly fall back in love? Why did any of it matter to me?

My thoughts darkened and spoiled the otherwise pleasant Faery evening. Morgan must have been struggling with her own inner voices. Neither of us said anything further as we trudged through the forest. When we came across a fallen tree not far from a small creek, I suggested we camp for the night.

"If we sleep next to the tree and cover ourselves with leaves, it'll reduce our visibility and keep uninvited visitors away."

She eyed the log with uncertainty, remaining where she stood.

"Is there something wrong?"

She pursed her lips and sighed. "No, I suppose not. It's just the log looks so ... icky. There's no telling what lives underneath there."

"Let me get this straight." My eyes narrowed, and I

prowled over to where she stood. "The mighty Morgan Le Fay is scared of a few bugs?"

She crossed her arms over her chest in a huff. "Snakes, spiders, there could be anything under there."

I leaned in close and whispered in her ear. "Don't worry, I'll protect you." I winked when I pulled away, hoping to elicit a smile from her but received a frown instead.

"Actually, I thought about that a lot as we walked," she explained. "The other day, you mentioned your magic needed to be charged. While I'm not a fan of you getting to use magic when I can't, I realize now that it was idiotic of me to keep us both powerless. I abhor having to rely on you for protection, but I suppose I have no choice. If that's the case, you need to have use of all your powers. Dying before I ever reach the cauldron does me no good." Her eyes lowered for a moment before she met my gaze again. "When the Spriggans had me just before you showed up, I thought I was about to die. It was the closest I've ever come to death, and I never want to experience it again. If that means helping you recharge your magic, I'll do it."

Her speech was unexpected and took me a moment to cipher through. I liked the idea of being intimate with her —my wolf fucking howled at the thought—but I wasn't sure I was thrilled with the circumstances. I didn't want her to feel forced because she needed protection. For the first time in my life, the concept of feeding magic with sex was unappealing. I wanted her to truly want to be with me. I wanted her to suck my cock like she couldn't get enough. I wanted her to scream my name as I brought her to climax. I wanted her...

Fuck.

I wanted her. Period.

I closed the distance between us and lifted her chin up so she'd meet my gaze.

"You sure about that?" I asked in a deep rumble.

"Yes." Her eyes bore into mine, no sign of wavering.

The tenacity in her voice made my dick hard. The woman was unlike anyone I had ever known. She was fire and ice, satin and steel, all in one delectable package. She had me turned around so completely, I couldn't tell which way was up or down.

Turnabout was fair play.

She might not have been as affected by me as I was by her, but if I was going to feed from her release, I would make it mind-bending. Give her a taste of what she had served up to me ever since the day we met.

I lifted her up against me, delighting in the way she wrapped her toned legs around my waist. With her arms around my neck, I walked us to an area clear of plants and lowered her to the ground. She shoved off her backpack and lay back on the cool dirt.

"Knight," she said uneasily. "We don't have any protection. I want to charge your magic, but I'm not willing to risk a pregnancy."

I settled my weight above her, lowering my face to within inches of hers. "Oh, no. I'm not going to give you my cock until you beg for it—until you moan and writhe and ache for it. This right here is just a temporary fix, a taste of what's to come. You and I both know that's where this is headed, whether we like it or not."

Her blue eyes widened, but she didn't argue.

The caveman in me beat his chest wildly at her submission.

Raising up on my knees, I pulled her shirt over her head, then did the same with my own. Before Morgan could lay back down, I placed her shirt behind her and wrapped mine around her face to cover her eyes. Her hands flew up to remove the obstruction, but I grasped them firmly before they could get too far.

"Hands down, Morgan," I warned her.

"Knight, I can't. I need to be able to see—we're out in the middle of a Faery forest," she argued.

I lifted the shirt and held her cerulean gaze. "You don't need to see. You just need to feel. I won't let anything hurt you, but you have to trust me. I know that doesn't come easily to you. Just try."

Her breath caught, and her pulse pounded at the base of her neck. She licked her full lips as her eyes flitted about. With a hesitant nod, she slowly reclined back onto the ground.

"Good girl," I hummed as I resumed securing the shirt to restrict her vision. "Now, it's time to eat."

CHAPTER
TWELVE

MORGAN

Never in my life had I let a man blindfold me. Closing off my senses and handing over that kind of control—I would have laughed in the face of anyone who had suggested it.

Knight was becoming the exception to many of my rules.

Any kind of intimacy with him had initially been off the table, considering we stood on opposite sides of an electrified fence. I wanted to kill his precious queen. He wanted to keep me locked in a glorified prison. Neither of us had any business getting into bed with the other, and those glaring facts suddenly bore little weight.

I tried to tell myself that there was, in fact, logic to my decision. If Knight had use of his magic, he could help keep me alive—nice, neat, and practical—it made perfect sense. Enough sense that I was able to feed the story to Knight, but that wasn't the truth. If it had been,

I simply could have brought myself to orgasm and allowed him to feed. Fae magic didn't require penetrative sex in order to feed, just a release. In theory, it could be done in an almost clinical setting, but that's not what I wanted.

After almost being killed, I wanted to feel alive, and I wanted Knight to be the one to breathe me back to life.

Something about him spoke to me on a primitive level. If he ordered me to jump, my usual hesitations didn't kick in—I simply asked how high. He slipped under my skin, trampled my walls, and made himself comfy in the blackest part of my heart.

I should have evicted him. I should have been petulant and refused to cooperate at every turn, then rebuilt my walls and rallied my defenses. There were so many things I should have done differently, but I was tired of doing what I should. As long as I still accomplished my mission, was I not allowed to do what I wanted every now and again?

The moment I made the offer to fuel his magic and his eyes went molten gold, there was no going back. Knowing I could bring that hungry look to his face was a heady rush I wanted to experience over and over again. I didn't want my release to be a product of my own doing. I needed to feel Knight's touch, needed to see his eyes dilate as his arousal coursed through his veins.

That was the other reason I wasn't crazy about the blindfold. I wanted to see every curve of his flexing muscles and every heated gleam in his eyes as he moved above me. That way, when this was all over and we went our separate ways, I could replay each delectable moment in my mind.

The fact that I wanted to hang onto the memories was a dangerous sign—one I was evidently going to ignore.

Before I lay back down, Knight had spread out my shirt beneath me so that my back wasn't flush on the dirt and rocks. As the coolness from the ground seeped into my back, I waited in breathless anticipation of what he would do first.

Without warning, feather-light fingers grazed along the outside of my breasts, over my ribs, and down my belly to the button on my pants. His searing touch had me arching off the ground and made my breaths come in shallow pants.

"Morgan, you need to hold still," he cooed as he glided one finger back and forth, just inside the waist of my pants. "Do I need to tie you down as well?"

I shook my head and tried to be still, but my chest heaved as I struggled to get enough oxygen to my racing heart. As I slowly regained control of my faculties, Knight unclasped my pants. With his fingers hooked into my panties on each hip, he glided my clothing down my legs and off my body.

"This is a lovely patch of strawberry hair you have," he mused as his hand slid back up my leg and toward my sensitive core. "I take it this is your natural color?"

"Yes. My mother and I had ... have the same hair color. The older I got, the more I resembled her, so I started to bleach my hair." I had hated seeing her image in the mirror every day, being reminded of all I had lost.

Knight lowered himself until his body hovered over mine, and I could feel his breath against my neck. "It suits you." His heat radiated down to me, and my body ached to feel him against me like a sunflower seeking out the sun's rays. He gripped my wrists firmly on either side of my head and grazed his teeth along my neck. "Before a wolf mates, he claims his female by biting her neck from behind in a show of dominance." He grazed his teeth along the length of my neck enough to make me squirm but not enough to break the skin. Then with one sultry swipe, he licked over the area to soothe the ache. "This beautiful neck begs to be bitten."

His words ignited a fire in my belly.

"Knight, touch me," I urged with a moan.

He bit and nipped his way down to my breasts, where he sucked each peak into his mouth through my lace bra. A surge of need shot straight to my core, and I arched my hips in search of friction to ease the ache.

"Ah, my girl likes that. Good to know these are sensitive. We can have a lot of fun with that." His words were laced with a devious smile I didn't need eyes to see.

Over and over, he tweaked my tightly pebbled nipples between his teeth, pulling them away from me, just to release the pressure and have them bounce back. I groaned a frustrated plea, but instead of stopping, he gave each peak one more taut pull.

"I'll move on when I'm damn well ready. Don't think to top me from down there," he warned. His voice was coarse, the vibrations like velvet drifting over my heated skin.

He spread my knees wide, and my heart rate picked up in anticipation.

This. *This* was what I wanted, needed. His touch on my most sensitive flesh.

A fire began to rage inside my veins, threatening to consume me. His hands squeezed my inner thighs and caressed in and around everywhere but where I needed him most. My clit pulsed angrily, swollen and begging for attention. Before I could vocalize my frustration, a puff of warm breath blanketed my pussy.

I went absolutely still.

Not until his tongue swiped a long searing lick from my opening all the way to my slit did I suck in a lungful of air. I had wanted to feel alive, but that wasn't an adequate description for what I experienced when he touched me.

I became sensation.

I was blinding light and scalding fire. I was the pounding rhythm pulsing in my ears. I was the forest of trees and the soil and the setting suns.

I was nothing and everything in this man's arms.

He licked and sucked and teased, torturing me with endless pleasure. Just when the pressure would build to the point of boiling, he would change his angle or the pressure of his strokes. Tears streamed from the corners of my eyes into the fabric of my blindfold.

"*Please, let me come,*" I whimpered when I feared my mind would shatter if I wasn't allowed to release the devastating pressure building inside me.

"That's what I want to hear. The next time I hear those beautiful words fall from your mouth, it will be my cock you're begging for." He slammed two fingers inside me and ravaged my clit with the merciless assault of his tongue. He didn't just finger me aimlessly like so many clueless men I'd encountered. His fingers hooked inside me and electrified that bundle of nerves.

Almost instantly, I was back on the precipice, but this time, he sent me flying into the abyss. Just barely holding back his name from my tongue, I screamed out into the chill evening air as my body twitched and contracted from waves of orgasmic bliss. Weightless and buoyant, I became a fallen leaf floating along the swift current of a winding river.

Gradually slowing, he continued to milk every single ounce of pleasure from my vibrating body.

"You taste even better than I had expected, which is saying something because I had a feeling you were going to be irresistible." His words followed after the distinct smacking sound of his lips sucking my essence from his fingers. Knight lifted his shirt from my face and gazed down at me with hooded eyes. "I like hearing your cries echo through the woods, but next time, it had better be my name you're screaming."

"What makes you think there's going to be a next time?" I smirked up at him lazily.

He dropped his torso to hover just over mine, his sinewy shoulders flexing with the movement, and lowered his face to my ear. "Your pussy clamped around my fingers like they held the secret to the universe. It doesn't matter what you say. That told me everything I needed to know."

Fuck.

His dirty mouth was even more alluring than his gorgeous body.

Time to practice some serious self-discipline. A taste of his man candy, and I could find myself hopelessly addicted.

That was not an option. I had to get a grip on myself.

Knight helped me dress then gathered some nearby berries to add to our meager supper. An hour later, we'd eaten and cleaned up for the night. With nothing more to do ensconced in darkness, we lay down next to the fallen log. He positioned himself closest to the log in a gallant gesture that did not go unnoticed. The moment I lowered myself to the ground, Knight yanked me back against his large frame.

"This isn't a good idea," I said with less conviction than I wanted. "I told you I'm not going to run. I couldn't even if I wanted to. I'm exhausted." I weakly attempted to pull free of his hold.

"This has nothing to do with you running," he replied mid-yawn, not giving me an inch of leeway. "It's going to be cool out here in the open. Just relax. It's not a long-term commitment. We're staying warm out in the woods at night. That's all it is."

I hated to admit it, but he made sense. I stopped struggling and forced myself to lie back against him. "You say that, but people grow attached rather quickly," I grumbled.

"And what part bothers you more—the possibility I'll become hopelessly addicted to your sweet charms or the other way around?"

His ability to zero in on my precise fear unsettled me, but there was no way I was going to tell him how right he'd been.

"My concern is all on your behalf, Rin Tin Tin. The last thing I need to deal with is overgrown puppy love." I forced playful bravado into my voice to conceal my unease. Knight may have been teasing, but his question struck closer to home than he realized.

Love inevitably led to loss, and I'd had enough loss in my life to last a thousand lifetimes.

"IF YOU DON'T REMEMBER your life before the Red Caps, and you didn't have your powers during your captivity, does that mean you don't remember what your powers are?"

The thought occurred to me as I listened to the forest come alive in the minutes before dawn. I stayed there longer than I should have, enjoying the sounds of nature and the heat of Knight's warm body at my back. When he began to stir, I forced myself to sit up and prepare for the day.

"That's exactly what it means." His voice was coarse with sleep as he stretched out along the forest floor.

My eyes wandered to his long, lean body as the muscles flexed and elongated.

"I think it might be best to have a refresher course on using your magic before we head out for the day."

"I was thinking the same. Give me a minute to get going, and we can get started."

Once he dusted off most of the leaves and dirt from our bed and relieved himself behind a nearby bush, I handed him the canteen. "Here, start with this."

He removed the lid and took a long drink.

"I didn't mean drink it. Use the water to see if it's your element."

He lifted an impatient brow at me, then poured some

water onto his palm. "Are you always this demanding in the mornings?"

"Are you always so grumpy in the mornings?"

Knight released a long sigh and dropped his eyes to stare intently at the small pool of water on his hand. "Nope. Not a water elemental." He shook out his hand, wiping the excess moisture on his pants.

"Air?"

He closed his eyes and held out his hands, but nothing happened. "Nope."

"Earth?"

He bent down and dug his fingers into the soft soil. The ground stayed perfectly motionless, but Knight's eyes began to glow as he stared at a pile of leaves.

The dry debris burst into flames.

"Fire," he breathed. "I can feel each of the flames like they're a part of me."

Goose bumps danced down the length of my arms.

"Not many have that power." My lips pulled back in an excited grin. "This is phenomenal news. What can you do with it?"

The flames were suddenly extinguished, leaving only ash and wafting gray smoke. Knight opened his hand where a glowing ball of fire formed, then flung the orb at a nearby tree, where it disintegrated upon impact.

"I may not have remembered my powers, but my body knows. It's like the muscle memory is all there; the magic feels second nature." When he opened his hand this time, twin flames began to dance around each other on his palm. The image was mesmerizing, and I had to force my eyes away.

"Alright, pyro boy. What else can you do?"

A brilliant smile spread across his face like a child at Christmas. It was charming and endearing and made me want to wrap him in my arms. Instead, I wove my fingers together and forced my feet to stay exactly where they were.

Knight practiced casting an energy shield and tracing without the use of the enchantment Merlin had given him. I adamantly refused to allow him to practice mental suggestion on me. He would have to practice that skill on an unsuspecting human when he was back on Earth.

Seeing him explore his powers when they had been dormant for so long made my chest hum with the unmistakable feeling of happiness. I had only been without my powers for a month, and I missed them dearly. I couldn't fathom being powerless for centuries.

Knight sauntered over, flames extending up off each of his fingertips. "I have to say, I was a little worried my magic might not come back after being gone for so long. I had a lot of time to adjust to the idea, so I would have been able to handle it, but it still haunted me."

"I had wondered the same," I admitted.

"I knew a certain amount of my Fae traits still existed because I remained immortal, but there was always this uncertainty lingering over me. I think Merlin's enchantment helped keep my powers alive. I may not have been able to use them, but I think the spell was like a lifeline, providing enough charge to keep my magic from fading entirely."

"Of all the people to come across, you're pretty lucky he's the one who found you."

Knight closed his fist, dousing the flames. "I'm well aware. I owe him everything, which is why this little escapade was such a betrayal and why those cuffs will remain exactly where they are. It's not like I could get them off anyway. My magic won't work on the iron. Fortunately, that's no longer an issue. I can protect you from anything that comes our way."

"Yeah, yeah." I rolled my eyes with a sigh. "We better get moving." As much as I wanted those damn cuffs off, I understood the issues. Having my magic would have been helpful, but it was minor in comparison to getting the cauldron. As long as I got that, nothing else mattered.

As we walked throughout the day, we discussed random topics of no great importance. Knight explained why the makers of dog food needed to be shot, and I listed my favorite restaurants across the world. Our discussions were lighthearted, and our periodic silences were companionable. The day passed rather quickly, and I had to reluctantly admit I'd enjoyed Knight's company.

Soon the evening hours cast long shadows across the forest floor. We spotted an enormous tree in the twilight that instantly snagged our attention because of its unique features. The thick trunk was over ten feet in diameter. Twenty feet away, it was encircled by a dozen gnarled gnome trees, which were given their name because each bore a knotted face in its textured bark. Floating within the ring of trees were thousands of Will-O'-Wisps with their glowing lights illuminating the area. They were simple Fae creatures of the forest, not at all dangerous, and known to be a good sign the area was safe.

"A Dryad circle," said Knight. "Whoever lives here might be inclined to let us stay the night." Dryads, or tree faeries, lived deep in the woods. Their magic was connected to the trees in their forest home, and they lead simple, peaceful lives.

"I've never seen quite so many Will-O'-Wisps in one circle. Granted, it's been a while since I've seen a Dryad at all, but this is spectacular." My words were no more than a murmur as my eyes followed the floating lights.

"Not just that, but the circle is particularly well-guarded by gnome trees. Most Dryads are lucky to have five or six—this one has been around a while. It would be enormously helpful if he or she would allow us to sleep inside the safety of its circle for the night." Knight stepped forward and passed through the barrier of gnome trees.

The knotted eyes on the tree faces swiveled to follow him as he crossed their perimeter. A shiver cascaded down my spine. Despite my wariness, I followed Knight into the circle. He was right. A night of rest, protected from the nasties in the forest, would be priceless.

"Hello? Is anyone home?" he called out.

For several pregnant seconds, we waited in silence, our eyes cautiously scanning the area.

"Why, hello friends," a woman said in a serene voice from behind us.

I jumped out of my skin, but Knight swiveled gracefully like the consummate predator.

A woman glided around from the other side of the tree to where we stood. She was about four feet tall and rather wide with deep brown, weathered skin. Her black hair was wound into a loose bun on the top of her head, and she wore a long dress that was masterfully sewn together from a beautiful array of multicolored leaves. Her face was kind, but my initial instinct was to be somewhat wary after so many years dealing with Unseelie and Shadow Fae.

Knight and I both bowed our heads respectfully.

"Madam Dryad, my name is Knight, and this is my companion, Morgan. We're on a journey and have spent the past three days in the forest. We would be grateful if you would allow us to spend the night inside the safety of your circle."

Her thick brows lifted in surprise. "That is a good deal of time to spend in these woods far from home. It sounds like a thrilling adventure." She peered over at me, her eyes dropping almost imperceptibly to the iron cuffs on my wrists.

My hands flew behind my back as if that would undo what she had seen. "I suppose it is an adventure. One that was unexpected, which means we had little time for preparation." I wasn't about to spill our secrets, no matter how harmless the woman appeared.

She offered an understanding smile. "My name is Magda, and I am happy to help you. My sentinels allowed you to pass." She tilted her head toward the gnome trees surrounding her home. "That tells me you do not wish me harm. Come inside and tell me more about yourselves while you have supper, then you may rest comfortably in my home."

"That would be wonderful, Magda. Thank you," said

Knight, laying the charm on thick. I shot him a knowing look as Magda turned her back, and he flashed a rakish grin.

The Dryad woman waved her arm in a large circle, inches before the tree. The bark faded away to reveal a portal doorway into a cozy living area within the tree. I had no idea how we would fit in her home, especially Knight who was almost twice as tall as the woman. However, as soon as we passed through the entrance, the room seemed to expand and adjust to our size. The spatial distortion was disorienting, making my head spin for a moment. Once everything settled, the room appeared as any other living area might in a small cottage.

"Your home is beautiful," I offered.

"Why, thank you. Follow me back to the kitchen, and I will prepare some food." She continued on to another room, which never should have fit inside the confines of the tree.

The kitchen was a small affair with one curved wall of shelving and a table with four chairs in the middle of the room. Knight and I took a seat while Magda began to flit about gathering supplies.

"Please don't go to any trouble for us," I said, feeling uncomfortable with her being put to work after we had intruded on her evening.

"Nonsense," she quipped with a glance in my direction. "I don't get visitors often, and I enjoy hearing new tales. It's been years since someone arrived at my doorstep."

"Years?" I gawked with surprise. "I hope you haven't been all alone since then."

"I do have some family who visit on occasion, but we Dryads prefer a solitary life with our trees. But enough about me, tell me what brings you to these parts." She began to mix a salad with crisp greens along with nuts and berries.

My eyes sought out Knight's, attempting to communicate he was *not* to tell Magda about our purpose. He motioned at the corner of his mouth as if he were turning a key and remained silent. Looking back toward Magda, I attempted to offer a vague response.

"It's just a little something I've wanted to do for a very long time, and Knight here has been good enough to accompany me."

She glanced at us with a curious gleam in her eye that made me a tinge wary. "That's lovely, such a fine young man."

Knight grinned smugly, and it took all my control not to roll my eyes.

When Magda brought over the large bowl of salad and several plates, I thought perhaps the interrogation was over, but I was mistaken. I had barely swallowed my first bite when she continued her prying.

"Tell me, were you running from something or toward it?"

Her forwardness stunned me motionless, and my utensil froze in the air before me. "Toward?" I offered in what sounded like a question. It wasn't my most impressive evasion, but her question had caught me so off guard that little else came to mind.

"Are you sure?" She assessed me with those ancient dark eyes. "I'm rather adept at reading people, and I could have sworn you were running from something monumental in your life."

I glanced at Knight who was staring at me curiously, then back to Magda, hoping an answer to her question might magically appear. "I suppose you could say, in a way, it was both."

She nodded with a smile. "Life is rarely black and white," she sympathized. "Oh, silly me. I forgot our drinks." She hurried over to a closed cabinet and pulled out a lidded jug. "This is some of my specialty wine I save for guests—you must have some." She displayed the jug aloft with great pride before pouring us each a glass.

I didn't think wine was a good idea after our night in the cave, but I wasn't about to offend our host. I sipped a small amount of her brew, pleasantly surprised at the refreshing burst of flavor. Knight wasn't burdened by the same sense of restraint as me. He downed his cup as we finished our meal and described to Magda the current state of human culture on Earth.

As the minutes flew by, an enchanting melody began to swell in the air around us in a gradual crescendo. I peered about in surprise but couldn't distinguish the music's source.

"The Will-O'-Wisps," explained Magda. "They play each night to call forth the moons."

"I've never heard of Will-O'-Wisps creating music, let alone anything so exquisite. I can almost see the melody in the air around us." I gazed about the room, wide-eyed at the dips and swirls of color that kept pace with the changing rhythm.

"The melody is something only we creatures of the

forest share. Here in my home is one of the few places you would be able to experience their song." Magda's voice was distant compared to the intoxicating melody. With the colors, sound, and vibration of the music, we didn't just listen to the song, we became one with the music. Each refrain had its own texture and emotion. The soulful strains of bass made tears gather in my eyes, and the spirited cadence of melodic staccato had me rising to my feet.

Knight's hand took hold of mine, and when I met his eyes, he whisked me into his arms to dance. The magical walls of Magda's home stretched and expanded until we appeared to be in a modest ballroom. As Knight led me in a breathtaking waltz, I could almost feel the swoosh of an elegant ball gown glide about my legs.

We transitioned effortlessly between pieces—from the waltz to a polonaise to a quadrille—dances I hadn't even known that I knew. We gazed into each other's eyes, and I counted the flecks of deep amber that sparked in his golden irises. There was no need for talking, both of us too absorbed in the moment to sully it with words.

The richness of emotion coursing through me as I glided across the dance floor was addicting. I could have danced forever, wrapped in Knight's arms, carried by the lilting melody. I was weightless and free, unencumbered by my worries, and unrestrained by any burdens.

I was an eagle gliding on a rising thermal, soaring to new heights, exploring new lands.

Lands.

Seelie Lands. I was on Seelie Lands.

Somewhere I had wanted to be for so long.

Why had I wanted to be on Seelie Lands?

Did it matter? I was there, and it was everything I had dreamed it would be. So many dreams. It was all I ever wanted. Planning and plotting, maneuvering and scheming, all for the cauldron.

As confusion settled over me, the music wobbled. My steps faltered, but Knight continued to lead me from a slide into a spin without hesitation. I followed his steps as I struggled to recall what I had been thinking. Like waking from a dream, my thoughts were an amorphous mass just outside of my periphery.

Like a dream—something about my dreams.

And then I saw it. The foggy cloud in my brain coalesced to form a dark, solid object.

A cauldron.

That was what I had remembered. I was not there to enjoy the music—I was there to get the cauldron.

I ground to a halt, and Knight wrenched from my arms, sashaying into the next stanza.

"Knight!" I hissed hysterically. "Stop dancing. We've been tricked; something's horribly wrong."

He never acknowledged my words. Hands held out as if dancing with an invisible partner, he continued his graceful steps.

I rushed over and pulled at his arms.

"Knight, wake up!" I battered his chest with my fists and slapped his bearded cheek. Aside from interrupting his steps, he showed not the slightest evidence I had broken through his trance. I stopped my assault, and my companion drifted away with the music.

"Magda!" I bellowed angrily. "Stop this *now!*"

"This is a most pleasant surprise," mused the ancient woman.

I whipped around to find her seated not far away in a chair along the ballroom wall as if she were a spectator at a sporting event.

"Make the music stop," I demanded in a tone that carried the bite of a thousand winters.

"I will in a moment, but first, you and I need to talk."

Uninterested in taking her bait, I held my ground. "I have nothing to say to you."

She gracefully rose and glided toward me. In response, I clenched my fists and prepared to defend myself, but she made no move to aggression.

"You, dear child, have passed the first test." She peered up at me with a small smile, eyes crinkling in the corners. "I know you are upset and confused—it is understandable. However, this exercise is essential in determining one's dedication to their cause. You have fought off my magic even with the iron on your wrists disabling your powers. Your devotion is ... impressive."

She had been testing my resolve? My resolve on my quest? I was wrought with confusion until the answer hit me.

"You're the gatekeeper," I whispered.

Magda bowed her head. "I am sorry to have tricked you, but that is a necessary part of my job. You have earned passage to the next leg of your adventure."

I glanced over to where Knight continued his enchanted dance.

"And what about him? Is he allowed to go with me?" I wasn't sure how I felt about the implications of my question. If she said no, could I force myself to leave him there? Should I not be relieved if he was denied passage? I should, but that wasn't the case. Trepidation at her answer had me gnawing on my bottom lip.

She glanced at him with such warmth, he could have been her own son. "He has suffered more than most in his lifetime. Nonetheless, I have been appointed to ensure only those who have proven their dedication may pass this point. His purpose is far less defined than yours, which made him unable to see beyond my magic." Her eyes came back to mine, and in their depths, I could see a world of mischief. "However, I am but a mere Dryad who cannot leave her circle for long. Should someone follow you on your journey, it would be out of my control," she noted mournfully.

"Life, as you say, is not always black and white. Thank you, Magda." I nodded gratefully, understanding her unspoken words.

She walked to Knight and placed a hand on his shoulder. Like bursting a bubble, he instantly ceased dancing, and the room morphed back into her simple kitchen.

Knight shook his head, attempting to free himself from the cobwebs.

"I suppose it's getting late," declared Magda. "Let me show you to a room, and we can get you on your way at first light." She led us to a small guest room off the main living area and provided a basin of fresh water to clean up. With a polite bow, she left us alone for the night.

"What the hell is going on?" demanded Knight tersely. "I'd swear we were dancing in a ballroom, but that doesn't make any sense. I don't like this place. I think we need to leave."

"Magda is the gatekeeper!" I hissed, rushing to Knight's side. "She enchanted us, but I was able to see through the magic and remember my cause. It was a test, and I passed!"

"She enchanted us?" His eyes narrowed, and his shoulders grew taut with tension. "And you still want to stay here?"

"She's harmless, mostly. In the morning, she's going to reveal the next step to finding the cauldron," I explained, eyes wide with excitement. "Now, here's some water to clean up. The sooner we get to bed, the sooner we can get back on the road."

His eyes warmed to a melted honey, and he took my hands to pull me in close. "You know I won't argue when a beautiful woman tells me to get in bed."

I wasn't sure if it was his damn persistent charm or the fact I had passed Magda's test, but I had to fight off a smile.

"Don't be absurd. I'm not having sex in Magda's house, and I told you it wasn't happening again, anyway. I only agreed to fuel your magic that one time, nothing more." My smile died as the words came out, and Knight's playful manner charged to something visceral.

The air in the room thickened, and my heartbeat hammered in my throat. Knight's lips lifted seductively as he placed the pad of his thumb against the pulse point on my neck.

"That's not what this says. The thrumming of your heart tells me just the suggestion of having me inside you excites you. You want me as much as I want you. Lucky for you, I had no plans of ravaging you tonight. The noises you'll make when I'm inside you would terrify poor Magda."

I took in a steadying breath through my nose, trying not to broadcast how profoundly Knight's words had affected me.

"I don't think we need to fear her, but I also don't think she's so meek as she would have us believe. She knew about you and that you had suffered. I have no doubt she knew plenty about me as well."

His features hardened, jaw muscles contracting. "Even more reason to be on our guard. Now, get ready for bed—the sooner this is over, the sooner I can fuck you properly." He spun me around and placed a sharp swat on my rear.

I yipped in surprise and glowered at him, which only spurred him on. We washed up, and while I stayed in my clothes, Knight stripped to his underwear. Had he been any other man, I would have openly gawked without any problem. Considering our unique situation, I didn't want to give him any ammunition to use against me. He already knew he affected me. The last thing I needed was for him to catch me openly ogling him.

Same as the night before, Knight yanked me against him as soon as I crawled into bed. I glared back at him with as much annoyance as I could muster.

"You know, not everyone likes to sleep all smashed together."

"Whatever," he murmured into my hair. "You slept so soundly in my arms last night. Your snoring could have woken the dead. It was a miracle we survived at all."

I elbowed him in the gut with indignation. "I do not snore, you giant fleabag."

Knight burst out laughing and pulled me in even tighter. His soft chuckle close to my ear made my skin prickle with awareness. I attempted to remain stiff and surly, but Knight had a way of withering away my resolve. With his thumb lazily stroking back and forth across my belly, he whispered to me softly.

"Not only do you not snore but you're also even more beautiful when you sleep. I hadn't thought it was possible, but when you're drifting peacefully, you look like an angel."

For so long, I had accepted my reputation and played my part well. I fed into the rumors, and people saw me as a heartless bitch, treating me as such.

To some extent, I'd begun to believe it was true.

Until I'd met Knight.

He made me remember the person I used to be. Even more confusing, he made me wonder if I wanted to be her again. He made me think and feel a lot of things—all of them complex and terrifying. I wasn't sure what to do with any of it. I certainly wasn't ready to share those feelings—nor the tear that slipped from my eye at his words.

CHAPTER

THIRTEEN

MORGAN

Early the following morning, while the first rays of light were just peeking over the horizon, Magda led us toward the next leg of our mission. Not far from her tree home, we approached a dense, solid thicket of sharp holiander bushes standing taller than Knight and stretching at least twenty feet in either direction.

Knight and I slowed our pace at the sight of the formidable wall while Magda continued unfazed. When she was within inches of colliding with the prickly barrier, the leaves and branches withdrew, slinking back to create a tunnel and allow her passage.

She glanced back at us, clearly tickled to reveal her little trick. "Come on, you two, stay close to me. It won't allow you through without me."

We leaped into action, shadowing Magda's every move. Inside, no light penetrated the thick weave of needle-sharp leaves. It was impossible to see, but Magda had come prepared. She reached inside her flowing morning robe and withdrew several Will-O'-Wisps. The tiny creatures floated into our cavernous walkway, providing just enough light to see.

What had seemed like a simple thicket from the outside was, in actuality, something much more complicated and ominous from the inside. As if swallowed by an enormous snake, we were processed through the body of the beast. The path revealed itself as we walked and closed behind us, making it feel like we were walking in place for countless minutes until we were spit out on the other side.

The hedge not only acted as a barrier but also a portal. From the dim stirrings of the forest at dawn, we were transported to the brilliant midday landscape of a tropical beach.

I looked in awe at the crystal-clear water, my feet sinking in the silky-white sand.

"This is incredible." I stepped out from under the canopy of palms into the penetrating heat of the suns in a cloudless sky. We were still in Faery, but where was anyone's guess.

"Too bright for me, I'm afraid," said Magda with a cringe, not straying from the holiander.

"You're not leaving already, are you?"

Magda tilted her head toward a spot along the tree line to our right. There, on a set of rails, was a small wooden boat. Had it not been for the ornately carved figurehead, I might have thought it was a simple dinghy cast off from a larger ship. There was no mistaking the rearing stallion that morphed into a great mer-beast, its front hooves dancing over the water.

"I see you recognize it," Magda mused in a delighted tone.

I peered back at her, eyes wide and mouth gaping. "Is that truly what I think it is?"

"Anyone care to clue me in?" asked Knight, brows narrowed.

"That's *Wave Sweeper*, the infamous ship given to Lugh by his foster father, the sea god Mananaun," I explained.

"Lugh—the man who conquered the Formorians and took back the cauldron and spear?" he asked, recalling the tale I'd told him earlier in our journey.

"The very same," Magda confirmed.

"I'd say that's a good sign we're headed in the right direction. Let's go check it out." Knight took two steps when Magda called out behind him.

"I'm afraid this is as far as I can go. It has been a great honor to have met you both. I have seen only a handful of seekers make it even this far in my long years as the gatekeeper—know that I will be rooting for you to find what you seek."

I stepped toward her and took her hands in mine. "Thank you, Magda, for all you've done. You can't know how much this means to me."

"I had little to do with any of this. Your single-minded focus is rather unusual—it has brought you this far, and no doubt will help you in the challenges to come. But remember, the end of your quest will not be satisfying if it comes at the cost of everything else you hold dear. Your objective is admirable, but it is not who you are." She squeezed my hands firmly as she offered her warning.

Her advice was wise, but at that point, I was afraid it had come too late. A man didn't run a marathon only to give up when the finish line was in sight. Plus, nothing was so dear to me that I would regret sacrificing it to achieve my goal.

I bowed deeply to express my heartfelt respect for the Dryad woman before she disappeared back into the living thicket.

"I still don't trust her," grumbled Knight at my back.

I turned to him with a pointed look. "Be nice. If it weren't for her, your ass might still be back at her place, dancing the night away."

He hmphed and stomped off toward the boat. I hurried after him, a tidal wave of excitement bubbling up inside me. The boat only seated two and appeared rather sturdy, considering its age. There were no sails, paddles, or other typical sea-faring equipment—just a simple wooden boat with an ornate figurehead rearing out from the bow.

"Tell me again how this rowboat is supposed to get us to the cauldron?" Knight glared at *Wave Sweeper* as if riddled with holes and covered in barnacles.

"The boat is self-sailing. It's a sea-born chariot, drawn by the horse Enbarr. All we have to do is get in, and it will take us where we want to go. In the legends, it could accommodate however many men were needed—or in our case, however few. Don't let its simple appearance fool you. This is one of the greatest treasures of Faery." As I spoke, I stroked my hand over the smooth wood of the ship's rail.

Knight gazed out across the endless open waters, seeming to contemplate our odds, then glanced back warily at the boat. Releasing a long sigh, he relented.

"I suppose we ought to gather some supplies before heading out."

"Already ahead of you," I replied in a sing-song voice. "While you were getting your beauty sleep early this morning, Magda helped me replenish my provisions." I poked my finger into his hard chest, smirking up at him like the Cheshire cat.

Lightning fast, Knight snapped his teeth at me, a wicked glint in his softly glowing eyes. I yanked my hand away but didn't otherwise retreat. Instead, we locked gazes in a silent battle.

He wordlessly challenged me to poke him again.

I assured him I would have if there hadn't been more pressing matters than his manly ego.

He offered to show me just how manly his ego was.

I swallowed thickly and dropped my eyes to the boat.

"Time to get her launched and on our way." My words were breathless, but I refused to otherwise acknowledge how easily Knight affected me. Thankfully, he let me slink away from our standoff.

"Let's get on either side of her and push her along the rails."

Whether owed to its magic or the beauty of its design, the boat was lighter than expected. It launched with little effort, gliding along the rails, then sliding smoothly through the soft sand when the rails ended. We both jumped inside once the ship was afloat in the calm shallows.

"Hurry, sit down," I urged him. "I have no idea what to expect." If I had thought the boat would rocket forward, I had worried for nothing.

Knight raised a brow as the craft eased ever so gradually toward open waters.

"Excuse me for trying to make sure you didn't end up overboard."

"As if that wouldn't have made your day."

"More like my year."

"Sorry to deny you."

"There's always tomorrow."

He lounged backward on the seat, arms draped casually over the rails, legs extended out and crossed at the ankles. A satisfied smile spread wide across his face. "I wouldn't hold my breath if I were you."

I rolled my eyes but was unable to suppress the smirk on my lips. My blood thrummed from the excitement of being aboard the legendary vessel. Building in momentum, the boat headed toward the endless horizon. The land behind us grew smaller and smaller until we were surrounded by deep turquoise waters.

Each time my heart rate began to settle, my eyes would fall on Knight, and a new burst of electricity would jolt my system back into overdrive. The sexual tension simmering between us was palpable, and I wondered how we would keep ourselves apart for a prolonged period in such close quarters. I had no idea how long our water voyage would last, but there was no question the charged chemistry between us was growing.

As it turned out, I need not have worried.

After only a couple of hours on the open water, our steady progress halted as if the breeze had died and left our invisible sails drooping. We both searched the horizon, wondering what had happened. Was another boat approaching? Was there a challenge we would face at sea?

The suns bore down on us in a cloudless sky as long minutes passed, and it became evident that nothing was happening. We had simply stopped.

"Is this thing broken?" Knight eyed the boat with distaste.

"How the hell should I know? I've never sailed on a magic boat before," I spat back, taking my frustrations out on him.

"I thought you said it was self-sailing."

"It *is*."

"Well, it's not sailing," he ground out.

"Don't you think I've noticed? I have no idea what's wrong—maybe it ran out of gas. Why do you expect me to have all the answers?" I raised my arms out in surrender.

"You're the one who is supposed to be this great sorceress. You apprenticed with Merlin and studied every sort of magic—*that's* why. I thought somewhere in that vast knowledge of yours, you might know something that would help us." He stood midway through his speech, spewing his frustrations down at me.

Not one to be talked down to, I flew to my feet and put my hands defensively on my hips. "You're absolutely right. I know exactly how to fix this—I'm a water elemental. All I need is for you to take these damn iron cuffs off my wrists, and we'll be on our way in no time." I held out the offending cuffs, my eyes cut in angry slits.

"You know I can't do that. Merlin trusts me, and I'm not going to let you disappear on my watch." His voice lowered to a warning growl.

"Well, marvelous. What are we supposed to do then? Sit out here and bake to death?" I plopped back down on the slatted seat. "I can't imagine your fire abilities will help us."

"Even if my powers could move us along, where would I take us? The boat is the only one that knows where we're going. Don't go blaming me. You're the one who said you knew how to get to Castle Corbenic. *I've been there before; I can find my way back.*" He tossed my own words back at me in a snotty falsetto.

"I thought I'd have the use of my magic." I gritted my teeth so hard that my jaw began to ache. I envisioned launching myself at him, hands wrapping around his thick neck and squeezing until he had nothing else to say.

Instead of sleeping with him, I was now worried I would lose control and throttle him to death.

I drew on years of practiced restraint to keep from murdering my obnoxious companion. Lowering myself to lie against the curved inside of the boat, I crossed my arms over my chest and refused to look anywhere near Knight.

I lay there for hours, analyzing why *Wave Sweeper* might have stopped. I envisioned the castle as I remembered it, pictured myself with the cauldron, and focused all my thoughts on where I wanted to be. The boat dipped and swayed in a steady rhythm as we drifted along on the waves—no momentum, no direction.

Why would the boat have traveled smoothly for hours, then suddenly stopped? What changed? Was there some test or objective I was supposed to accomplish while at sea? Nothing I had studied had mentioned any tasks outside three specific challenges, none of which involved being on a boat. Could the problem be the fact that I had brought Knight with me when he had not passed Magda's test? If that were the case, why would the boat have worked at all? It didn't make sense for the boat to bring us out to the middle of the sea, then quit.

Each time I tried to puzzle out an answer, I ended up at a dead end.

Eventually, I closed my eyes and let myself drift with the sway of the gentle waves. We floated aimlessly for the rest of the day and through the long, starlit night. Neither of us said a word. By the middle of the next morning, we had finished our meager water supply. While we didn't have to worry about sunburn as Fae, dehydration was just as debilitating for us as it was for humans. Granted, the onset of the effects was more drawn out, but the condition was equally problematic.

I had not planned for an overseas voyage when I had packed supplies the day before. If Magda had known what we would face, she gave nothing away. Faery was known for its multitude of lakes, rivers, streams, and water sources of all types. There was no such thing as a desert in Faery. It had never occurred to me we would need to carry more than a couple of hours' worth of water at any given time.

As the evening hours descended upon us, after well over a full day of being adrift, Knight stood and lifted his shirt over his head. When he began to undo his pants, I started to panic. "What are you doing?"

"I'm hot, so I'm going for a swim," he grumbled as he dropped his pants and stepped out of the legs, then reached for his boxer briefs.

My gaze dropped to my hands lying in my lap. Watching a man undress before sex was one thing, perving on someone who had no choice but to undress before me was totally different. I doubted it would bother him, but something about staring felt dirty. However, that didn't stop me from peeking at his muscled backside when he launched himself into the water.

For a moment, I considered joining him.

Before I could make a move to stand, the boat stirred to life. My body swayed as the craft pushed forward.

"Knight!" I cried out, whipping around to where he bobbed beside the boat.

His eyes flashed with furious urgency. "Morgan, wait!" His strong arms plowed into the water, propelling him toward me.

"I'm not doing anything. You need to hurry!"

He didn't answer. He was too engrossed in swimming as hard as he could to catch up to where the boat had eased past him. The rolling sea waters that had rocked me to sleep made swimming exceedingly difficult. Transporting onto a moving object was next to impossible. His only chance was to catch the boat.

I hurried to lean over the back and reach out for him, extending as far as I could without putting myself at risk of being dragged into the water. His first lunge at my hand only grazed my fingertips. Not giving up, he pushed himself to swim harder and harder until he could reach out and grasp my wrist. I flung myself backward, pulling Knight with me until he grabbed the back of the boat with his other hand and hoisted himself inside. As soon as his glistening body came to rest against the hull, *Wave Sweeper* lost its drive and slowed to a stop.

"*No!*" I slammed my hands against the wooden rail. "Why are you doing this? Why can't Knight be in the boat?"

The only response was Knight's puffing breaths as he struggled to recover from his sprint. I bellowed in frustration, screaming a curse to whoever had set the rules of the game I was forced to play. My cry flew out across the water, then resounded long after in the quiet of my head.

"Thank you." Knight's gravelly voice broke through my mini meltdown.

The depth of emotion stirring behind his golden eyes made me forget my angry tirade. He knew I could have left him. It would have been a simple thing to let the boat take me far away from him, leaving him helpless in the vast sea. I would have been free to continue my quest and disappear from Merlin's clutches—but I hadn't. And now, it was evident to both of us that his presence was keeping *Wave Sweeper* from functioning.

"I don't understand," I whispered through building tears. "If you're the problem, why would the boat have taken us out to sea? Wouldn't it have stayed dormant back at the beach? Why bring us out here, then reject your presence?"

Had this been part of the test? Was I supposed to choose between Knight and the cauldron?

Magda's words came back to haunt me.

The end of your quest will not be satisfying if it comes at the cost of everything else you hold dear.

I had been naïve enough to think there was nothing left in my life I held dear. I was being forced to face that very decision. Could I leave Knight for dead in order to get myself to the cauldron?

If only I had been as heartless as everyone claimed, there wouldn't have been a problem. The answer would have been simple, and I would be safely on my way to the next test. But I couldn't even contemplate abandoning him to such a horrible death. What did that say about me? What did that say about my feelings for Knight?

Panic infected my thoughts like an insidious virus. I could feel its poisonous effects toying with my emotions, and I tried desperately to calm my thinking before I spiraled out of control. This was not the first seemingly impossible problem I had faced in my life. There was a viable solution. I would just have to find it.

Magic was not willy-nilly. There had to be a reason for the boat's peculiar actions. Magda had said Knight didn't pass the test because his purpose was not pure. He was not totally committed to our mission. His presence itself had not affected the magic, but something he did affected the boat.

Wave Sweeper was spelled to take its captain wherever he or she wished to go. If two people were in the boat who wanted to go different places, how would the boat decide which to follow? Had Knight's wavering commitment altered our course?

My eyes flew to his, and he cocked his head in question.

"Knight, where is it you want to be most?" I asked him urgently.

Knight had his pants back on and sat bare-chested against the side of the boat. He narrowed his eyes, sensing the importance of my question.

"I want to be at Castle Corbenic. I want to be wherever the cauldron is located."

Nothing. We simply rocked on the ever-rolling waves.

"That's not enough." I shook my head frantically. "It's not enough just to say it. You have to want it with all your heart."

He lifted himself to the seat across from me and bore into my eyes. "I *do* want it."

"No! Don't you see? The boat will take us where we want to go, but with you on board, that confuses the boat because we want to be in two different places." My eyes pleaded with him, desperation and exhaustion bringing me near tears. "I didn't leave you, and I'm not going to, but if we have any hope of getting out of here and finding the cauldron, you have to *truly* want what I want. You have to want the cauldron."

Knight reached out, and with his hands behind my neck, he pulled my lips to his. I wound my fingers into his thick, long hair and reveled in the taste of his tongue against mine. Unlike our other kisses, this one held meaning. This was not merely a lust-filled joining.

His reverent lips apologized and thanked me. They pled forgiveness and demanded patience. Everything about the kiss was a maelstrom of emotion, bombarding me until I could do nothing but revel in the onslaught.

When he pulled back, he kept his hands at the nape of my neck and rested his forehead against mine. Feeling his scorching stare, I opened my eyes and bore the full brunt of his gaze. Flames leaped in his eyes, and his nostrils flared from whatever thoughts had stirred his heated response.

As my pounding heart battered the walls of my chest, the boat surged forward.

FOURTEEN

KNIGHT

I wasn't lying intentionally.

I firmly believed I wanted to find the cauldron more than I wanted anything else. I had no secret agenda or other unspoken aspirations clouding my intentions. Even after the boat began to move, I still had no idea what about me could have been confusing its inner compass.

I wanted the cauldron.

I wanted my memories.

But as Morgan ardently pled her case, and I witnessed her turmoil over our predicament, all I wanted at that moment was her—passionate, complicated, breathtakingly beautiful Morgan. I couldn't have kept my lips from hers had Merlin himself commanded me not to touch her. I wanted to calm the distress I had caused. I wanted to ease her fears. I wanted to give her whatever it was she wanted.

I wanted Morgan.

She wasn't the hateful woman people described her to be, and I wanted to find out why. How had she gained such a bad reputation? I witnessed her honest reaction when the boat began to move while I was swimming. She never even considered leaving me behind. There was only fear and urgency in her eyes. I was willing to bet the woman hadn't committed half the atrocities attributed to her name.

Granted, I knew some of them to be true. Rebecca had witnessed Morgan kill the Erlking Alberich with her bare hands. There was no sugarcoating that one. How did I reconcile such disparate facts? The woman who killed a man in cold blood had put her own life at risk to save me, and it hadn't been merely to keep her protector alive. There was desperation in her voice. She had been terrified for me—for the man keeping her imprisoned in iron cuffs.

Nobody with that kind of goodness inside them could be entirely guilty of her rumored behavior.

Did that mean she was a good person who had done bad things? Or was she a bad person who was capable of good things?

I got the feeling Morgan was far too complicated to be labeled as good or bad. She was every shade of complexity, and it made me want to dive under her skin and see exactly what lay beneath.

As the boat picked up speed, I pulled Morgan down to lay with me on its wooden bottom. For once, she didn't argue. I rested on my back, gazing up at the first few twinkling stars visible in the evening sky, and Morgan lay alongside me, her head resting against my chest. Between our relief to be moving, the rocking of the boat, and our exhaustion from two long days at sea, we were asleep within minutes.

I awoke to the sound of my name being repeated on urgent cries. It played perfectly into my dream—I had Morgan pressed up against a tree and was thrusting into her from behind. I held her arms stretched high above her head and had the small skirt she'd been wearing bunched at her hips. She arched her back, presenting the pale globes of her perfect ass for my possession. I pounded into her relentlessly, but as her cries of pleasure morphed from sexual to something more tangible and urgent, they drew me reluctantly from my sleepy haze.

"Knight! You big oaf, get up. There's land!"

Morgan's words finally penetrated my sleep-fogged brain. I lifted up and squinted at the dark line on the dusky horizon. Still too far to see much of anything, I plopped back down and groaned as my cock pulsed with angry need.

"Why are you up so early? There's nothing to do; you might as well sleep."

She was quiet before murmuring, "I had to go to the bathroom."

I cracked one eye open. "And how exactly did you do that?"

"You don't want to know," she grumbled.

Even at the bloody crack of dawn, she had a way of making me smile. I was in over my head, and I knew it. Eyes wide open, I was walking straight into a cataclysmic storm bound to leave me in shreds. Retreat wasn't an option. All I could do was batten down the hatches and hope for the best.

As we drew closer to the growing landmass, Morgan refreshed my memory on the history of the Isle of Man, where Castle Corbenic was rumored to reside. If I had been educated in Fae history at some point in my earlier life, the knowledge had been lost, along with my more personal memories. My years as a wolf had not lent themselves to much studying, nor had I had any reason to seek out the knowledge. The more information Morgan conveyed, the more I realized how much I must have lost.

And now, the answers were literally on the horizon, mere minutes away.

The town of Corbenic sat on the edge of the water and was surrounded by an enormous stone wall. Marking the entrance was a formidable wooden gate, flanked by two stone lions, all facing a single wooden pier. There were no boats or sailors in sight. I would have assumed a mythical town did little in the way of trade, but it was still odd to see a port city with only one pier. It made me curious what we would find inside the city walls.

Around the outside of the gate was a smattering of apple trees, their crimson blossoms waving in the sea breeze. The scene was picturesque but in an odd way— like photographic art of ancient ruins.

There was not a living soul in sight.

"Would now be a good time to ask what we're about to face?" I asked as a growing sense of unease settled in my gut.

"There are three tests that must be passed in order to

obtain the cauldron," she answered quietly, never taking her eyes from shore. "The first was the test of heart, which was Magda's challenge as the gatekeeper. The next is the test of strength, which we should find here at the entrance to Corbenic. The final test we will face at the castle. That will be a test of wit. If we pass all three and prove ourselves worthy, the cauldron will be revealed."

I didn't miss the fact that she explained the tests in terms of "we." When had she gone from seeing this quest as her solitary plight to something we were doing together? I had an interest in the cauldron, and Morgan had used that interest to get herself out of her prison, but I never believed she saw me as equally vested in the quest. At some point, she had legitimized my desire to find the cauldron and viewed me as more than just her jailor. She didn't want me dead—her actions on the boat had made that clear. But seeing me as her ally was an entirely different situation.

I tucked away the information to be assessed at a later time, needing to focus on what we would be facing on the Isle of Man.

The boat seamlessly guided itself to the pier and slowed to an easy stop. Morgan and I stood and scanned the area, our eyes falling on a troll standing guard outside the gate. The stocky Fae man was broad but only about five feet in height, wearing tattered clothes without shoes. His skin was a sickly gray, hanging in heavy wrinkles, and his deep-set eyes tracked our every movement. I had no idea where he'd come from—he seemed to have appeared from thin air.

"Morgan, get out your knife," I ordered under my breath.

"Already in my hand."

"We can take a single troll, but I doubt that's the extent of the test."

"Agreed. Unfortunately, there's only one way to find out." She climbed out of the boat onto the wooden dock, using my hand to steady herself.

Still clasping her hand, I made to step onto the dock but met with an invisible barrier. I kicked my leg out and felt all around me with my hands—a seamless wall stood between me and the pier.

Eyes wild, I looked up at Morgan, whose face hardened with determination.

"No, Morgan, you're not doing this alone," I barked furiously. "Step back!" As soon as she cleared the edge of the pier, I blasted the invisible wall with waves of blinding flames. Morgan retreated from the scalding heat, but the wall remained intact.

"Knight, *stop*. Nothing can be done. I'm the one who passed the first test. I'm the only one who can take on the next challenge." Morgan stepped closer but not within my reach. She knew me well enough to know I wouldn't hesitate to pull her back onto the boat where she was safe.

"That's bullshit. You don't have your magic. I'm not letting you take on a troll by yourself."

Her eyes softened, and she smiled sadly. "You don't have a choice."

"I could make you get back on this boat." My eyes glowed with the power that begged to coerce Morgan to safety. It wasn't easy to coerce another Fae, but with her magic inaccessible, I could do it.

"If you did that, I'd never forgive you." Her soft plea tore at my conscience.

I bellowed in frustration, sending a giant ball of flame careening into the gentle blue water.

Morgan pressed a firm kiss to her fingertips and lifted her hand to me in a gesture that was both an apology and a farewell. As she turned toward the troll, the two stone lion statues on either side of him began to vibrate and crack. She halted, and we both watched in horror as the heavy stone crumbled away from two living, breathing lions. They were both golden with jet-black manes, each weighing hundreds of pounds, and their predator's gaze was trained on Morgan.

"Under the apple trees are fallen branches—use them as spears," I called out from the boat, feeling as helpless as a child.

She didn't turn back at my words, but her spine stiffened, and she gave a single nod of acknowledgment before she continued down the pier. She dropped her pack along the way, never taking her eyes from her opponents.

As if being kept from the fight wasn't torture enough, I had a perfect view of what was about to unfold. The giant creatures shook off the remaining bits of dust and released thunderous roars that would have set fear into the hearts of the bravest men. Upon Morgan's approach, the lions stepped forward in front of the troll and lowered their heads aggressively.

I reached out with my mind to try to control the animals, hoping there might be something I could do despite being physically restrained to the boat. The lions roared their aggression, unfazed by the touch of my magic. I wanted to scream, but I didn't want to distract Morgan. All it would take was one mental slip, and she would be instantly killed.

Why had I been so insistent Morgan keep on the cuffs? Merlin would rather Morgan escape than be killed. I had made the stupid assumption she wouldn't need her magic with me around. That I would protect us both with my magic. Now I was stuck on a boat while Morgan walked headlong into danger.

While I was busy berating myself, Morgan made a sudden dash for one of the closest apple trees. The lions leaped after her, charging with predatorial grace. Every muscle in my body coiled, and I leaned against my prison wall as I watched, air frozen in my lungs.

With her pursuers just ten feet behind her, Morgan flung herself into a diving roll, twisting as she rose to fling her knife with exacting precision into the neck of one of the lions. It reared up upon impact with a rumble of surprise, crimson quickly dripping onto its obsidian mane. She'd struck an artery. The injured beast wouldn't survive long, but its partner continued to surge ahead.

I was aware Morgan had been trained in combat, but her agile skill was mesmerizing. Her flawless movements were calculated and efficient. The knife hadn't been the throwing sort, yet she had done so as if it were a perfectly weighted. I felt a small modicum of relief she had evened her odds, assuming the troll didn't enter the fray. However, the remaining lion wouldn't make an easy target now that Morgan had lost the element of surprise.

As the enormous animal barreled toward her, Morgan braced herself with a large branch in her hands. She had used her diving roll to snatch a second weapon, knowing she would need something once she no longer had the knife at her disposal.

The lion pulled up before her, avoiding the branch she jabbed in its direction, and slashed out viciously with its savage claws. The branch was of little use with a blunted end. She poked at the lion, attempting to keep it outside her circle or reach, but the lion's swipe grazed Morgan's outstretched arm.

The wounded lion, who still carried Morgan's blade deep in its throat, made one more gurgling cry. It slumped to the ground, drawing its companion's attention. The brief reprieve was just enough time to allow Morgan to snap the branch over her knee, creating a sharpened tip on one end. When the lion turned back, it opened its wide jaw in a vicious hiss.

"*Come on*, you overgrown alley cat. You think I look like lunch? Well, come and get me!" she screamed at the crouching beast.

For an eternal second, nothing happened.

The trees swayed in the warm summer breeze, unaffected by the deadly battle being waged down below. The two combatants stared each other down, and time seemed to pause in anticipation.

As tension reached its boiling point, Morgan and the lion both unleashed savage battle cries.

The lion launched itself toward Morgan.

Its body arched up and over her, pouncing directly on top of her until I could no longer see her petite frame.

Rage and fear propelled me forward. I slammed against the magical wall just before it suddenly disappeared, sending me stumbling forward. Scrambling onto the pier, I raced toward where the lion lay slumped over Morgan. The beast was clearly dead, but I couldn't tell what had come of Morgan.

Fear had my heart pounding in my throat as I circled their mangled bodies. The beast covered her, undoubtedly crushing whatever was left of her.

I didn't want to hurt her but knew of no other way to get her free than to use my powers. I had to get the lion off her.

Raising my hands, I blasted a fiery ball of energy at the lion's corpse, sending it rolling in a lifeless heap. Morgan lay motionless on her back.

"*Fuck*!" I spat out desperately, rushing to her side. "Come on, baby. Breathe for me." I wove my fingers together and did compressions over her chest. I may not have been able to talk while I was a wolf, but I'd learned plenty from observing people in my years on Earth.

One, two, three, four, five. Then I breathed my air into her lungs.

I repeated the process twice when Morgan took a gasping breath and bolted upright. I pulled her into my arms and barked out a relieved laugh.

"*Christ*, woman. You scared me," I breathed in her sweet, feminine scent, my face buried in her hair.

"Owwww," she groaned weakly.

When I pulled back, she lifted her shirt to expose her belly, where the beginnings of an angry bruise had colored her skin a bright reddish-purple.

"The stick," she explained in a strained tone. "When I impaled the lion, its momentum drove the branch back into me and flung me to the ground. The lion was so heavy ... I couldn't breathe."

"How bad is the pain?" I held her gingerly and swiped the hair off her face. "Do you think there's internal damage?" My stomach rose in my throat. If she had been wounded internally, there was little I could do to help her, and I didn't know if the cuffs would impede her natural healing abilities.

"No, it's just bruised. Help me up." She bent her knees, but I pressed her back down.

"I don't think that's a good idea. You're hurt."

Her eyes pleaded with me, crumbling every ounce of my resolve.

"Knight, I haven't come this far just to give up now."

My lips pursed firmly together, but I gave her a nod and helped her to her feet. She gave a new meaning to the word persistent. Never had I come across a person with more drive and single-minded focus than the beautiful blonde at my side.

Clasping my forearm for support, she led the way toward the gate where the troll stood guard. I had forgotten about the angry-looking man. There was no way I was letting her fight another battle. We stopped ten feet away, and I glared at him with the wrath of all seven hells.

Little good it did.

He ignored me as if I weren't even there. Much to my relief, it seemed he wasn't there to fight. The troll bowed, eyes never leaving Morgan.

"Proceed directly through town on the main road and

exit at the far gate. Speak to no one and do not deviate from the path. Is that understood?" He spoke in a deep rumble that sounded more like distant thunder than a man's voice.

His mandate begged the question why, but I stifled my curiosity and nodded in agreement along with Morgan. He opened the large gate and glared at us in warning as we walked through. As soon as we had passed, the gate closed behind us with the troll securely on the other side.

Looking around inside the wall was like falling through a vortex to a different time. Faery culture had retained its old-world style, but it was nothing compared to these people. The structures and people of Corbenic had been lost in the ages.

The road was not fortified with pavers, and the buildings were constructed from rudimentary materials. The inhabitants gawking at us wore clothing made of rough-hewn fabrics sewn together in an archaic fashion. Every one of them cowered away in terror of our presence. Mothers shoved their children behind them, and as soon as the adults snapped out of their shock, they scurried inside to safety.

"I don't think they get many visitors," I noted under my breath.

"That's an understatement." Morgan snorted, then grimaced from a twinge of pain.

We pressed forward, keeping our word to refrain from all interaction with the people of Corbenic. It took all of five minutes before we came to another gate. A large man with wide, brown eyes verified with his sentries above that there were no threats outside the wall, then opened the wooden latch to allow us passage, keeping his eyes cast down at the ground.

Unlike the rocky seascape on the other side of Corbenic, this gate revealed trees blanketing the landscape as far as the eye could see. And on the distant horizon were the unmistakable stone turrets of a castle.

CHAPTER

FIFTEEN

MORGAN

CASTLE CORBENIC, THE CASTLE OF SLEEPLESS DREAMS—IT WAS just as I remembered it. I had only been there once when I was a young child, but it was the sort of place you never forgot. A stone fortress looming over the treetops, the castle got its name from the powerful illusions that affected its visitors. Inside the castle, it was hard to know what was real and what was not. It had been known to drive men mad.

As we started to walk along the path through the woods, the trees obscured a vastly different land from the first forest we had traversed. Evergreen trees grew close together, keeping the undergrowth manageable but also filtering out much of the sunlight. The most ominous distinction was the unnatural quiet. The sea breeze didn't make it far enough inland to rustle the leaves, and the forest creatures were impossibly silent.

I was oddly comforted because, in that way, it was similar to my home in the Wilds. But that preternatural silence also conveyed warning. Nature only went to such lengths when danger was about.

Both sensing the gravity of our situation, we continued without speaking. We had walked for a little over an hour when Knight finally spoke in a hushed whisper.

"This place gives me a bad feeling." His eyes scoured the area for threats in an endless sweeping pattern.

"Yes and no. It feels like home—but home was definitely dangerous."

"If by home, you mean the Wilds, then our perceptions differ. My time there was less ... peaceful than yours. I constantly feel as though I'm being hunted."

I glanced at him, my chest constricting for what he had suffered. "I suppose you have a right to be somewhat paranoid."

"It's only paranoia when..." His voice trailed off, and I realized he had stopped walking.

I glanced back to see what had happened, spine-tingling fear wrapping its fist around my throat.

Knight stood ram-rod straight, eyes wide with terror. Tremors began to wrack his body as I rushed to his side.

"Knight," I whispered soothingly. "What's happened? What's wrong?"

His eyes darted down, frantically scanning the forest floor before lifting my arm to display the cut where the lion's claws had gouged me. The wound was still open, and large red droplets dotted the ground.

"It's still bleeding," he murmured to himself. "They've

caught the scent; they'd never miss it. They'll be here any moment." His words were choppy and incoherent, like a child lost in their imagination.

I placed my hands on Knight's cheeks and forced him to meet my gaze. "Knight, who's coming?"

His Adam's apple bobbed, and his breathing shuddered. "The Red Caps. They're coming."

My eyes darted to the castle that now loomed not far away. We had made good progress and were almost halfway through the forest.

"We need to run. We can make it." I clamped my hand around his wrist and pulled, but he wouldn't budge.

"Can't run. Never run." His words were nothing more than wisps of air as he was sucked further into the recesses of his mind.

Unsure what else to do, I reared back and slapped him. When his eyes came back around to mine, they held none of their usual warmth. He was a cold shell of the man I had begun to know.

"Come on, Knight. *Please!*" I urged him along as I continued down the path, waving my hand for him to follow, hoping he would give in to the need to catch up.

Ten, fifteen, twenty feet, but he never moved.

A twig snapped just out of sight, and I slid behind a nearby tree trunk, my pounding heart creating a stifling pressure in my head.

"Look what we have here," a garbled voice said.

Adrenaline coursed through my veins as I realized Knight had been right. There were Red Caps in the forest, drawn to us by the scent of my blood. I peeked around the tree to see three of them surround my incapacitated companion. Physically, he was fine. He had his magic and the use of his body, but his mind had betrayed him. The memories of his years of torture had swallowed him whole, casting him back to a time when he was powerless.

Rage vibrated through my body.

I removed my pack and pulled out the knife we had retrieved from the fallen lion. Without giving it a second thought, I stepped out from behind the tree.

"You need to step back. He's *mine*," I commanded with absolute authority.

In the laws of the Wilds, might was everything. I might not have had the use of my magic, but they didn't know that. I drew on every ounce of self-assurance and confidence I could manifest and let it ooze from my pores. It wasn't a guaranteed win, but it would plant a seed of doubt, and I was going to need all the help I could get.

Knight had dropped to his knees, eyes staring vacantly ahead as the small band of Red Caps circled him menacingly. If they were intimidated by my claims, they didn't show it.

"We found him first," the leader growled back at me, angling himself possessively in front of Knight.

They might have had numbers, but I had several inches on them and a lifetime of combat skills. Red Caps were known for their immense strength, but they were also small, unintelligent, and possessed little other magic outside of their ability to trace. They were each only eighty pounds at best, clad in filthy rags with crusty blood-soaked caps atop their overly large heads.

As I approached them, I flipped the knife in my hand casually, going from handle to blade and back without glancing down. "You're truly ready to die for him?" I asked with feigned amusement.

The two underlings glanced at their leader who narrowed his eyes at me angrily.

"Fresh meat in these parts is hard to come by. You can't scare us away so easily."

Rallied by his braggadocios posturing, the two flunkies grinned and hissed in my direction.

"Have it your way," I replied nonchalantly before landing a wicked roundhouse kick to the leader's head. In one clean motion, I exited the kick with a thrust of my knife into one of the Red Cap's bellies. Careful to keep my weapon gripped in my hand, I yanked the blade free and stepped farther from Knight to draw the fight away.

The Red Caps followed my lead, stalking toward me on three sides. "You may be able to fight, but there are three of us, little girl," the leader hissed around his jagged teeth.

We were in front of Knight, but his unseeing eyes stared through us. I, on the other hand, was well aware of his presence and the crucial importance he not fall into the hands of Red Caps again.

I would kill him myself before it came to that.

In the blink of an eye, the melee began. All three launched their attacks simultaneously, and while I could handle two, three was a stretch. Fortunately, the one I had already stabbed in the gut had been substantially weakened. Spindly fingers clawed at my arms as I kicked and swiped with the knife. One of their fists collided with my head and sent me reeling against a tree.

Black dots danced around the edge of my vision as I struggled to stand. I exaggerated my staggering, drawing closer to one of the creatures. As intended, he dropped his guard enough that I was able to slash out with lightning speed, slicing the knife across his throat.

His hands flew up protectively to his neck, but it would do him no good. Blood gushed and spurted through his fingers as he fell to the ground. An enraged yell pulled my attention away just as the other lackey rammed his head into my gut, sending us both careening to the ground in a heap.

Until that point, I had attempted to keep my cries muted, hoping to maintain my illusion of superiority. However, his blow landed on the exact spot I had been injured by the branch and ignited a searing pain in my belly that I couldn't ignore. I let out a mournful wail as the Red Cap landed on top of me.

It was the one I had stabbed in the gut. He lifted up, straddling my torso, and plowed his fist into my cheek. I lifted my hands feebly in an attempt to protect myself, but it was no use against his unnatural strength. I had lost the knife when he had taken me to the ground and was helpless beneath him.

"You killed my brother, and now we will eat you *and* your friend." He lifted his hand again.

Unadulterated fear fluttered in my chest.

All I could think was that I had been so close to the cauldron. So close, and now I was yet again facing my own death.

His fist came flying at me only to slam prematurely against an invisible barrier. He studied me in confusion, and I looked back at him, equally baffled. As one, we both swiveled our heads down the path to where Knight now stood, back on his feet, eyes glowing a fierce orange I hadn't witnessed before. They'd been golden, liquid honey, and even amber, but never the deep orange of pure flame.

His hand was held out, casting a shield to protect me. In a flash, his other hand burst forward to project a ball of flame into the Red Cap above me. Unlike the flames I had seen him create before, this one did not disperse upon impact. As soon as the creature was clear from my body, the flames hungrily consumed him.

The creature screamed in torturous pain, writhing on the ground as his flesh melted from his bones.

I considered telling Knight to stop, but decided it was his right to exact revenge. These may not have been the same individuals who had hurt him before, but they had the same makeup, the same mindset. They would have eaten us alive if given the opportunity. Perhaps standing up to the ghosts from his past was exactly what Knight needed. Who was I to deny him that?

The leader of the small band of miscreants began to slink backward into the trees.

One after another, small bits of flame leaped from the burning corpse of his brethren and rushed toward the fleeing man. Dozens of tiny dancing flames surrounded him, halting his progress. When he lifted his leg to try to step over them, the flames flared to life, caging him in place.

Knight prowled closer, glaring ruthlessly at his captive.

"Please, let me go. I'll leave immediately, I swear it."

The Red Cap's begging fell on deaf ears. Knight turned

his eyes toward me, and I could feel the cool caress of his gaze as it touched my swollen cheek and each of the numerous cuts and bruises that now marred my exposed skin.

Judge, jury, and executioner.

He commanded the flames to engulf the man's body.

Watching the first man burn had been manageable, but I wasn't up for a second. I turned my head away and took a deep breath to calm my heaving stomach. Averting my eyes didn't stop me from hearing the excruciating cries and crackling flames as the Red Cap burned alive.

I only opened my eyes after Knight dropped to his knees on the ground next to me. His eyes still glowed but had returned to a more normal shade of amber. In their depths, I witnessed an expanse of emotions so vast, it wiped away all thoughts of the burning creature.

"I abandoned you. I'm so fucking sorry." He choked on the words, and his turmoil drew tears to my eyes.

I shook my head and began to argue there was nothing to be ashamed about, but he wouldn't let me, holding up his hand to silence me.

"You had every right to leave me and save yourself. In fact, when I was stuck there inside my head, I begged and pleaded for you to run. What you did for me ... I'll never forget." He held my eyes, his brimming with fierce devotion.

"Don't look at me like that." I couldn't remember ever being on the receiving end of such a look, except for perhaps from my mother. "I may not be all the things people say, but I'm also no saint. Don't put me up on a pedestal like one."

"I'm not going to argue over this," he cut in. "What you did was a pure, selfless act. It was my life you saved, and I can choose to honor that if I want."

I lifted a brow, attempting to lighten the mood. "Please don't tell me you owe me some kind of life debt and will follow me around until you repay it."

My effort at levity was wasted. The intensity in Knight's gaze never wavered.

"I'm not looking to become your bodyguard, but I need you to understand this changes things. I can't see you the same way I did when we started this journey, and I hope you don't see me the same. You may be trying to bring back your love from so many years ago, but that doesn't change the fact there's more here between us than prisoner and guard, and we both know it."

The sincerity in his words made my heart swell and break at the same time. What exactly was he saying? Did he have some grand delusion of us falling for one another? We hardly knew each other, not to mention his friends wanted me dead. Surely, he didn't believe there was a chance for something between us.

"I can't—"

He held his fingers to my lips, barring my words. "Just think about it. That's all I'm asking."

I was too stunned and exhausted to argue. I acquiesced with a nod, and he helped me to my feet, tearing off the bottom section of his shirt and wrapping my bloody arm with the fabric.

"I wish I could do something to heal your bruises." His fingers glided down my temple just outside the swelling around one eye. "As soon as we reach the castle, I'll ask for help removing the cuffs."

"*No!*" The word rushed from my lips without thought. "I mean, that's very generous of you, and I appreciate your trust, but there's little point once we reach the castle—magic won't help me there. Let's just get the cauldron, then we can deal with my cuffs."

He studied me beneath a furrowed brow, frustrated I would resist his offer.

"Please don't argue. Just help me get my jacket on." My eyes pleaded with him until he begrudgingly conceded.

An hour later, we cleared the trees and entered the castle grounds under the waning afternoon sun. There were no gardens or signs of habitation aside from the fact the grasses were kept well-manicured. Excitement and trepidation tied my stomach into angry knots as we neared the castle portcullis. Although we had not seen a single guard, the gate began to retract up into the castle wall, permitting us entrance. We proceeded cautiously through a tunnel and into the main courtyard where a man stood waiting for us.

He was younger-looking than I remembered—most likely the eyes of a child warping my perceptions at the time. He had sandy-colored hair that fell in waves and wore archaic leather armor fitted to his strong frame.

"The Fisher King," Knight gasped.

"It's the leg, isn't it—it always gives me away," the man teased dryly, giving me a wink. His right leg was missing below the knee, a wooden peg taking its place.

I laughed and ran to him, throwing myself into his arms.

"Easy, love. You're a bit bigger than the last time you came," he laughed out jovially.

I grinned at him, then glanced back at Knight to make introductions. My poor companion wore a flabbergasted expression that made me giggle.

"Knight, I'd like to introduce you to Bran, my father."

"You're *what*? How?" he stuttered, eyes dancing between us.

"Well, you see, young man. When a man and a woman come together..."

I burst out laughing. "Father, please. Don't tease him, he's been through enough today."

"I get so few guests—allow me some fun, daughter."

Knight crossed his arms over his broad chest and glared at me expectantly, still waiting for his explanation.

"My mother was the original Lady of the Lake. She met Bran before he became the Fisher King, which is a long story in itself. When I was just a baby, Bran was tasked with becoming the cauldron's warden, which meant he had to live here as its protector. My mother considered moving to the island so that I could be near my father, but there are no lakes or bodies of fresh water nearby. As a Water Nymph, living near fresh water was a necessary part of life. There was nothing she could do. When I was a young girl, she brought me once for a visit to meet my father, but I haven't been back since."

Bran placed his arm around my shoulder affection-ately. "It has indeed been too long. But now that I have you here, we can get reacquainted. You can start by telling me why you look like you've been beaten to a pulp."

"A bit of a mishap with some Red Caps in the woods just before we arrived. I should have known the wall around Corbenic was there for a reason. Nothing to worry about, I'll heal soon enough." I tugged at my jacket sleeves, ensuring they covered my cuffs.

"Ah, yes, devilish little creatures. I'm terribly sorry you had a run-in with them. Join me in the kitchen—I'll get us some refreshments. I want to hear all about your mother and what brings you here for this unexpected visit."

I had been so caught up in my desire for the cauldron, I hadn't considered having to tell Bran about my mother. I glanced back at Knight, surprised to find myself seeking him out for reassurance. Knowing I had him at my side bolstered me in a way I hadn't anticipated.

Bran had a kitchen hand prepare an early supper as I told him about my life growing up and the unfortunate circumstances of my mother's illness. As expected, he was visibly shaken to hear she'd suffered such a terrible fate.

"And is that why you came here—to bring me this news of Viviene?"

"Not exactly." I glanced at Knight warily. "We're here for the cauldron."

"I see." Bran lifted his chin sagely. "And you understand you must pass the test just as anyone else would, regardless of our relation?"

"Of course," I assured him.

"I have no doubt you'll do just fine. I'm impressed you made it this far—the both of you, no less!"

"Actually," Knight cut in sheepishly. "If it weren't for Morgan, I'd still be back dancing at Magda's house."

Bran burst into a fit of laughter. "Ah, the gatekeeper. She's a wily one, is she not?"

I narrowed my eyes at Knight. "She seems to have a soft spot for flagrantly flirtatious men."

More laughter from Bran. "Well, whatever the reason, I'm glad you've had company on the journey. I know it's not an easy one. And on that note, I should probably show you to your rooms. Tomorrow, I will present you with the final challenge." He rose from the wooden bench, but I simply stared up at him in shock.

"Tomorrow? Why not now?"

"Why have tests at all? It is the way of the cauldron. Seekers must pass the night in the Castle of Sleepless Dreams before they can be presented with their final task," he explained.

I nodded reluctantly and followed my father to the guest quarters where he showed us to rooms across the hall from one another. Mine was a beautiful emerald green, containing a four-poster bed lined with rich velvet curtains. Both the bed curtains and the matching drapes, which hung over leaded glass windows, were pulled back with golden ropes. Tying the room together, a rich tapestry rug covered the cold stone floor.

I had just begun to explore my room more closely when the door opened, and Knight slipped in.

"Is everything all right?" I asked, suddenly concerned.

"I don't trust this place."

"You shouldn't. This castle is enchanted—don't trust what you see. We could have a long night ahead of us."

The corners of his mouth lifted lazily as he ambled toward me. "Is that right?"

"That's not what I meant, and you know it."

"It seems I know very little anymore. Were you planning to tell me your father was the Fisher King?" His voice rumbled in the quiet space as he backed me into the room.

I lifted my shoulders noncommittally. "It's not that I didn't tell you—it just never came up."

"I take it that's why you didn't want me to mention your cuffs."

I bit anxiously on my bottom lip. "My father is one of the few people not influenced by the rumors and whispers. I didn't want to have to tell him about the cuffs because then I'd have to tell him why they were in place."

The back of my legs hit the bed, and Knight pressed himself against me.

"Is there anything else that hasn't … come up?"

I could feel his hard length against my belly, and it made my breathing grow shallow as words evaporated from my mind. "Um … no. Nothing else … up. You should probably go back to your room—propriety and all. I'd hate for my father to get the wrong impression."

That was just about the lamest excuse ever.

My father was Fae, after all. There were no wrong impressions about sex in Fae society.

Knight flashed a wicked grin, no doubt enjoying his effect on me. "There's no way in hell I'm leaving here tonight. You said yourself this castle is enchanted. I'm not letting you out of my sight." He spun me around and slapped my ass. "Now get ready for bed."

I yipped at the sharp slap and glared back at him. "Would you stop doing that?" I hissed.

He launched himself backward onto the bed, arms crossed behind his head. "Never."

The image reminded me of the first night we had met when he was still a wolf and had usurped my bed. I had cursed, bribed, and pushed to get him off, but he never budged. In a matter of a week, he had done the same to my life as he'd done my bed—forced himself right into the middle and refused to leave.

Arguing would do no good, and more to the point, would have been counterproductive because there was no place else I'd prefer him to be than beside me on the eve of the most important day of my life.

CHAPTER
SIXTEEN

MORGAN

Haunting strains of music drew me from sleep. It was the lullaby my mother once sang to me as a child. Its sad melody called to my heart in a way I couldn't ignore. Just like a particular smell could trigger memories more than a picture, the sound of my mother's song elicited a startlingly clear image of her in my mind as she sang in her garden.

I rose soundlessly from the bed and followed the unforgettable tune. When I arrived at the curving staircase that wound down to the first level, I stepped onto the first step but found the stairs were an illusion—my foot met with smooth stone colored to look like stairs. I slipped onto my backside on the steep, flat incline. Squealing in surprise, I flew down the slick surface. Instead of landing on the first floor, however, I was deposited into deep water, plunging beneath the surface.

I pushed back up to the open air and coughed out a sputtering breath. The fall itself had been disorienting, but when I was met with the midday sun as I floated in the middle of a large pond, I felt totally beside myself. What had happened? Had it not been the middle of the night when I had woken? Where had the pond come from?

I hurried to the water's edge and pulled myself up on the grassy bank. The rear of the castle stood not far away, but I couldn't see any doors to return inside.

High up in one of the windows stood my father. I waved my arms frantically, and though he appeared to look right at me, he made no move to acknowledge my presence. My arms drifted down to my sides in bewilderment. What the hell was happening?

I knew the castle was enchanted, but I'd never considered what that meant. Were its effects all inside the visitor's head, or was it all real? It sure felt real. If that was the case, could a person disappear forever inside this shifting dimension of alternate reality? Would I be the only one at risk, or was Knight trapped in a maze of his own?

KNIGHT

As soon as I closed my eyes to sleep, I found myself back in the forest I knew well. I pressed forward through the thick foliage, an unshakable drive pushing me to know what was on the other side of the dense vegetation. Despite the familiarity of the dream and my staunch certainty that nothing good would come from proceeding, I continued to push forward.

In an odd way, it was a relief when I came to the beautiful red flowers. They were there, just as they should be—deep crimson petals inviting nature to partake in its sweet nectar. The moment I stopped to admire their perfect design, the vines began to advance. Like a whip cast around a tree branch, the vining tendrils clasped around my ankles.

I reassured myself it was only a dream.

Even when the vine snaked itself around my neck, I didn't panic. I knew I would wake alive and well. As ardently as I tried to convince my body there was no danger, however, the perceived tightening around my throat felt impossibly real. I gasped for air and began to pull against my restraints.

The vine squeezed tighter.

Unable to shake the sensation, my body exploded into full-blown panic. I thrashed and flailed, my survival instincts kicking in with a vengeance.

I flung open my eyes to find I was lying on the castle bed. Just as I had expected, it had been a dream; but when I made to inhale much-needed oxygen into my burning lungs, nothing happened. The crippling grip of the vines still circled my throat.

Trying to free myself, I yanked my arms toward my neck, only to find they too were restrained. This time, it wasn't the vines from the dream but the golden curtain ties that had wrapped themselves around me.

I pulled against their hold, and in a moment of clarity, I remembered Morgan had stashed her knife beneath her pillow. Reaching my hand as far as it would go, I dragged the blade close enough to grasp then sliced at the ropes. Once my hand was free, I made quick work of the other golden restraints. When they were severed, each fell limp as if they had been ordinary rope, but that was far from the case.

The curtain ties had tried to squeeze the life from me.

As I gulped in large breaths of air, it occurred to me that Morgan was no longer in the room. I leaped from the bed and frantically began to search for her. With no sign of her in the room, I checked my room to find it similarly vacant.

There was a chance she had gone for a drink or some other ordinary errand, but my instincts told me her absence was more troublesome. She had mentioned the castle capable of illusion, but those ropes had been a hell of a lot more than illusion. If the bedding had attacked me, what danger might she have encountered?

I hurried into the hall toward the main stairwell, racing past door after door. After running longer than should have been necessary, I realized I could see no ending to the hall. When the Fisher King had shown us to our rooms, we had only gone some twenty feet from the stairs to the bedroom doors.

My steps slowed, and I examined the hallway intently. Each door was closed as far as the eye could see. Altering my tactics, I opened the door closest to me. I was stunned to see the sun shining through the window. I felt an unshakable certainty that it had been deep into the night when I'd woken.

What the hell is going on?

I stepped toward the window for a closer look and spotted Morgan outside by a small lake. I slammed my palms on the glass, hoping to draw her attention, but she wasn't looking direction. When that didn't work, I desperately tried to open the window, but it was hopelessly stuck shut.

Running from the room, I bolted down the hall, intent on finding a way down to Morgan. However, each stairwell I came upon only led up.

Morgan

WANTING to get back inside the castle, I hurried toward the building with the intent of walking around to the front, where the gate was located. As I neared the stone structure, the world seemed to tilt on its axis until the wall itself became the ground. Curious, I lifted my foot from the grass and stepped onto the castle wall.

My head spun fiercely as my mind battled to reconcile what was happening.

I'm walking on the wall! This is utter madness.

Step by step, I moved cautiously across the stone toward the window where my father had been standing, only to find it empty. I knocked on the glass without any response. In hopes that he might still be nearby, I stepped to the next window over. When I peered inside, Knight was there in an elegant bedroom.

I banged on the glass as I had done before, but he never flinched. I couldn't imagine how he hadn't heard me, yet he walked from the room without a glance in my direction.

Irritation etched away at my composure.

What's the purpose of this? What does the damn castle want from me?

The challenge of whit wasn't until morning, so what was the point of this exercise in madness? A frustrated scream clawed at my throat, begging for release, but I kept my lips sealed. I was so close to gaining access to the cauldron. Giving into weakness now wasn't an option.

Knight

REALIZING the never-ending hallway wasn't going to produce a set of stairs to the first level, I again turned to the only avenue remaining—the endless stream of closed doors.

I opened the next one I came upon to find yet another bedroom, this one decidedly more grandiose than the others. I scanned the furnishings only briefly before I caught sight of Morgan out the window somehow standing on the outer wall of the castle.

She peered inside the room as if looking down inside a hole in the ground.

For a moment, I stood stunned.

When she started to walk away, I rushed to the window and slammed my hands against the glass, but she didn't hear me.

There's no way she can't hear all the noise I'm making.

Fed up with whatever joke was being played, I stormed to the vanity and lifted its ornate bench overhead. Returning to the window, I launched the bench at the leaded glass, which shattered into thousands of tiny pieces.

Along with the glass, the image of a sunny afternoon disintegrated. Instead, the window now opened to the pitch black of a moonless night. Had both sightings of Morgan been an illusion? Was my running around searching for her just making matters worse? Could I even find her room again if I tried?

Morgan

AFTER FAILING to get Knight's attention, I wandered farther upward toward the roof of the castle. Just as the ground had tilted for me to walk onto the wall, it righted itself as I approached the roof, allowing me to transition back to a normal gravitational pull.

From up high, I admired the vast forest and could see the town of Corbenic in the distance. As I gazed out at the horizon, daylight faded to darkness at an unnatural rate, and the sun morphed into a brilliant full moon.

I had never seen anything like it.

My mind bent and stretched to adapt to the parameters of the reality I was experiencing. How was I supposed to know where to look or what to do in a world with unknown rules?

Frustration and a tinge of fear sped my heart rate to a

fiery pace. My hands tingled with sweat. I was on the verge of a full-on panic attack when I spotted a metal wind vane in the shape of a raven. The body was black velvet, the beak a brilliant gold, shimmering beneath the glowing moon.

Something about the artistic metal carving called to me, just as the strains of music had when I'd first woken. I couldn't deny its mesmerizing pull.

Without realizing I had moved, I suddenly stood just inches away.

Hesitantly, my hand reached out and touched the spellbinding bird.

Knight

I grew more agitated by the second. If I wasn't supposed to run and couldn't find my way back to where I had been, what was I supposed to do?

I had a brief glimmer of hope when I realized I hadn't tried my magic to help me, but that was quickly dashed. Whatever enchantment I had fallen victim to kept my powers inactive. I tried to trace myself somewhere, anywhere, but not even the spell on my chest, given to me by Merlin, was working.

My eyes danced around the room, searching aimlessly for an answer when they fell upon a small figurine of a black raven with a golden beak perched on a branch. A calm clarity fell over me as I approached the statuette. Inexplicably drawn to it, I reached out my hand, and the second my skin connected to the raven, a jolt of power raced from my fingertips through every cell of my body.

I barely had time to process the shock when suddenly Morgan was there before me, her hand in mine. Her astonishment mirrored mine as we stared at one another, bewildered, but only for a second. Morgan launched herself against me, wrapping her arms around my neck as if she were afraid I might disappear.

Immense relief at having her near washed over me, and I held her tightly against me. When she pulled her head back, arms still snug around my neck, she peered anxiously back and forth between my eyes.

"It's really you, isn't it? This isn't just another illusion?"

I smiled at her, but on the inside, I crowed proudly that she was so genuinely relieved to see me.

"You tell me." I sucked her bottom lip between my teeth and nibbled on the soft flesh.

She responded without hesitation, wrapping her legs around my waist, kissing me with the desperation of a woman starved.

"I was so worried ... I would never reach you," she shared between breathless kisses.

"I know exactly what you mean. Now that I have you, I'm not letting go."

We were back in her original bedroom, and a glance at the golden ropes still tied neatly around the bed curtains made me wonder if we had been there the entire time.

Damn castle had been in our heads, taking us on a demented joyride.

Shoving the thought aside, I wrenched the clothes

from our bodies and carried Morgan to the bed, lowering her down to the pillows.

I was done waiting.

"Morgan, I need to be inside you." My words were guttural. Commanding. I was no longer capable of civility. "I don't give a fuck what you've done or haven't done in the past. I don't care about your reputation or my lack of history. The only thing that matters is that I want you. Each time you're in danger, it makes me insane with rage. When those Red Caps attacked you, I was ready to burn the whole damn island to the ground. You may be here for another man, but I'm here for you. Fuck the cauldron and fuck my memories—all I want is to call you mine."

My eyes burned brightly as I presented what needed to be said. She could easily walk all over my flowery words, but she was too important to let slip away. I was man enough to express my feelings—my pride was an easy thing to risk if it meant claiming what was mine.

CHAPTER
SEVENTEEN

MORGAN

He didn't know what he was saying, but I wanted the words to be true—wanted so desperately that I couldn't contradict them. It was selfish and brash, but at that moment, that was who I was. I needed that one window of time to be solely about want and pleasure—no thought to consequences or reasons, no worries about plans or implications.

Just Knight and me.

His hard body rested over mine, his eyes searching my face for a response to his declaration. I sucked in a fortifying breath, then turned my head to the side, presenting the delicate length of my neck.

A rattling growl rumbled from his chest as he flipped me onto my stomach and lay fully over my body. Knight gently pulled my hair away from my face before his breath ghosted over the sensitive skin on my neck. His nose traced a slow line up toward my hair before his lips retraced his path back down, sending a cascade of goose bumps down my arms and legs.

"Tell me you want this," he whispered next to my ear.

"*Yes.*" My voice cracked as I said the word, and I hoped he would see it as a product of need and anticipation. The truth was, my niggling conscience was rising to the surface.

Knight leaned around to meet my eyes. "If I do this, there's no going back. Tell me you understand."

I admired his sentiment, but I knew better.

Nothing was forever.

"I understand your meaning, but life is dynamic. There may be no going back, but there is always change. You want me to be the hero—the misunderstood girl who's been painted the villain. That's not the case. When you understand fully, things will change. They always do. I'm willing to give myself to you with the understanding nothing is permanent. If you hear my meaning and want me regardless, I'm yours."

There. I had done what I could to ease my conscience. Let no one say I tricked him into my bed. I may not have told him everything, but I had given him enough to know there was more to my story.

His eyes blazed, but instead of the wariness I had expected, there was only triumph in his golden gaze.

Knight snaked his hand under my hips and yanked my backside in the air. His throbbing slid along my folds for only a moment before he bit down on the base of my neck and thrust himself inside me.

Both intrusions walked the line between pleasure and pain.

I cried out from the overwhelming intensity. I had no doubt he'd broken the skin on my neck, and it thrilled me. I'd had men bite me before, but never like that—never with such possession.

Knight began to move inside me but didn't release his grip on my neck until a long moan of pleasure was drawn from my lips. Only then did he lick at the wound to soothe the ache. His enormous body curved around mine, arms wrapped beneath me, holding me to him tightly. As he filled me, surrounded me, claimed me, I realized I wasn't the only one who was more than they seemed.

This man was still part wolf, and it only stoked my lust further.

Let him be wild and free, unconstrained by the bindings of society. In that way, we were more alike than I had known.

Deep inside, a small voice wondered if perhaps he did see me—all of me.

Perhaps he did see what was underneath, and he wanted me anyway.

Dashing away the foolishly hopeful thoughts, I pressed my ass up and languished in his punishing thrusts. A sheen of sweat coated my body, and I lost all track of time and meaning.

Knight flipped me back around so I could see his glorious chest flexing and straining as he hovered over me. He stayed upright, holding my legs far apart as he focused all his attention on where we were joined. Languidly, he rolled his hips, pressing inside me before gliding back out.

"I could never tire of watching my cock fill you, those pretty pink lips open and begging for more."

I whimpered with need. He was right. I needed more—harder, faster. The easy pace was sensual, but I needed the bruising assault of his claiming.

"I told you what you'd have to do, Morgan. If you want my cock, you need to beg for it." His voice was a gruff rasp, the strain of holding back just as punishing for him as it was for me.

I might have been proud, but in this one case, I was not above begging. I needed his cock like I needed to breathe.

"*Please*, Knight, fuck me. Fuck me hard."

His eyes lit with satisfaction. He lowered himself and sucked my breast into his mouth. Clamping down his teeth, he didn't break the skin, but he no doubt left a mark on the delicate surface.

Grunting with pleasure, Knight resumed his relentless siege on my body. His punishing thrusts created the perfect pressure inside me while his body angle built a delicious friction against my clit. Together, the two sensations were cataclysmic.

"That's it, come for me," he rumbled in my ear, the vibration of his voice only adding to the coursing pleasure.

Arching my back in a tight contraction, I felt my body ignite with pure energy. I cried out and sank my nails into his back, seeking purchase as my body attempted to drift away on a tidal wave of bliss.

Knight roared his release, pounding relentlessly into my battered body until his thrusts slowed, and his muscles began to relax. He didn't roll off me. Instead, he rested the bulk of his weight on my side and kept the rest of his body draped over me. His hand ran lightly over my skin, paying special attention to the marks on my breast and neck as we both recovered.

I'd had plenty of sex in my life—sometimes for the release, sometimes to feed my magic. What I had just shared with Knight was different. Terrifying.

Instead of the goodbye I had envisioned in my head, it felt like a beginning, the creation of something new. With one look in his eyes, it was clear he believed this thing between us was unbreakable.

I shuddered to think how wrong he was.

He gazed down at me with raw hunger. Would his look turn to disgust when he learned why I wanted the cauldron? I almost wanted to tell him right then and there, to be done with the uncertainty, but I couldn't.

He would try to stop me, and I couldn't take that chance.

Instead, I took his hardening length in my hand and stroked firmly, eliciting a growl from him.

"Again," I whispered.

There was no need to ask twice—he was on me in an instant.

We spent the hours leading to dawn exploring and sating one another. It would likely be the last chance I had for something so pure and uninhibited, so I reveled in every touch and whispered caress.

When the sun finally rose, we made our way downstairs, the castle having returned to its natural state. My father waited for us in the great hall, a roaring fire burning in the hearth.

"I'm relieved to see you." His features were twisted in worry as if he'd been up all night.

"The castle isn't exactly easy on its visitors, is it?" I noted wryly.

"There have been some who never returned after their night in the castle." He gave a tight smile. "Nothing about this place is easy." A shadow fell over his features as he gazed at me with something akin to regret.

"Is there any way you might be released from your service here, aside from dying?"

"Perhaps. You never know what each day might bring."

"That's the truth," Knight huffed.

"On that note," my father continued, brightening his tone. "Am I correct in assuming you're ready to finish your quest for the cauldron?"

"Yes, thank you."

"I must remind you that Knight cannot help with the final challenge. I will give you a riddle, and you will have one guess to answer correctly. Do you understand?"

I nodded as my fingers fidgeted anxiously.

Before my father could begin, Knight came to stand before me, eyes boring into mine. "I know I can't help, but we do this together. No matter what happens, I'm here beside you."

Unable to speak, I nodded and squeezed back the tears that filled my eyes.

He placed a kiss on my forehead, then stepped aside to allow me to fulfill my lifelong mission.

My father cleared his throat, then voiced my final challenge.

"*Alive as you but without breath, as cold in my life as in my death, never a thirst though I always drink, dressed in mail but never a clink.*" The words echoed off the cavernous walls, staccato and abstract as my mind struggled to give them meaning.

I chided myself to calm down, taking several deep breaths to steady my heart rate.

Think about the words, one line at a time.

Alive but no breath—something that doesn't breathe? Something cold but alive. Not thirsty but always drinks. A flower? No breathing but they require air—alive but cold and drinks. Did a flower get thirsty? Possibly. And what about the mail? Armor? Plants didn't have armor.

Think, think, think, Morgan.

It's a riddle, it won't be obvious. You must be clever.

The armor seemed to be the key. Dragons, insects, armadillos, all types of sea creatures ... what else had armor? Did I need to think more abstractly? No, the thing was alive, not an abstract concept. My eyes danced around the room, unseeing until they landed on my father. Standing stately beside the fire, he clasped his hands behind his back, clad in his leather armor.

Then it hit me. The answer.

He had warned me there would be no free passes as his daughter, but he'd picked a riddle I was bound to guess.

My father, the Fisher King.

I turned hopeful eyes on him with a giddy smile I couldn't contain. "Fish. The answer is a fish."

He smiled broadly and opened his arms for an embrace. I flung myself at him, a sob tearing from my throat. I could hardly grasp the magnitude of what I'd done. Centuries of work, and it was at an end—I had earned the cauldron.

My father lowered me to the ground, and when I stepped back, the cauldron itself appeared in his hands. It was larger than a chalice but not so large as a cooking pot. The dark metal was engraved with intricate Celtic swirls that seemed to move as they reflected the light from the fire. He extended the cauldron toward me, but I stepped back, looking over my shoulder at Knight.

"Am I allowed to use it on more than one person?" I asked nervously, realizing I hadn't considered if there were restrictions to its use.

"Of course, there are no limits to how many may drink from the cauldron," replied my father.

Knight stepped forward and extended his hands with a noticeable tremor. I encouraged him with a nod, and he brought the cauldron to his lips. After two gulps, he brought it back down, his eyes closed on a shaky breath.

I sucked in a lungful of air, realizing I had been holding my breath in anticipation. "Did it work?"

When his eyes opened, there was a darkness to them that had not been there before. Not just darkness but hatred.

I knew the look well. It was one I had seen in the mirror my entire adult life.

"Yes," he replied, his voice devoid of emotion. His head

slowly swiveled toward me, drowning me with his violent stare.

What had he remembered to bring on a look of such vengeful wrath? Had I somehow played a role in his transformation and torture? I didn't see how I could have been involved, but I racked my brain for details I might have forgotten.

"It was Guin," he finally explained in a hollow voice, a stark contrast to the emotions raging behind his eyes. "I remember every vivid detail like it was yesterday. We were in her throne room as she sat upon her throne of vines, red hair cascading down in waves over a vibrant red gown. Her usual throngs of courtiers were absent, the halls of the palace startlingly silent. Durin stood to one side of her, and on the other was Mordred."

My initial self-righteous response that it was Guin at fault was washed away with confusion. "What? Mordred was an enemy to the Court—Arthur was fatally wounded killing Mordred. Why would he have been at Guin's side?

"This was after Arthur's death. It appeared Mordred was being kept alive with the use of blood magic. He was bound to her, though his mind was warped and grotesque. She kept him caged, only allowing him out to perform her darkest deeds. He was the one who turned me into the wolf. He also began my torture, but Alberich delivered me to the Red Caps at Guin's command."

So much information to process. It was overwhelming.

I'd known Guin was evil for a long time, although I had not suspected her depravity had gone so far as to keep her own blood mage as a pet. If Mordred was still alive, killing Guin might be harder than I had planned.

Knight was visibly shaken.

We both knew the story behind his torture would not be pleasant, but it had affected him far more fundamentally than we had anticipated. Similarly, I was surprised to feel my own measure of guilt. The woman I had been hunting had been the source of his pain. Had I stopped her long ago when I'd first tried to kill her, perhaps his trauma could have been prevented.

Nothing I could say would fix what had been done or ease the pain of his discovery. Opting to give him time to process, I returned my attention to my father.

"I need the cauldron for one last purpose, but the person who needs it could not make the journey."

The Fisher King's forehead wrinkled, and he tilted his head with confusion. "The cauldron cannot leave this castle."

"But it must." My pulse began to pound in my throat, panic coursing like an electric surge to all my nerve endings. "I've earned the cauldron, and there's someone who needs it desperately. Please, Father, there must be a way." The last words broke on a ragged sob as a wall of tears blurred my vision.

How could this be? How could I have gotten to this point and never found a word, in all my studies, limiting the cauldron to the walls of the castle? It was hidden there, yes, but that didn't mean it couldn't be removed. Of course, there hadn't been a *Cauldron for Dummies* book. I'd had to gather what limited knowledge there was through stories and ancient texts.

"Is this about your mother?" asked my father.

"No." I shook my head, then paused. "But yes. I'd love to help her as well, but there's someone else."

"Is this about him?" Knight's hard voice bit out behind me. "About Lancelot?"

"*No!* This has nothing to do with him." I turned back to my father. "Please, is there anything you can do? I've spent centuries trying to get here. Don't send me away empty-handed." Tears streamed down my cheeks, and my legs shook with the strain of keeping me upright.

He thought for a moment, choosing his words carefully. "I am the guardian of the cauldron, protecting it here until my death." He gave me a pointed look as I choked on a sob. "However, there is one possibility I might offer. You may take a single vial of the elixir from within the cauldron, but the cauldron itself cannot leave these walls. Bear in mind, there is no guarantee the elixir will work without the cauldron."

I buried my face in my hands and allowed the tears to flow, unsure if I was elated or devastated.

My father pulled me into his arms, and while I appreciated his comfort, a part of me desperately wished it was Knight. He stood cold and distant, too absorbed in his burdens to help me shoulder mine.

Once I had regained control of myself, my father provided me with a vial of elixir from the cauldron. I cursed my shaking hands as I took hold of the small glass bottle, terrified I would accidentally drop it. Unwilling to part with the lifesaving elixir, I placed the vial inside my bra, close to my heart.

"*Wave Sweeper* should be waiting to take you wherever you need to go," explained my father. "I truly hope this works for you. I want nothing but happiness for you, daughter. Your visit has been an unexpected delight." He dropped his chin, becoming somber. "I am sorry I wasn't able to be there for you … for your mother."

As I glanced around awkwardly, uncomfortable with his apology, my eyes fell on a large painting over a wooden buffet. The primary subject was a man resembling my father, standing with a raven on his shoulder. A raven with a beautiful golden beak.

"That's a beautiful painting," I said absently, wondering just how far my father had gone to help us.

Had he provided us with a means for escape from the castle's clutches?

My father followed my gaze. "Ah, yes. An old family heirloom." He dismissed the artwork as if it were inconsequential, but his eyes gleamed with mischief.

"Thank you, for everything." I wrapped my arms around him in a tight hug.

We said our goodbyes before Knight and I headed back into the forest on our journey home. As deeply affected as he'd been by his newly acquired memories, a part of me half expected him to transport himself away to deal with his demons.

I wouldn't have blamed him.

However, Knight was not the type to let his problems get in the way of his responsibilities. He may not have been his normal playful self, but he also didn't abandon me. We had started our journey together, and so it would end.

CHAPTER

EIGHTEEN

MORGAN

KNIGHT'S EYES BLAZED A VIBRANT ORANGE THE ENTIRE TRIP through the forest. Whether there were more Red Caps or other nasties about, I never knew because nothing dared to approach. We walked the entire distance uninterrupted and in complete silence.

The gate into Corbenic opened upon our approach. I had expected our walk through town to pass as uneventfully as our trip through the woods but was surprised when Knight pulled aside a guard as soon as we passed through the gate.

I yanked on Knight's arm before he could speak. "We aren't supposed to talk to them. Remember the troll's warning?"

"Fuck that. We have what we came for. Now, I'm getting those cuffs off your wrists." Dismissing me, he turned back to the guard. "Do you have a smith?" he asked in a commanding tone.

When the man nodded, Knight instructed him to lead the way.

Remove my cuffs? Knight was going to have my cuffs removed? No matter how I thought the words, they didn't seem to make sense. He had been so adamant the entire trip that it hadn't been an option—that I couldn't be trusted. We'd shared something special that morning, but he'd glared at me like he couldn't stand me ever since. He'd hardly spoken a word to me in hours. Now, he was going to free me? None of it made sense, but I wasn't going to argue.

We were directed to a building that stood off to itself, billowing steam wafting out of one window. The air in the single-room structure was sticky with an oppressive heat, and the man inside was coated with a sheen of sweat over a layer of dirty black smudges. Breathing in the stifling air was a chore—I couldn't imagine working in such conditions.

"Good day," offered Knight. "I need you to get the cuffs off her wrists."

I shook off my surprise and lifted my wrists to expose the cuffs. They weren't thick, just solid enough to require the use of a tool to remove them. In hardly any time at all, he had clipped through the iron and freed me.

My magic flared to life as it rushed from its prison deep within me. Though it was weak after not being fed, it still provided enough strength to make my skin buzz with power.

As I rubbed the raw area on my wrists, I offered Knight

a grateful smile. I debated hugging him, which had been my first instinct, but decided against it when I met his stoic features.

"Thank you," I whispered.

He merely nodded, lips set in a grim line. "We'd better get going."

We thanked the smith and continued through town toward the pier where *Wave Sweeper* still waited. What I would have given to have Merlin's ability to trace long distances. It was a skill he had never explained, and I never mastered on my own. Instead, we would have to take the long trip home the same as we had come.

We climbed aboard the small boat, and I wondered if it would have issues determining a direction. Knight and I had not discussed where we were headed. My desired destination was clear in my mind, but I had no clue where his thoughts would take him.

To my relief, *Wave Sweeper* came to life as soon as we were seated and carried us out to sea. We both reclined against opposites sides of the boat, legs extended next to one another. For hours we rode, each lost in our own thoughts.

When the sun fell toward the horizon, and the first stars twinkled in the sky, I broke our long silence. I hadn't planned to tell him my secrets while there was still a chance he could get in my way, especially considering how distant he'd been since recovering his memories—but none of that stopped me. Before I knew what I was doing, the story tumbled from my lips.

"This all began after the birth of my son." The salty sea breeze quickly swept away the words, but their meaning hung heavily between us. "He was tiny and perfect in every way. Those first few weeks of his life were the happiest I've ever known. But the joy was short-lived. Just weeks after he was born, he grew sick. It took me a while to figure out what was going on. As you know, Fae infants are dependent on their parents' magic for protection in the first weeks of life. Being immortal, infant death owed to loss of a parent is rarely a problem. When he continued to grow more and more sick, I realized something must have happened to his father. I was torn between tending to the sick infant and going in search of his father, but when it came down to it, I couldn't leave my baby alone. I watched helplessly day after day as he grew weaker. Before my son took his last breaths, I placed an enchantment over him. I entombed his tiny body, frozen in a magical spell where the effects of time couldn't touch him.

"After entrusting him to a close friend, I went in search of answers. I learned that Guin had killed his father. I was so enraged that I attacked her. I was still young, and my emotions made me sloppy. She overcame me with little effort and had the Erlking Alberich escort me to the Wilds to be exiled. Somehow, she erected wards around her lands specific to me alone, keeping me from re-entering. I couldn't get back to my child nor get to the cauldron to heal him. I've been searching for a way back to him ever since. Merlin had supported Guin in my banishment. Between that unfathomable betrayal and his staunch belief as a Seer that there is a natural order in life that should not be disrupted, it was clear he wouldn't help me. I considered telling him the truth about what had happened, but he would never have condoned my plan to bring back my son. He would see it as a violation of nature. But how could I not? My boy is everything to me. He's all I have left. Everything I've done has been for him—that and to bring down Guin."

Relieving myself of the burden of my story was a balm on my ragged soul. As much as I feared Knight's reaction to learning about my past, it was also an enormous relief to finally have it out there. Let him do with the information what he would. Another mother might understand the lengths to which I had gone through to get my child back, but many others would not. I couldn't force him to see from my perspective, nor would I apologize.

"You've been kept outside of Seelie Lands for so long. Do you have any idea if your son is still where you left him or if the spell has kept him safe?" Knight asked quietly.

He hadn't immediately cursed me and thrown me overboard, so I took that as a good sign. His words had been more clinical than anything, consistent with his demeanor all day.

I swallowed hard before my answer, the words no more than a whisper. "No. I don't."

I lifted my gaze to find his penetrating eyes locked on me.

Throughout the time we had spent together over the preceding days, Knight had been unerringly transparent. It hurt my heart to see him so guarded and withdrawn. His features were masked in impassivity, leaving me grasping at straws for clues as to his state of mind.

The emotions dredged up from my story and the tension with Knight began to overwhelm me. My chest constricted into an angry knot, and my eyes began to water.

"Come here," he said gruffly, lifting his hand out to draw me in.

As if I'd been anticipating his invitation, I jumped into action, scurrying from my side of the boat to his. Knight drew me into his side, holding me close with his arms wrapped tightly around me. He held me like that for the rest of the night, and neither of us said another word.

Midway through the next morning, we approached a familiar landscape. I knew instantly where *Wave Sweeper* had taken us. Unable to contain my excitement, I threw my arms around Knight.

"We're home! My house isn't far from here. I can't believe it. I can't believe I'm here." I had envisioned my small house, but that had been no guarantee we wouldn't be deposited back on the beach where Magda had left us or wherever Knight's thoughts had taken him.

My stomach was a roiling pit of nerves.

My father had sent us out with replenished supplies, but I hadn't been able to force down a bite of food. The moment we touched land, I hurried ashore and raced in the direction of home.

After just an hour's walk, we were there.

I burst through the trees into the clearing where my childhood cottage sat next to a small lake. Despite so many years of absence, I knew every inch of the property by heart. My mother's garden was overgrown, but other-wise, just as I had left it. The dark lake waters were serene and reflected sunlight onto the weathered cottage. Knight and any other visitor would likely see an uninhabitable heap, but to me, it was beautiful.

I ran toward the lake's edge, never slowing as my feet carried me into the cool water. When I stood waist deep, I lay my hands flat against the surface and mouthed the words of the summoning spell that would bring my child to me.

For long minutes I waited, each passing second speeding my heart rate to a frenzied pace. Again, I performed the spell, eyes flitting about the surface in growing panic.

Why isn't it working? He should have come to me already.

I lay my hands flat again, ready to say the damn spell as many times as it took when bubbles began to rise near the middle of the lake. A moment later, a figure emerged from the water.

"Odiane!" I cried in utter shock.

The female Selkie I had left as protector of my newborn son glided toward me in the water. In her arms was a tiny child, its fingers waving in the air.

"I had started to wonder if you were coming back at all. I was days from sending out a search party." She smiled broadly at me, but I only had eyes for the tiny bundle in her arms.

He was alive. Without the cauldron.

I was utterly dumbfounded and overwhelmed by emotion. My mouth hung gaping open, tears pooling in my unblinking eyes.

"I'm not sure what you did, but some days ago, he began to cry out of nowhere. I thought you told me he had passed. It had been so long since I'd even thought of him

—I had no idea what to do." As she approached, she gently transferred the baby into my shaking arms.

He was exactly as I remembered him, only alive and well.

"I don't understand. How did this happen?" I whispered in awe.

"What do you mean? I figured you were returning after undoing whatever spell had harmed him." My dear friend cocked her head in confusion.

"No," I shook my head. "I have the elixir here with me —I had planned to use it on him. I had no idea he had been revived on his own."

His tiny hand clasped around my finger, and a sob tore from my chest, unleashing an onslaught of tears. I hugged him close to my chest, swearing I would never let anything happen to him again.

My loss of control instigated his own newborn cries, and I quickly calmed my sniffles and walked from the water, rocking him and cooing softly. He quieted and peered at me through his warm brown, tear-filled eyes.

I felt like I could smile every day for the rest of my life.

"Knight, this is my son, Galath." My voice shook with a swell of immense love and relief.

His face morphed from impassivity to confusion and on to horror as he stared down at the baby.

Even if he hadn't been bothered by my intent to bring back my son, finding out I had a child might also push him away. However, I had not expected such extreme emotion. I pulled Galath close to my chest and stepped back from Knight.

"What the hell is wrong with you?" I demanded.

"He's got my eyes." He staggered back a step.

"What do you mean? His eyes are brown, not golden."

His gaze darted around in confusion before returning to me. "I thought when you said there was a child, you had moved on."

"Moved on? Moved on from what?"

"I didn't know how to tell you." He paused, his mouth opening and closing with uncertainty. "I remembered Guin turning me, but I also remembered the day we first met in the garden—the smell of the flowers and the way your long golden hair waved in the wind."

"What are you saying? We met in my bedroom when you were turned back into a man."

"No, that wasn't the first time." His wide eyes met mine. "It's me, Lance. I mean, I *was* Lancelot."

I stumbled back a step, hugging Galath securely to my chest.

"Why are you doing this?" I breathed.

"All the memories, they were too much to process at first. Then in the boat, when you said you had a child, I assumed you had found another man after I disappeared. I didn't know how to tell you. I remember, Morgan. I remember how we met and the depth of our love. I remember our time in Avalon, then the months we spent together at your cottage home. I recalled being sent away, but I had no idea about the child." Knight fell to his knees, his chest heaving with strangled breaths.

I stepped back farther, needing space from his outlandish claims. "How can you say that? Lancelot was killed. I know he was killed—not only did I perform spells to verify the fact, but that was the whole reason Galath became sick. Plus, you look nothing like him. How can you say such a thing?" I spat out my words, shocked and confused by his implications.

"I don't know how it's happened. Maybe your magic couldn't find me in wolf form. I had no magic, maybe I wasn't even Fae any longer, and that's why the child became ill. My hair was solid brown, and I had chestnut eyes, just like him." His voice cracked as he returned to his feet and pointed at my son. "His face is mine—I see it. I know my eyes have gone golden, and my hair has streaks of white, but it's *me* underneath. I am Lancelot, and he is my son."

I urged my breathing to calm so that I could think rationally. Knight's long hair and beard concealed most of his face. What was left, those golden eyes, had seemed so different from my Lancelot. But I supposed it was possible. Had Galath been revived when Knight was made Fae again? Had I inadvertently fallen in love with the same man twice?

To have my son back was a gift greater than I had dared to hope for. To be reunited with my lover as well? It was preposterous. I didn't know what to say or what to think. Each time I opened my mouth, nothing came out.

"It's me, Morgan. *Please*, believe me. I know all the rumors about you were lies. You never tricked me into your bed to lure me away from Guin. My time with her had been long over. Arthur had discovered that Guin intentionally prolonged The Great War; it was why he left the Court and formed the Hunt. She seduced me after Arthur commanded that none of the Huntsmen were to go near her. I was cast out of the Hunt because of her. I couldn't fathom why I'd ever broken Arthur's trust. I hated myself. As a way of atonement, I swore to stay close to her and learn her secrets. Arthur might not have wanted me close to him, but I could still feed him intelligence. When he died, I was enraged to learn Guin was at fault. The knowledge of what she did to Arthur was the real reason I was exiled."

My breaths became shallow pants as I struggled with disbelief.

He knew.

He knew our history. The things no one else knew, no one else would believe. The reasons Guin had to be stopped. He knew it all.

"Lance?" The word fell from my lips breathlessly as I dared to believe it might be true.

He stepped closer, stroking my hair as his eyes bore into me imploringly. "I haven't been that man for a very long time. I'm not sure I'll ever be him again—I'm certainly not ready to be called by that name—but in every other way, yes, it's me."

"Why didn't you tell me back at the castle? Why have you been looking at me like you can't stand me?"

"I just learned I'd been keeping the woman I loved imprisoned. Shamed her for her actions while I was the one who left her alone to be victimized by a vengeful queen. For years, I've been alive and well, couch surfing and eating my way across the world while you were fighting for your life. I've never hated myself more."

"You couldn't have known. Your amnesia wasn't your fault."

"Doesn't mean I'm not still furious with myself." He

slammed his fist against his chest. "If I had fought harder for my memories years ago, or if I'd been strong enough not to lose that part of myself."

"Knight, you survived two years with the Red Caps. How much stronger were you supposed to be?"

"Strong enough to be there for you." His perceptive eyes scoured my face, still searching for answers. "All these years, you've faced such insurmountable odds, yet you never gave up. You devoted your life to saving your son ... *our* son."

I nodded, unable to speak.

"I never imagined I would have a child. To discover I bore a son and he'd been in trouble all this time ... I owe you everything." He shook his head slowly, still processing his shock. "It just makes everything I've done that much worse."

"What you've done? I'll tell you what you've done. You were the first person to see past the rumors and truly see *me*. Not only have you saved my life on multiple occasions but you also gave me a reason to hope things could be different. Don't discount that because you're upset."

His jaw muscles twitched with tension as his gaze bore into mine. "You said you confronted Guin. Did you tell her there was a child? She would have known her actions against me would have condemned the child to death."

My response would provoke his wrath, but I could not lie to him. "Yes. I went to her twice. The first time while I was still pregnant when you had just been exiled to Earth. I begged her to allow you to live with me. She banished me to the Wilds. At that time, her wards weren't as strong, and I was able to sneak back onto Seelie Lands. I came back here to have Galath at home. When he grew sick, I knew something awful had happened. I confronted Guin, and she laughed when she told me you were dead."

Knight's body locked down stiffly, and his eyes lit with golden flames.

"This ends now. The bitch is dead."

CHAPTER

NINETEEN

MORGAN

"WE NEED TO DISCUSS OUR PLANS WITH MERLIN. I'M GOING TO bring him here. I'll be back in just a moment."

"Knight! *Wait*, you can't do that. He'll just put me back in his prison."

He placed his hands on my cheeks and stared confidently into my eyes. "No one is ever putting a hand on you again. Do you hear me?"

I bit down on my lip, unused to relying on anyone else for my safety. Knight was telling the truth. If at all possible, he would keep me safe. I doubted he could control Merlin, but if he believed Merlin wasn't a threat, I would try to trust him.

I gave a small nod.

He kissed my temple, then hesitantly placed a kiss on our son's head before disappearing from sight. I had little time to panic before Knight returned with Merlin at his side.

I tugged Galath close to my chest reflexively, fighting off a strong urge to run. When Merlin's eyes landed on the baby, they swirled with a storm of emotion. Normally, the Fae sorcerer was a lesson in impassivity, but seeing my son had triggered a well-spring of emotion.

"Morgan, what is the meaning of this?"

Together, Knight and I launched into the tale. By the time we finished, Merlin's expression had recovered its inscrutable mask.

"Your life has not been an easy one, and for that, I will be forever sorry. I had thought my sister to be my one great failing in life, though I am beginning to see my oversights were more extensive." His gaze drifted to Galath. "I have worked endlessly to right the wrongs tied to my name. I know I wasn't always the parent I should have been for you, and I am not sure how I could have failed you so drastically—to have been so wrong in certain beliefs—but you have proven to be a magnificent woman despite the adversity you've faced. I'm so proud of you, Morgan." Sadness tugged at the corners of his eyes, and his voice carried an unusual solemnity.

For years, I had hated him. Hated him for not supporting me. Hated him for not seeing me, for not seeing through the lies. But as I stood with my precious child in my arms, everything else suddenly became trivial in comparison.

Who was I to condemn him eternally for actions he believed were just? Had I not committed my fair share of atrocities in the name of good intent?

"Perhaps this might be a good time to start over," I offered hesitantly.

"I would like nothing more." He smiled, but his eyes clouded with an oppressive sadness. "Actually, there is one thing." He disappeared and, in an instant, was back, this time hand in hand with my mother.

Laying eyes on her for the first time since I was a child was surreal—both because it had been so long and because of the vacant look in her eyes. I had no idea my heart could be mended and shattered at the same time.

When Merlin had first captured me and deposited me in his wooded prison, I had just discovered my mother had not been killed centuries before as I'd been told. Merlin had tried to explain to me that he had kept her a secret because she had suffered irreparable damage, and he didn't know if she'd ever heal. I had scoffed at him, adding the lie to the list of reasons to hate him.

But seeing her now, I realized how wrong I'd been. She stared through me as though I didn't exist.

My mother was utterly broken.

Merlin had been trying to protect me. I had only been twelve when I learned she was dead. That had been hard enough, but if I'd had to suffer her loss on a daily basis, it would have been immeasurably harder. That was what it was to see her—to see her body but know the woman inside was gone. To have her and lose her over and over in an endless cycle of pain.

Unable to help myself, I tried to reach out to her. "Momma?" It was the hopefulness in my own voice that cut most deeply. How I desperately wanted her to see me. "Momma, this is my baby boy. This is Galath."

Nothing.

Merlin placed an arm around my mother's shoulders, his lips pulled down in the corners. "I'm sorry to have to hurt you by bringing her, but I've wanted to reunite you for so long. I never wanted to keep you apart, despite what you may have thought. In light of what I now know, I realize this reunion is long overdue."

I peered up at him with tear-filled eyes. "I understand. I never thought I would, but I think I do now."

"Morgan," Knight cut in from behind me. "You're forgetting something. The child ... Galath ... didn't need the elixir. You still have it to be used."

"How could I have forgotten!" I cried out, eyes bulging with realization. "There was just so much to absorb—I wasn't thinking." I juggled Galath ineptly, being centuries since I'd held a baby, as I tried to retrieve the vial from inside my shirt.

"Here, let me," offered Knight.

I slowed my movements but didn't offer up the child. "Are you sure?" If it had been a while since I'd held a baby, it had to have been eons for Knight. Not just that, but I was reticent to let Galath out of my arms. I trusted Knight, but I'd only just gotten my son back.

"Yes, Morgan, I'm sure," he said softly, the first hint of humor resurfacing in his eyes.

I finally acquiesced and handed over the baby, then located the small vial and turned to Merlin. "We don't know if this will work, but it was the best we could do. We made it to the cauldron, but the Fisher King couldn't allow us to take the cauldron with us. This is the cauldron's elixir."

Merlin took a shuddering breath, more affected than I had ever seen him. He took the vial from me with trembling hands and removed the stopper. His eyes fell closed on a silent plea as we all held our breath anxiously. Merlin lifted the vial to my mother's lips and poured its contents into her mouth.

She swallowed obediently, then pinched her eyes shut, her brow furrowed in pain. Merlin helped keep her upright when her legs began to give out and whispered soothing words near her ear.

I stepped closer to Knight for support, terrified to hope.

After endless seconds, she gulped in a tremendous lungful of air and flung open her eyes—vibrant blue eyes, just like mine. Vibrant blue and *alive*. Her arms circled her middle as her gaze danced about, disoriented.

"Morgan?" she asked in a hoarse voice wrought with confusion as she scanned me from head to toe.

For a record third time that day, I began to sob.

I hadn't cried since I was a child, but now, I couldn't seem to stop. I stepped forward, and my mother and I clung to one another in an embrace that filled the last of the empty holes in my heart.

This day had made every other day from the past century worth every minute—every struggle, every obstacle, every endless trial.

Worth it.

Eventually, my mother pulled back and searched my face. "Morgan, my baby girl. I'm so confused. You're a beautiful woman now. Where has the time gone?"

"Try not to worry. It's a long story, but we have plenty

of time to explain." I smiled reassuringly. "The first thing I want to share with you, though, is your grandson."

I lifted Galath from Knight's arms and brought him around to my mother. Her lips parted in surprise, and she reached out a trembling hand for Merlin's arm.

"I've never seen anything more perfect in my life," she rasped, love brimming in her eyes. She was the kindest, most peaceful soul I had ever known. The world was a better place with her in it.

Hand over her mouth to contain her happiness, my mother turned back to Merlin, then seemed to realize just who she'd been leaning on. Her hand lowered to reveal a brilliant smile spread across her lovely face.

"Merlin." She exhaled the word like a benediction, and he gazed down at her, equally enchanted.

Merlin traced the contours of her face with the delicate touch of a butterfly's wing. "My Viviene."

When he turned his turbulent gaze back to us, his arctic eyes were glassy with emotion. "You have accomplished what I could never have done alone, and because of that, we have both been reunited with our loved ones. Though that entailed more than even I could have foreseen." He peered down at the wriggling bundle in Knight's arms. "Now that things have been set right, I need time with Viviene, and you need a moment with Knight. Revel in that opportunity to reconnect. Life will not always be so simple." His stare grew weighty with the burden of knowledge only he possessed. Then he disappeared.

My mouth bobbed open and shut like a fish stranded on shore. "What? He took her so soon?" *What the hell was wrong with him?* "What about Guin? What about the blood mage? Merlin, you bastard, get back here!" I screamed out to an empty sky.

Silence followed.

"He knew," Knight mused softly.

"He knew what?"

"He knew all of it. He knew who I was and that together, we could retrieve the elixir to save your mother. When I first turned back, I went to him to ask how I could get my memories back. He knew the cauldron was the only way Viviene could be healed and told me he had tried to acquire it but couldn't."

"Are you suggesting this was all a part of his plan?" My face contorted with confusion.

"I think it may have been."

"And just how far back does this plan go?"

"I doubt we'll ever know."

The implications hung heavily between us until Galath's small flailing hand caught our attention.

"I guess that means he got what he wanted, and the rest is up to us." I gathered my resolve, drawing on my years of practiced determination. "I'd rather not take on Guin and her mage alone, but I suppose we don't have a choice."

"There are always choices, but there's no need to tackle them this second. For now, we'll take his advice and head inside to get some rest." He swatted my backside, drawing a yelp from me.

"I told you to stop that," I fussed at him, an easy air of playfulness resuming between us.

"And I told you *never*."

"That was when I had no magic," I cooed devilishly. "I could do very naughty things to you now."

"Promises, promises." He peered at me through his thick lashes, eyes hungrily devouring me.

For the next several hours, we spent time with Galath. Odiane came back to bring the baby supplies, then we simply watched our son sleep. He was the most perfect creation I had ever witnessed. I could spend every minute of my lifetime watching him and never regret a second of it.

Knight was also taken with his son but had more diverse plans for our time. When night came, and Galath had fallen asleep, Knight pinned me against the back of the sofa.

I had been pleasantly surprised to find Odiane and her friends had kept the inside of the cottage in a livable condition while I'd been gone. The furniture was old but not as musty as I had expected. It was no five-star hotel, but it would do for the night.

The day had been emotionally exhausting, but being near Knight sent a renewed energy through my veins. His hard body pressed against mine, and his hands bound mine behind my back. His playful manner sobering, he stared deep into my eyes.

"You expected me to stop you from trying to save your child?" His gravelly voice sent a shiver cascading down my spine.

"Not everyone is as accepting of a woman bringing her child back from the dead. Plus, I had no idea he was your child as well."

"Perhaps," he mused.

My head fell to the side invitingly, and I basked in the feel of his lips against my skin. "After you got your memories back, I was worried I had done something to hurt you. That something about your memories made you see me differently."

"You're still worried I'll change my mind."

"I'm not that young woman from the garden so long ago. I have blood on my hands no soap will wash away." I held his gaze pointedly. "As you know, not every story about me is false. While I believe my actions have been justified, many would see things differently. You don't have to be a part of that. I can raise Galath on my own."

Anger flashed in his amber eyes, and his hands squeezed mine behind my back. "You think I would leave my son? That I would leave you?"

"It's not that I think you'll leave. I don't want you to stay because you feel like you have to. Don't do this tonight out of some misplaced sense of guilt or a need for penance. There's a reason I'm not involved with anyone. My life is dangerous and challenging, and now, there's a child to raise. Nothing about me is casual or easy. If you do this, you agree to accept everything that comes with it, everything that comes with me."

"First, that is *my* son, and I will never walk away from him. Second, you are the only woman I have ever loved. Twice now, I've fallen madly, deeply in love with you. It doesn't matter what time or space comes between us— our souls belong together. You are mine, and I am yours, and *that* is the last I will say on the matter. Is that understood?" Orange sparks danced in his scalding gaze.

Each word he spoke became seared into my heart,

fusing the broken organ back together in a way I had never dreamed possible.

I gave a jerky nod, too stunned to say more.

"Good." His voice deepened, and his features took on a different kind of heat. "Now, I'm going to show you just how this tight body belongs to me. There's no doubt about who I am or who you are. We are Morgan and Knight. Tomorrow, when your body aches and my cum drips down your legs, you'll remember exactly who you belong to. I'll make sure neither of us ever forgets again."

CHAPTER

TWENTY

MORGAN

"Oh, *hell* no." That was Knight's grand plan? He wanted to call a meeting with a huge group of people who wanted me dead in the hopes that we could work through our differences. Was he delusional?

"We need them. It won't be a problem, I swear. I'll keep everything civil. Once they hear what we have to say, they won't harm you."

I wasn't buying it for a second. "And if they kill me before we even get a word out?"

Knight brought his face a breath away from mine, his hands cupping my cheeks. "I did not get you back just to lose you again. Please try to trust that I would never put you in danger."

I let out a ragged sigh and nodded.

Knight pressed his lips against mine in a passionate kiss before pulling away.

"Let's get this over with," I grumbled half-heartedly. "How do you propose we have this meeting? I'm not sure I can get to Earth. Even if I could, I'd have to use one of Guin's portals. I doubt that's an option if we want to go unnoticed."

"I'll gather them and bring them here."

"*Here*? To my home?" *Yup, he was delusional.*

"Yes, to *our* home."

"How will you even get them here?"

"I think I know a way." He placed a tender kiss on my temple and smiled. "Try not to worry. I'll be back shortly." Then he was gone.

That seemed to be a common theme lately with the men in my life—popping in and out of existence at their leisure.

I huffed with annoyance and took Galath inside to wait for Knight's return. Several hours later, movement by the water's edge caught my eye. I watched out the window as a large circular portal appeared and Knight stepped through, followed by a swarm of familiar yet wary faces.

He reappeared more quickly than I had expected, considering he had to explain who he was and convince his friends to come to Faery in addition to figuring out how to get them all here. Aside from Merlin, Fae couldn't trace other people with them. He later explained that he'd shown Rebecca my home using her dream walking ability. Once she knew where she was headed, she could circumvent the Seelie Queen's wards via the Twilight Realm and bring the others.

A part of me had hoped his plan wouldn't work. That

the others would refuse to join him, or he'd be unable to bring them. For better or worse, he'd succeeded.

Galath slept in my arms. I considered laying him down, but I couldn't bear to part with him. No matter how much these people hated me, I still felt the safest place for him was with me.

Taking a fortifying breath, I clutched my baby close and slowly stepped outside.

Knight instantly traced to my side, angling himself protectively in front of me. The looks of wariness and anger morphed to skepticism and confusion at the sight of Galath. I wasn't sure what all he'd told them, but it didn't appear to be much.

In all, eight of Knight's friends came to his aid—Lochlan and three other men I assumed to be Huntsmen, along with Rebecca. In addition, a human couple and a blond Fae woman were among them.

I tried to keep my face impassive, but it was hard not to posture along with the rest. The sky darkened with distrust and animosity, making an otherwise sunny day feel oppressive.

Knight made the first move, bowing to Lochlan and initiating our summit. "Thank you for coming together on such short notice. I know everyone is uneasy, but I ask that you suspend your judgments and hear us out." His eyes traveled over the group, ensuring his message was understood.

Lochlan nodded. "This was highly unexpected."

"You're telling me. I'd love to give you the full story, but it's all rather complicated. For now, an abbreviated version will have to do. My name was originally Lancelot, and you know Morgan already. This"—he motioned to the baby—"is our son, Galath."

The group descended into stunned silence.

"You're *Lancelot*?" The blond woman balked. "I gave tummy rubs and fed sandwiches to *the* Sir Lancelot—the famous knight of the round table?"

My spine stiffened at the note of implied intimacy, even if he had been a wolf at the time.

"Yes, and each was much appreciated." Knight chuckled. His eyes cut over to me, and I scowled as he continued. "A very long time ago, I learned that Queen Guin had aided a man named Mordred in killing the Erlking Arthur. To keep me silent and partly out of jealousy, Guin exiled me to Earth. When Morgan learned that I'd been exiled, she went to court to beg for my return. Guin wasn't sympathetic, even after being told about the pregnancy. In fact, she banished Morgan to the Wilds."

"I remember this. I was there that day."

We were all stunned when Casek spoke up.

"Morgan sobbed in fear for her unborn child. Guin ordered Alberich to take her to the Wilds." His brow knotted as his unseeing eyes searched the sky for understanding. "I don't know why I didn't remember this earlier."

My teeth clenched at the reminder.

"What do you mean Guin *ordered* Alberich?" asked Lochlan. "He was the Erlking; he didn't answer to the queen."

Casek glanced at his leader with a touch of unease. "It

wasn't long after Guin had killed the Erlking Odin in the war between the Seelie Court and the Hunt. Alberich hadn't wanted to enter another war with Guin. I can't say why for certain, but he bent to her will, perhaps more than he should have."

We all glanced between Lochlan and Casek, wondering how Lochlan would take the less than flattering news about his adopted father. Before Lochlan could respond, Knight drew everyone's attention.

"We've all made mistakes in our lives, some more impactful than others. We've all done the best we could with the limited information we had. Meanwhile, Morgan has been forced to go this road alone. Despite being banished, she found her way back home and had her baby here in the family cottage. During that time, Guin sent her Valkyrie guards to bring me back from Earth. This is where things begin to grow problematic. As it turned out, Arthur's great enemy, Mordred, was not killed in the battle of Camlann as we were all told. Guin has been keeping him alive as a blood mage."

The group exchanged horrified glances, finally realizing that I might not be their greatest threat.

I continued the explanation. "Guin used Mordred to curse Lancelot. When Galath grew sick because of his father's transformation, I enchanted him into a timeless stasis in the hope that I would be able to one day revive him and provide a cure. I went straight to the palace and confronted Guin, but she laughed as she informed me Lancelot was dead. I became insane with rage and attacked her. Guin overtook me and exiled me to the Wilds again. Only this time, she erected insurmountable wards to keep me out of Seelie Lands. She could have killed me too, but she was too malicious for that. She preferred to keep me alive, tortured by the knowledge of what she'd taken from me."

"That's why Guin refused to believe you were a threat," Rebecca surmised. "We warned her over and over, but she refused to admit you or your rebellion were a problem."

"Her wards were exceptionally thorough. The only way I could get past them was to have Guin killed, so her existing spells would fade. I've spent my life working to get back on Seelie Lands to save my son."

Rebecca held my eyes with surprising confidence for someone so young. "It sounds like there's a lot we don't know, and you've suffered far worse than we had imagined. However, that doesn't excuse what you've done."

Before I could respond, Lochlan cut in. "You killed my father. He may not have been perfect, but his missteps did not justify killing him." His tone was as frigid as his arctic-blue eyes.

I had known the incident would be one of my greatest obstacles to overcome in winning their cooperation. It was likely a waste of time, but I attempted to explain.

"I'm willing to admit I acted hastily. Unfortunately, my actions cannot be undone. What I ask is you try to understand that your father essentially helped kill my son. He was there the day I begged for my child. Instead of helping, he cuffed me, ignoring my cries, and deposited me into the Wilds."

"Lochlan, I know this isn't easy," offered Knight from beside me. "But Morgan isn't lying. When I was turned into the wolf, Alberich was the one who delivered me to the Red Caps. I don't know if he was aware of Mordred, but he knew I had been a man, and he still handed me over to those creatures. Doubtless, he thought he was keeping the peace. Just like Morgan here, sometimes we do horrible things in the name of the greater good."

The group was quiet for a moment.

Lochlan didn't look convinced, but he also hadn't tried to kill me.

Baby steps.

"And what about Ronan?" asked Rebecca defiantly. "You sent him to kill me."

I sighed deeply, holding my son close as my heart ached for the other boy I had tried to nurture. "Knight told me what Ronan did. You may not believe me, but I had no idea he was so damaged. When he first came to live with me, I was still raw from the loss of my own son. I tried to be a good mentor to Ronan, but he had already gone through a great deal at a young age. He wanted nothing more than to help me, so I allowed him to infiltrate the Hunt with the intent of gathering information. He never knew my background. Not only was that something I kept private because of its personal nature, but the Huntsmen were too linked to their leader for me to allow Ronan any knowledge of my purpose. He would have inadvertently given away my secrets.

"All I can figure is he misconstrued my motives and used them to fuel his own hate. I never told him to kill you. I never even sent him after you. I know I've committed my share of unforgivable acts, but I wouldn't have harmed a soul if it could have been avoided. Guin's malignant reign over the Seelie Court must be stopped. Now that I have my son back, removing her from the throne is the only thing that matters."

"What about the assassin at the palace?" Rebecca continued her interrogation, arms crossed and lips thinned.

"What assassin?" I regarded Knight with confusion. "I have no idea what you're talking about."

"That would explain it," Casek murmured to Lochlan.

"Explain what?" Rebecca bit out with growing frustration.

Lochlan turned to her placatingly. "Casek's contacts at the palace were never able to question the man who tried to kill you because he disappeared. I never said anything because we had more ... important matters at the time." He glanced at me as he spoke. "We had no idea how the man might have escaped, but if Guin had been responsible for his attack, his disappearance from the palace makes much more sense." Lochlan dropped his chin and took a cleansing breath before turning back to me. "All these years, the rumors about you stealing Lancelot from Guin, that you were the reason Arthur was killed, and that you had become a recluse after his death out of guilt—none of it was true, was it?"

I shook my head.

"Morgan was shattered by Arthur's death. I was there just after. He was the last family she had alive. Guin made up all the lies to sully Morgan's reputation and keep anyone from asking questions about her disappearance." Knight spoke fervently in my defense.

"You don't have to convince me the queen is evil."

We all turned to the unfamiliar man who had stood quietly in the back of the crowd with the redheaded woman.

"That's Fenodree," explained Lochlan. "Another long story, but he was Fae originally. Guin killed his human wife and exiled him to the Shadow Lands, where he lived alone for a thousand years until Rebecca helped him escape. He lost the use of his magic while he was there and has since become human now that he's on Earth. The redhead beside him is Cat—she descends from the Druids."

Cat stepped forward tentatively. "My ancestors were Guin's handmaids. The Hunt killed them after Odin claimed Guin had sanctioned their deaths. Guin denied the claim and killed Odin. We had surmised perhaps you had a hand in tricking Odin into killing the queen's friends."

"At that period in time, I wasn't even pregnant yet," I explained. "I had no vendetta against the queen."

"I was with Morgan every day at her home by the lake," Knight offered. "She was never even at court when the handmaids were sent back to Earth and the portals between worlds were closed."

"It wouldn't surprise me if the entire situation with Odin was orchestrated by Guin as a means to crush the newly formed Hunt. She always hated that Arthur drew away her best warriors. She could easily have started a war with the Hunt in the hopes of ending the brother-hood." My theory was just a guess, but it made sense.

Everyone was speechless.

So much of their past had been a web of lies. It was a lot to process.

Knight broke the heavy silence. "Many of the facts you considered truths have been manipulated. Now that we've started to put all the pieces together, we're discovering it's far worse than we ever imagined. Guin has a blood mage under her control, something we didn't know was even possible."

"I'm sorry," the woman named Cat cut in. "Can someone tell me what exactly is a blood mage?"

"It's a person who has lost their soul to the use of blood magic," Fenodree explained. "Usually, a person who uses blood magic loses their mind to the craving for blood. They become mindless and uncontrollable. They are extremely powerful but sloppy. Most are killed on sight."

Cat glared at Fenodree.

Interesting.

Lochlan grumbled. "Not only has she been manipulating us like puppets but she now has the Sword of Light. If truth is what we're after, that would be the best way to get it."

"I thought we had the sword," Knight said.

Lochlan shook his head. "While you've been gone, we were forced to surrender it in exchange for Fenodree's life."

The somber mood of the room thickened with trepidation.

"Have you reached out to Merlin to ask for his assistance?" Rebecca asked.

Knight sighed deeply. "Merlin is gone. Morgan's mother, Viviene, has been revived, which appeared to be his only concern. The two have disappeared."

"That sounds about right," mumbled Casek.

"Maybe it's naïve," Cat spoke up again. "But is there any way she'd step down if her lies were exposed?"

I had intentionally remained quiet knowing I was the outsider, but her question caused a visceral reaction in me that I couldn't set aside.

"Never. No Seelie monarch has ever stepped down voluntarily, and Guin is too attached to the power of her rank to ever surrender. No incentive would ever be great enough to force her compliance. The only solution is death." Anyone who believed differently was deluding themselves.

"Agreed," Lochlan said, much to my relief. "If Guin is too corrupt to rule, she will have to be forcibly removed."

"So how do we do it?" Rebecca asked.

Casek was the first to answer. "A surprise attack is our best hope of overcoming her. Stealth. We strike while she has no idea we plan to rise up against her. I'd suggest some of us use a pretense for a visit while the others infiltrate the palace behind the scenes. Lochlan and Rebecca would likely raise the least suspicion."

"I don't know about that," Rebecca murmured. "She won't be too happy to see me after helping Fen escape."

"Maybe that's exactly why you go. Tell her you're there to make amends. Although pissing her off might even be a good distraction."

Rebecca shrugged, and though Lochlan's features hardened, he didn't argue.

"What about the blood mage?" asked Fen.

"She keeps him secreted away," said Lochlan. "She would have to, or people would learn what she'd done. I would think he would need to be restrained, but then again, I didn't think someone with blood lust could be controlled at all. He's a wildcard that will be difficult to plan for. Let's enter the palace in the afternoon under the pretense of joining the court for supper. We could plan to conduct our attack during the hour before while the queen is in her chambers. She wouldn't have time to retrieve the mage."

Casek nodded. "Agreed, but I think we should have a backup plan in place should he come into play."

"If Rebecca could help us get him to the Twilight Realm, he would be removed from the equation for the time being," I offered. "He's powerful, but with all of us working together, we could do it. Once he was through the portal, his magic would no longer work there."

Rebecca's gaze met mine. I half expected her to contradict me, but instead, she gave a single nod. She wasn't my biggest fan. I got that and understood why she felt the way she did, but I also appreciated her ability to set aside the past and focus on the problem at hand.

The reality of our task struck home, and a deafening silence settled around us. That was until a hushed whisper rose from the back of the group.

"If I'm staying, *you're* staying," hissed Cat.

"I'm not the one who's *pregnant*," Fenodree clipped back at her.

The women gasped, and the men shuffled their feet uncomfortably while the quarreling lovers offered sheepish smiles to their friends.

"Surprise?" Cat lifted her hands out questioningly to the crowd. Everyone fell silent for a moment before a chorus of voices broke into congratulations, and she was enveloped in hugs.

"We only found out today," she continued to explain. "This isn't exactly how I envisioned telling you all, but none of this is quite how I saw our evening unfolding."

"This is such an incredible surprise," Rebecca gushed. "But I agree with Fen. I wouldn't be comfortable with you risking yourself." She looked at her friend pleadingly.

"I have a suggestion," Knight cut in. "We can't take our son with us either. Perhaps Cat would be good enough to stay here and watch Galath. That way, she will be doing us a great service by keeping him, and both of you will stay safe."

"Absolutely not," I spat out, drawing my son close to my chest.

Is he insane? There's no way I'm leaving my baby with a stranger.

Knight rounded on me, face unusually hard. "I've asked you to trust me, just as I've asked them to trust *you*. My friends will protect him with their lives. We need you with us, and you know as well as I do that we cannot take the boy."

Trust and fear—two great enemies.

The two did not coexist. If I feared these people, then I did not fully trust Knight and his pledge that his friends were safe. I had to make a decision. Fear or trust.

I searched the faces before me even though I knew I wouldn't find the answer anywhere but in my heart. When my eyes landed on Knight, my heart swelled with love. This man was my past and my future. He and Galath meant everything to me. I had to find a way to trust him.

With a tear streaking down my cheek, I nodded my assent.

I hadn't vanquished my fear, but I chose not to let it govern me.

Knight smiled back, his chest swelling with pride.

"I was just wondering," the blond woman spoke up for the first time since fawning over Knight. "What happens when the queen is dead? Will that bring down her wards?"

An ominous quiet descended upon us as though all of Faery quivered at the prospect.

"Yes," Lochlan said grimly. "Until an alternative can be put in place, the walls between Faery and Earth will fall, along with the borders isolating the Wilds and the Shadow Lands. All of the queen's spells will die with her, and the magic of Faery will choose a new monarch."

Rebecca's face scrunched in thought. "Could we safely keep her alive long enough for the new queen to instate her own wards, then kill her after so there's no gap in protection?"

"There can be no new queen until the previous has died. The magic won't transfer until that time, and such a tremendous spell could only be performed by someone entrusted with Faery queen's power."

"How is a new queen chosen?"

"The magic of the Seelie Queen will seek out the next most powerful Fae woman. It is the land itself who chooses." At Lochlan's explanation, everyone's eyes landed on Rebecca and me.

She and I both shook our heads adamantly.

"There's no way—"

"Absolutely not—"

"Ladies," Knight said, "we can worry about that once Guin is gone. There is no way to know who the magic will choose, so there is no use borrowing trouble. First, we bring down the queen."

CHAPTER
TWENTY-ONE

MORGAN

What a difference a week made.

I had gone from being locked in a prison and running dangerously low on hope to having everyone I cared about returned to me and marching into battle to take down my nemesis. Not in a million years could I have predicted the events as they had unfolded. In particular, the fact that my enemies had rallied at my side to help me in my cause.

I hadn't truly considered them enemies. To me, they had merely been yet another obstacle to overcome. I understood, however, why their campaign against me had been personal. I would have even understood if they had turned their backs on Knight's pleas because of me.

Even more surprising than their support was that for the first time, I cared what others thought about me. I wanted these people to see me as worthy, if only for Knight's benefit. I didn't want to hurt him by driving a wedge between him and his friends. They had given me the benefit of the doubt temporarily, but I knew my role in our makeshift uprising would forever fix my place in their minds.

After our planning session, everyone took a couple of hours to return home and prepare. I spoke with Odiane, who agreed to stay with Cat and the baby to help and act as an extra set of protective eyes. Knight and I quickly charged our magic together. While I would have enjoyed a more prolonged session in bed with him before our battle, my heart demanded I spend every possible second with my baby. I'd only had him back for a precious handful of hours, and there was a distinct possibility these would be the only minutes I'd ever have with him. What we were about to embark upon would be incredibly dangerous. I hated the thought of leaving Galath, but he was precisely the reason I needed to go. I didn't want him living in a world run by a tyrant.

Once everyone had returned to my cottage, we said our goodbyes to Cat and the baby and set out for the palace. There were a dozen of us in total. Our hour-long journey was a somber one. We spoke on occasion, but a majority of the trip was made in silence.

Having worked as a palace assassin a lifetime ago, Casek was familiar with a secret entrance into Avalon. Rebecca and Lochlan continued toward the main gate while the rest of us followed Casek into the bowels of the city. Still too large a group for comfort, we split further into two groups of five with plans to sneak into the palace separately, then reunite within. Moving undetected was paramount. Guin kept her Valkyrie guard scattered throughout the palace. The elite, all-female soldiers were known for their loyalty, ruthlessness, and unparalleled dedication to training. Each wore armored leather uniforms in the Seelie Court's color of forest green.

The warriors were both beautiful and daunting.

From the myriad of servant's tunnels, we were able to slink beneath the guard's notice. The lesser Fae conscripted as servants weren't powerful enough to prevent the alteration of their memories. Those we encountered had their memories wiped of our existence and were sent on their way none the wiser.

We snuck into the laundry facility and snagged servant's clothes to help us go undetected. Little attention was paid to the multitude of palace workers.

Guin was a ruthless monarch who had held her throne for centuries, but her ego would be her downfall. She thought herself better than everyone around her, giving little merit to potential threats. She was so self-assured of her lasting reign that it was almost impressive. Most kings and queens eventually fell to a level of paranoia, fearing usurpers and traitors. If anything, Guin had only grown more lax in her years.

Her loss, our gain.

Rebecca and Lochlan took their time getting to the palace, enabling us to infiltrate before they made their grand entrance into the throne room. The two were escorted in, flanked on either side by Valkyrie guards.

"I don't like it," said the Huntsman at my side. We'd been watching the room from behind a curtain, Knight and the two other hunters not far away. "Lochlan isn't normally received in such a manner."

"Could it be her dislike for Rebecca?" We'd known the queen was likely to bristle at her appearance.

"It could be. I'm just not sure."

We watched anxiously as the couple was paraded to the front of the room where Guin roosted on her dais. Once they were brought to a stop, she slowly rose and sneered down at them.

She was nothing if not theatrical.

"I should have thought after our last exchange, Rebecca, that you would have known better than to appear before me."

Rebecca bowed deeply. "I understand, and that's why I'm here. I want to make amends."

Guin whipped around, her sapphire gown swirling around her legs. "Amends? *This* is how you purport to make amends?" she sneered, then raised her hands to her sides. "Everyone out!" Her command barreled across the room, sending the throngs of courtiers scrambling for the exits.

Distracted by the chaos, we failed to notice the queen's guards approach us from behind until their spears jabbed at our backs.

"Out into the room," one of them ordered, pushing us forward.

Our entire group of five had been discovered and were being corralled toward Rebecca and Lochlan. As we walked, the other group of five was likewise forced from the shadows into the open.

She'd known we were there. Known we'd infiltrated her castle and orchestrated this grand reveal.

It was all a power play, and I hated it—hated her—but

not enough to overcome my devastation. I desperately clung to my hate to keep my spirits from crashing, but the stench of failure was too overwhelming.

We'd been stopped before we'd even gotten started. We hadn't had many options for a stealth attack, but I'd hoped we'd be given at least a small chance. Fate hadn't even seen fit to allow that.

My thoughts were a hurricane of questions and emotions as a parade of additional Valkyrie soldiers filed into the room from a side entrance with perfectly synchronized steps. They surrounded us in a large circle, spears pointed at the ready.

The culmination of a lifetime of plotting was being washed down the drain.

Hysteria threatened.

I desperately clung to my control, pleading with myself not to give up.

An eerily vicious smile spread across Guin's face. "I knew his attack two weeks ago wouldn't be his last. This is Merlin's doing, is it not? He thinks I have no power simply because he killed Mordred, but he's wrong." Her head tipped back and unleashed a maniacal tinkling laugh deep from her belly.

Mordred the blood mage was dead?

But I'd just seen Merlin, and he hadn't said a word. Could it be true?

We glanced at one another, trying to figure out what was going on.

"Did he not tell you?" She gaped at us, then leveled her eyes on Knight. "How did you think you miraculously transformed back into a man? *Luck?* What fools. The reason Merlin isn't here now is he knows I am the true threat. Mordred was useful, but his loss is not troublesome."

Knight had been right.

Merlin had orchestrated every bit of this. He'd known about Mordred and who Knight had been. He'd known Knight had transformed and that we would unite in our mission to find the cauldron. Had it all been to restore my mother's sanity? Did he even care about stopping Guin? Had he known about Galath and allowed me to be kept from my son?

I thought of the hint of heartbreak I'd seen in his eyes when he'd seen the baby, and my instincts told me that was the one part of this entire charade he hadn't predicted. For whatever reason, his gift of sight hadn't shown him my son, and for once in his life, he'd known the bitter taste of regret.

Good. He'd played us all like unwitting instruments. He shouldn't walk away from such a stunt without some form of remorse. If it weren't for the fact that I'd recovered Knight, Galath, and my mother, I'd have been even more pissed. If anything, learning the extent of Merlin's machinations lent me the vestiges of confidence I so desperately needed.

Merlin had set this entire showdown into motion. He knew we'd try to overtake the throne, and I would cling to hope that he hadn't let it all happen just for us to die.

Lochlan's booming voice drew me from my thoughts as he addressed the Valkyrie guard. "Did you hear what your queen has said? Is this dark sorcery what you pledged your lives to serve? How many of you knew your precious queen had fallen to the use of a blood mage?"

One at a time, the women began to glance around at one another in uncertainty.

The use of blood magic was a cardinal sin in the Fae world. There was no way Guin's soldiers had known about her dirty secret.

Guin watched Lochlan with a delighted gaze as if his speech was endlessly entertaining. I had to give the woman credit—she had balls. Nothing fazed her. Her mage was dead. Lochlan was rallying her troops against her. A powerful group, including the strength of the Wild Hunt, had come to overthrow her, and she stood casually on her dais, seemingly without a care in the world.

Lochlan continued his speech as Guin watched raptly. "You pledged your fealty to the just and benevolent rule of the Seelie Court, but that is no longer the woman who lords over this throne. Those of you who would not support the use of such dark, unnatural magic, you may excuse yourselves from this fight."

Again, more uncertain looks were exchanged at Lochlan's words.

"You tell them, Lochlan." Guin gave another laugh. "Tell them all about how wicked I am."

"No, you tell us, Guin. How extensive are your crimes? Would you admit your multitude of sins before your followers?"

"Absolutely. Where shall we start? Back when I prolonged The Great War? Casek, I believe your twin sister died in that little incident. Some of my best assassins were in that battalion. It was a shame, really, but necessary. Or perhaps I can explain how I intentionally started a war with the Hunt to kill the Erlking Odin. *Oh, I know!* Let's talk about how Lochlan's bitch of a mother ran from my service when I banished poor little Morgan. I had the woman killed. You would have been mine to raise if Alberich hadn't stepped in. It was the one time in his life he showed the slightest backbone. Call me benevolent, but I let him win that one. Most recently, I've been occupied with you, Rebecca. You're like a stain I can't exterminate. I even sent a Fear Gorda after you, certain that would do the job, but no. Somehow you managed to wriggle free yet again. Now, you all have left me no choice. I shall have to put an end to your rebellious nature once and for all."

A stirring of whispers and inhaled breaths filled the room.

I wasn't sure what was more terrifying—the fact she had committed so many horrible crimes or the fact she was confident enough to air them before us.

She rose to her feet, chin lifted, and glowered down her nose at the room. "I want to thank all of you for coming today to warn me about Merlin's recent exploits. It pains me to hear that he has been spreading rumors about me, but I appreciate your attempt to thwart his efforts. It could not have been easy to band together as you have to rise up against him." Guin's voice was melodic in a way that was warm and comforting. Her eyes glowed a gentle green as she addressed us, and I wondered if we could have been wrong about Guin. "I have sensed for some time now that Merlin has had designs on my throne, but I never imagined he had committed such atrocities in that endeavor and was circulating such lies. That he had blamed me for each of his unconscionable deeds."

Merlin wants the throne?

I wasn't sure it made any sense—women had always ruled the Seelie Court. Yet perhaps it was possible. Would he use us to further his aspirations? Why was he not here now to help us?

"Merlin Ambrosius has taken to the use of blood magic in his desperate search for more power. He must be stopped at all costs." The queen's words sank deep into my soul, cracking my heart wide open.

How could he?

I'd told myself for so long that I'd hated Merlin, but to find out he'd done something so unforgivable was heart-breaking. Sorrow like I hadn't known in ages coated my insides. Tears pooled in my eyes, and my breaths became shallow and pained.

Merlin had been like a father to me, and now, he had to die.

CHAPTER
TWENTY-TWO

FENODREE

No one laughed. No one argued.

The others stood motionless without any reaction at all as Guin spewed the most preposterous stream of lies I'd ever heard.

I chanced a confused peek at Rebecca beside me. She and all the others stared at Guin as though the woman walked on water. As though each of Guin's words were spun gold to be tenderly cherished.

What in the seven hells is going on?

If I hadn't known better, I would have said that Guin was enchanting everyone in the room, replacing their memories with her lies. But that couldn't be right. It was nearly impossible for any of our ... *their* caste of Seelie to enchant one another.

I was no longer one of them.

I contemplated the Druid truth run Cat had placed on

the back of my neck—a spell crafted by Guin herself to prevent her human handmaids from being compelled to betray her in any way. It gave humans the ability to see through a glamour and protected us from enchantment.

Could it be that I was the only one among us not affected? Was this how the queen had executed her heinous crimes through the years without the slightest bruise to her reputation?

One whisper from her forked tongue, and witnesses to her misdeeds simply forgot they ever happened.

It was no wonder her confidence was so absolute.

How will I ever get the others to believe me?

Cat would confirm my version of the facts, but would they discount her memories knowing she'd recently gone through brainwashing and psychological torture? If Guin's manipulation of the truth was easy enough to fix with a single voice of dissonance, she would not have prevailed with her lies for so long.

This couldn't be the end of our efforts. So many lives destroyed by that woman. I couldn't allow Guin to continue her corrupt reign if there was anything I could do about it. But how? How could someone as powerless as myself ever hope to conquer a Fae queen and her army?

You do have one source of power available...

The whispered words slithered through the back of my mind like a seductive caress.

No. I swore to Cat that I would never use blood magic again.

I cannot. I will not.

Then how? There had to be another way.

The Sword of Light.

An image surfaced in my mind of the shining blade as Lochlan handed it over to the queen in exchange for my life. I might not have had magic, but if I had the sword—an object containing ancient Fae power—then maybe I'd have a chance. At the very least, I could prove to the others I was telling the truth.

I had to recover the sword from the queen's possession. It would be here somewhere in the palace. I couldn't leave without at least trying to find it.

Once Guin finished her magical manipulations, our now demure band of would-be revolutionaries meekly followed orders to leave the castle. I acted as one of them, allowing myself to fall to the back of the group. Guin was so confident in her abilities to neutralize dissidents that she sent a single Valkyrie to escort us out. The second I had a chance, I slipped behind a curtain and disappeared into the palace shadows.

CHAPTER

TWENTY-THREE

ASHLEY

I should have known Merlin would grow corrupt. Anyone with such vast powers would be prone to greed and abuse. I'm just glad we found out now instead of later. It's a good thing the queen is so benevolent and looks after her subjects with such fervor.

We approached the enormous metal doors at the palace entrance, but instead of being met with the bright light of day, my vision dimmed and darkened. My magic was about to reveal a glimpse of the future!

I cleared my mind and allowed the image to take shape.

It was Fenodree and two others—Valkyrie. They were confronting him in a palace corridor, striking out and attacking. He was no match for them.

I cringed at the sight of Fen being brutalized, releasing my hold on the vision.

What the hell was that about?

I looked around for my friend, knowing he'd come with us on our visit to the Seelie court but unable to find him. I opened my mouth to ask the others where Fen might have gone but paused before I made a sound.

An overwhelming sense of wariness pricked at the back of my neck. I needed to keep my mouth shut, that much I felt in my gut, but I couldn't figure out why.

Closing my eyes, I focused on the feeling and asked my magic to show me the truth. A quick flash of two alternative realities unfolded before me. The one in which I kept quiet about Fen's absence resulted in a successful rescue, the other ended in death. Many deaths.

I shuddered.

Mum's the word.

I didn't know what the hell was going on, but I'd learned in the months since gaining use of my magic to trust my instincts. If I needed to go after Fen alone, I would do it.

Retreating back inside the palace entrance, I slipped away from the others and followed the pull drawing me back into a dark hallway and beyond to a small circular stairwell leading underground. The stone passage at the base of the stairs was murky, smelling of mildew and wet earth. When I passed a second corridor branching from the first, I caught sight of Fen squaring off with the two guards from my vision.

I raced down the hall, sending a blast of fire in their direction. Fen ducked at the last second, the magical flames obeying my command and leaving him unharmed.

The Valkyrie weren't so lucky.

They were flung back by the burst of power, slamming against the stone walls and falling to the ground unconscious.

"*Come on*, Fen. Let's get out of here," I hissed, grabbing his hand and tugging us back toward the stairs.

Fenodree refused to budge. "We can't. I know where the Sword of Light is located. I have to get it back."

"What? Why?"

He shook his head frustratedly. "I do not have time for this. Either help me or go back with the others." He cocked his head and stilled. "How did you know where to find me?"

"I had a vision. I have no clue why you decided to go on this little suicide mission, but I knew I had to help you."

Fen pulled me deeper down the hall to a thick wooden door covered in runes. "The Valkyrie were guarding this door. I believe the sword is inside."

"It's heavily warded." I grimaced.

"I know. We need Knight. He can walk through most wards."

"How would we get him here? It's too far to trace."

We stared at the formidable door barring our entrance.

"*Shit*," I hissed. "We don't have time for this, Fen. Those ladies are going to wake up any second, and we'll be screwed."

"I know, but this is important. We *need* to get that sword back."

I didn't understand, but I didn't have to in order to sense his urgency. Fenodree was almost frantic with desperation. Considering his normally perfect rendition of stoicism at all times, he was practically having a meltdown. Whatever was going on was important to him. I had to help.

Shit, shit, shit! But how?

Panic began to envelop me when my vision blurred yet again, and the hall around me faded to black.

CHAPTER
TWENTY-FOUR

"Wait." I stopped in the middle of the cobbled street on our way out of Avalon and looked around at each of the members of our group. "Where's Ash? She came with us today, right? I could have sworn she was with us." My head felt like it was filled with thick molasses, making every thought a challenge to free from the sticky substance.

"You're right," said Lochlan. "She and Fenodree. They both came with us to warn Guinevere about Merlin."

My heart sank as I recalled the horrible truths we'd uncovered about Merlin. All this time I'd thought we could trust him when he was the real culprit behind the scenes. He was nothing more than a power-hungry monster blaming Queen Guin for all his crimes in an attempt to turn us against her. I'd thought of him as a friend, making his lies an even greater betrayal.

"You don't think Merlin could have captured them, do you?" A spike of fear stiffened my spine. "Let me see if I can pull Ash into a dream walk." I closed my eyes and sought out my best friend, pulling her conscience into a waking dream. "Ash, where did you go?"

She peered around the imaginary room, which happened to look like her apartment only because that's what came to mind when I thought of her. When her eyes found me, they were wide with fear.

"Oh, Becca! Thank *God*, it's you!" She rushed over and clasped my hands. "We need you to do your portal thing and come here—bring Knight with you."

"What? Why? Where are you?"

"We're still in the palace. We need Knight to help us get the Sword of Light back." Her words were frantic, and her grip on my hands would have been painful had it been real.

What the hell is going on? Why would Ashley and Fen have taken it upon themselves to steal the sword from Guin?

I was totally mystified.

"Ash, we can't just steal that from the queen," I hissed at her.

"*Yes*, we can!"

"Can you at least tell me why?"

Ashley heaved an exaggerated breath. "I don't exactly know why. We haven't had time to cover that yet. I just know that Fen needs it, and I needed to help him—it's one of those strange Seer intuition things, okay? Are you going to help us or not?"

Crap. This is a terrible idea.

"Of course, I'll help. Show me where you're at."

"How?"

"Just think of the room you're in. I'm not sure this will even work, but I don't know how else to do it. I've never tried to portal to a place I've never been." I mentally turned over the reins to Ashley and watched as the room around us morphed into a dank hallway beneath the palace. "Oh, my God. I've totally been there before."

"You have?" Ash gaped at me. "When?"

"Long story, a palace maid was hurt trying to protect me. I went to check on her." I waved away her question. "Besides the point. I'll be there in a jiff."

I released our telepathic connection and gathered Lochlan and the others close.

"I'm not sure what's happening, but Ash and Fen are in the palace trying to steal back the Sword of Light."

"What the *fuck*?" Casek growled.

"They're in danger, so there's no time for questions. They need our help. Specifically, they need your help, Knight."

All eyes turned to the bearded man with glowing amber eyes.

"Take me to them, and I'll do whatever I can."

TWENTY-FIVE

KNIGHT

WE ALL RUSHED INTO A SUITABLY VACANT SIDE STREET BEFORE Rebecca opened a portal to the Twilight Realm. Lochlan, Casek, and Morgan all insisted on joining us; the remaining four Huntsmen likewise refused to be left behind. Once we were all through, Becca opened a second portal to a palace hallway. We quickly walked through, eyes scanning for potential dangers.

"Thank God, you're here," Ashley whisper-yelled from a connecting hall. "Come here! We think the sword is in this room, but its warded shut."

We hurried to where Fen stared at an ancient wooden door covered in runes.

"Can you pass through?" Fen asked gravely.

"I should be able to, but why? What on earth has possessed you to do this?"

Fenodree surged forward, his angry face inches from

mine. "This is of greater importance than you could possibly understand. I will tell you everything the moment we have time, but that is not now."

I nodded grimly and turned to Rebecca. "Once I get the sword, be ready to portal us back out of here."

Turning back to the door, I pressed my hand against the wood and felt the spell on my chest activate. The solid fibers of the wood gave, allowing me to pass through as if the door didn't exist. A wealth of artifacts lined the walls in the room. Some were expected—royal jewels and ancient weapons—and some were objects I didn't think wise for one individual to possess.

An eerie sense of unease clawed beneath the surface of my skin. Something odd was going on, but I wasn't sure what. The secrecy. The treasure trove of powerful objects. These were things we'd need to discuss, but not now. Time was of the essence if we didn't want Guin's guards to catch us.

I located the sword and passed back through the locked door. On the other side, Becca already had a portal waiting. We rushed through to the safety of the Twilight Realm. Once the portal was closed, and we were all ensconced in the twinkling starlight of the perpetually twilight skies, we all breathed deeply.

I lifted the sword, admiring the artfully crafted blade, then directed my stare at Fenodree. "We've done what you asked, so now it's time for some answers. Why the hell did we all just risk our lives for this?"

CHAPTER

TWENTY-SIX

MORGAN

I LISTENED TO FENODREE'S FAR-FETCHED TALE ABOUT GUIN having the power to enchant large groups at a time, and though logic told me such a feat would be impossible, a niggling sense of doubt chafed like a rock in my shoe.

I'd known Merlin all my life, and he adamantly refused to take any position of power. That was the reason he never joined the Hunt or took on an official seat at Court. Merlin prized his independence above all else. Why the hell would he suddenly set his sights on the Seelie throne, especially when the magic of the land had never once chosen a male receptacle?

The entire story didn't sit right.

As I looked around, I saw that the entire group was in various stages of confusion and disbelief.

"I understand your skepticism," Fen continued. "That was partially why I went after the sword. I knew it might be the only way you would believe me." He walked straight up to Knight, took the sword's blade in his hand and lifted it to his own throat. "Ask me anything. I will tell you nothing but the truth."

Knight's eyes flitted to mine. "I don't think it works here, like the rest of our magic."

Only a combination of light and dark magic worked in the Twilight Realm. That was what made the dimension so unique. The Sword of Light would not work without being comingled with a source of dark magic.

"We can portal home," I suggested.

Rebecca stepped forward and asked for the sword with her outstretched palm. Knight handed it over, and the second the hilt was in her hand, the markings engraved on the blade flared with light. Like the Twilight Realm, her magic was a mixture of light and dark. It was enough to coax the blade's magic to life.

"I'm sorry to do this, Fen," she said softly. "But it's the fastest way to the truth."

"Do not be sorry. This was precisely what I wanted." With the blade at his throat, he repeated everything he'd already told us, proving its veracity. The sword's magic never would have allowed any distortions of the truth to pass his lips.

Guin had lied to us, and even worse, she'd somehow made us believe it.

Upon Fenodree's explanation, the truth resounded in my ears, and a flood of memories broke free of Guin's magical manipulation. How could I have forgotten so easily? A lifetime of focus and dedication, wiped away with one swipe of her venomous tongue.

Fiery hatred coursed through my veins like liquid magma.

The dire reality of our situation settled heavily on our shoulders. It was more important than ever to stop her. Corruption like hers could not be tolerated.

"What do we do now?" Ashley asked quietly.

Rebecca looked back at Fen. "Is there any way you can give us all the rune you wear?"

"Cat is the only one who knows how, and I'm not sure it will even work on a Fae."

"We don't have time for guessing," Casek said gravely. "We need to end this while she thinks she has the upper hand. Guin believes we've all left with our tails tucked. The time to strike is now."

"Agreed." I turned to Rebecca. "Is there any way you could do what you did to me when we fought? Pull her into a dream without her knowing while the rest of us approach? That way, we could get to her without falling victim to her enchantment. We could do it tonight while she sleeps."

"Yes, that could work. I don't think I could hide my presence from her inside the dream, but hopefully she would believe I am a simple figment of her imagination."

"We'd need to lie in wait nearby," Casek mused. "I know where we can go."

We peered at one another, determination shining in our eyes.

I squared my shoulders and offered one last piece to the plan. "When the time comes, the bitch is mine."

CHAPTER

TWENTY-SEVEN

REBECCA

WE HUDDLED TOGETHER IN THE BACK OF A PALACE LARDER. Shelves loaded with food provisions stood between us and the door, protecting us from discovery. Sounds trickled in from the kitchens during the palace's ritual dinner service. Eventually, quiet fell over the servant's tunnels, but still, we waited. Only after night had fully descended did we make our move.

Once we'd all remembered the truth and recalled everything Morgan had suffered at Guin's hands, we agreed to let her wield the sword. Should our plan fail, and the queen attempt to enchant her attackers, we hoped the sword would keep Morgan from falling victim to her magic.

It was the Sword of Light and Truth, after all.

I wished I could join them on their mission, but my role demanded I stay in the pantry so that I could concentrate. I would need all my focus to keep the queen successfully preoccupied.

Lochlan stayed with me for protection and to help with communication. Casek would send word through the bond he shared with his Erlking when they were in place and ready for me to do my thing. Until then, we waited.

I wasn't sure I'd ever done so much waiting in my life.

It felt like an eternity passed in the dark before Lochlan finally got word that it was time. Closing my eyes, I envisioned the queen and gently tugged at her consciousness, trying to insert myself seamlessly into her dreams. I wanted to avoid doing anything that might draw her from sleep.

We appeared to be in the palace gardens. I did my best to disappear into the background, but the second I spotted Guin, her eyes collided with mine as though she'd sensed my presence.

"Rebecca." My name carried on the imaginary breeze. She didn't appear alarmed, but the eerie manner in which she'd zeroed in on me made me nervous.

I did my best to portray myself as the Rebecca Guin might see in her dreams. Benign. Simple. Vacuous. I waved and grinned, admiring the nearby flowers.

"How have the pixies been? Getting into any trouble lately?" I drew on a subject we'd discussed upon our very first meeting. We'd been in the palace gardens at the time, which made the topic a perfect extension of reality.

"Not lately, though it's only a matter of time with them." She eyed me curiously, slowly closing the distance between us. "I'm surprised to see you here. This isn't how you normally appear in my dreams."

"Well, you know how I love your gardens. The flowers are just so lovely. What's this one called again?" I leaned close to a deep yellow bloom, examining it more closely when a shriek sounded in the distance.

"What was that?" Guin looked about, her emerald gaze growing harsh.

"What was what?" I asked demurely. "Probably just those pesky pixies." I forced a laugh, desperately trying to keep her anchored inside the dream, but when another crash echoed around us, the distraction was too much.

Guin's consciousness slipped through my grasp, and our brief connection was severed.

CHAPTER
TWENTY-EIGHT

MORGAN

Sword in hand, I crept down the servant's hallways toward the queen's quarters. Casek led the way. He knew the palace well, which was a relief. I had spent little time there, and what time I had spent was a lifetime ago.

The team of Huntsmen silently disposed of every Valkyrie guard we encountered, Casek and Fenodree leading the charge. The two men were incredibly different but both lethal in their own right.

When the last of the guards had been neutralized, and we stood at the door to the queen's inner sanctum, it was my turn to take the lead. I clasped the ornate handle and pushed open the door.

From there, everything happened in a flash.

Two guards stationed inside the room jumped into action, but they had no chance against our numbers. They were quickly subdued, though not as silently as we had hoped. Their battle cries managed to rouse Guin from her sleep. She lurched upright, and while I expected her to spew her venomous words to twist our minds, she didn't. Instead, a single word burst from her lips.

"*Malagant!*" she screamed.

I'd never heard the name and had no idea what she was after until a dark figure appeared among us. He wore black robes with the hood down, enabling us to see his pasty white face and eyes ringed in deep purple bruising. He looked like death himself.

Seconds from his arrival, all the oxygen seemed to leach from the room. Each of us began to gasp and struggle for breath.

Casek stumbled forward, clamping an iron cuff over Guin's ankle, but she only laughed.

I clutched the sword as panic engulfed me.

What was this sorcery? He wasn't using any elemental magic I could sense. This was something darker. Something vile and unnatural.

Guin glided from the bed and looked down her nose at each of us, writhing in the darkness. "You thought you could sneak in here and kill me? How *dare* you!" Beneath the righteousness she projected was an ocean of rage. "Now you see why Merlin was a fool to think he could harm me by killing Mordred. I would never limit myself to a single weapon at my disposal."

She'd had more than one blood mage? Did her depravity know no bounds?

Across the room, Ashley fell to her knees.

The rest of us clutched our throats, clawing for air. I would not last much longer. As much as I wanted to use my final minutes to at least attempt an attack, my oxygen-deprived brain would not permit it. All I could manage was nihilistic desperation when a screeching wail tore through the room.

It was a haunted, mindless cry of tortured pain, and along with it came life-giving air.

The grip on my throat flickered and vanished.

Standing near the door, the cloaked mage raised his arm before him. His sleeve fell back to reveal nearly translucent skin streaked with tendrils of greedy black veins snaking their way up his arm. Branching and expanding at an incredible rate, his hand was almost instantly pitch black.

The man stiffened, his eyes rolling back in his head before he fell to the ground in a fit of convulsions. Seconds later, he ceased all movement, the cold chill of death settling over him.

We all stood in a state of shock, most of all, Guin.

As we watched, dumbstruck, the air beside the man shimmered before Rebecca materialized, her hand clamped over his blackened wrist. She slowly stood and turned to narrow black eyes on the queen.

"It's been you all along," Rebecca glowered, stepping closer.

Guin dropped into a squat, frantically clawing at the iron cuff Casek had so impressively thought to place upon her. He'd been just as choked for air as the rest of us, but he'd continued with his fight regardless. I'd have to give him my praises later, though.

It was finally time for justice.

In two swift strides, I had the Sword of Light pressed

to Guin's throat. She tried to push it away indignantly. I allowed the blade to slice her fingers rather than spare her.

"You can't do this," the queen hissed. "I have an army of guards."

"They aren't here right now. We're the only ones around to hear your screams, and once the world knows what you've done, none of them will care either."

Her eyes danced around the room, confusion knitting her brow. "I don't understand. How could this happen? How did you—?"

"Break free of your enchantment?" I asked snidely. "You have him to thank for that." I motioned to Fenodree, standing in the shadows.

"A *human*?" she sneered.

"Show her, Fen. Show her how her own magic brought her demise."

He stepped forward into a band of moonlight streaming from between the curtains and turned to reveal the rune on his neck.

"Remember that, Guin?" I asked with saccharine sweetness.

Her eyes narrowed. "How? My handmaids. That's the spell I used to ensure they couldn't be coerced to betray me. How could *you* possibly know such magic? I made sure every last one of them was killed."

Fen turned and slowly shook his head. "Not all. A few survived, and they've passed down their knowledge for centuries."

Guin's breathing deepened to furious huffs until a scream bellowed from her throat. "I'll kill you for this.

Every last one of you ... I'll..." She coughed and clutched at her throat. "As soon ... as I get this cuff..."

I lowered the sword and watched her struggle to speak.

My connection to water had always been exceptionally strong. It didn't require concentrated amounts—I could pull water from the air and other more solid objects ... like people.

I summoned the water from her mouth. Tongue. Cheeks. Throat. All completely dry. I was a water elemental, after all. I could drain every last ounce of moisture from her body, should I desire. It seemed only fitting, considering how venomous her words had been that her mouth be the first to go.

I wanted to make her suffer for ages like she'd done to so many of us.

"End it, Morgan, please. Let's put this behind us." Knight's pleading amber gaze enveloped me with compassion and understanding.

A quick glance around at the others told me they all agreed with him that a swift end would be better. It was easy to hold on to my anger. I'd done it for years. But when I looked at Knight and his friends—when I thought of my sweet baby waiting for me back home—a foreign sense of peace settled over me.

I was ready to let go. To release the pain and fear and hatred.

I was ready to live again.

"Guinevere, Queen of the Seelie people, you have been deemed corrupt beyond redemption. Your reign is over, you have no legacy, and even your memory will be but a dark blip on the map of our long Fae history. You will harm our people no longer."

I clasped the sword in both hands and swung my body in a full circle while lifting the sword high, then bringing it down through Guin's neck, severing her head from her body.

The unadulterated shock on her face was quickly hidden by the tangles of red hair as her head came to rest at my feet.

The queen was dead.

CHAPTER
TWENTY-NINE

MORGAN

I OFTEN WONDERED DURING THE YEARS WHILE I WAS IN EXILE why the magic of the Seelie Lands would choose such a horrific person in which to bestow its powers. It was easy to understand why a female would be selected—we tended to have a more nurturing nature, which was an important quality for a monarch—but just selecting the most powerful female seemed rather dangerous.

Shouldn't there be some set of qualifications or a series of tests that must be passed?

Maybe Guin had started out as a good queen and been corrupted over time. They say absolute power corrupts absolutely. Was that true? Was there a way for the ruler of the Seelie Court, someone who possessed such prolific power, to remain free of corruption?

I damn well hoped so.

The moment Guin took her final breath, my skin began

to prickle with energy. Every fine hair on the back of my neck stood at attention, and the murmur of voices from the room dulled to a distant hum. I could feel my energy funnel down deep into the ground, where it met with a vast aquifer of magic.

The sensation was beyond incredible as if I had become pure energy.

I could feel the life force of Faery. Not every individual plant and animal, but a conglomerate of each ecosystem. Their existence was the pulse of Faery, and I could feel that rhythmic beat. Just as I settled into the sensation, my consciousness was pulled back, slingshotting me into my body. My eyes flew open to find a room full of people staring at me in awe as I floated some ten feet in the air.

The reality of what was happening hit me like a physical punch to the gut.

The magic of the Seelie Queen had transferred to me.

"No, no, no, no, no!" I dropped like a rock to the hard ground, then stood in horror as every eye in the room gaped at me. "This is not happening," I barked, feeling like the butt of a cruel practical joke.

I found Lochlan among the sea of faces and stepped toward him.

"I don't want this. I'll give my powers to Rebecca—she's the idealistic, compassionate one. She has dark and light powers unlike anyone else; she's the one who should be queen."

"I don't think that's how it works." He smirked. "You know as well as I do the magic vests in the next most powerful female. It chose you."

"No one wants me to be queen. *I* don't want me to be queen." I pled with anyone who would listen.

"Maybe that's exactly why you were chosen." Rebecca. Was she arguing on my behalf? She should be the last person to acknowledge my reign. "You, more than any of us, know the ugly effects of the abuse of power—that would make you a natural choice to wield it. We may not ever be friends, but that doesn't mean you wouldn't make a good queen. You saw past Guin's manipulations and spent your life trying to free the Seelie people from her thrall. Who better to lead them going forward?"

The room became eerily silent.

One at a time, those who had gathered before us dropped to a knee, bowing their heads in respect. Stunned, I watched as Lochlan and his Huntsmen followed suit until the entire room before me bowed in a showing of allegiance.

I couldn't get enough oxygen.

Every bowed head sent me further into a spiraling panic until Knight stepped into my line of sight, blocking out everything else. Fingers woven into my hair, he pulled our faces together until our foreheads rested against one another.

"Look at me, Morgan. I'm here with you. It's just you and me." He soothed me gently. "You need to breathe." He led us in a series of deep breaths that helped clear the dizzying cobwebs from my brain. "We'll take this one day at a time, just like we have every other challenge. I'm going to take you to a spare room and get a bath running. I want you to relax while I get Galath. I'll make sure everyone leaves you alone, and we can talk when I get back. Alright?"

I nodded, keeping my eyes and thoughts focused solely on Knight as if he was a lifesaving bit of driftwood that would help get me to shore. He tucked me under his arm and led me from the room. Exactly as he'd said, he got me into the bath in a guest suite and left me to relax while he went for our son.

Not a single person came to my door. Whether I wanted to or not, I was alone with my tumultuous thoughts. No amount of meditation or distraction would save me.

A couple of hours later, the door to my suite opened, and Knight slipped inside. I sat curled in a chair in the dark room, staring out onto the well-lit gardens.

"Where's Galath?" I asked, alarmed when he returned empty-handed.

"He's with the ladies. They were more than happy to keep him for a bit while you and I had a moment to ourselves." Hands in his pockets, he came to stand by my chair.

My eyes strayed back outside in hopes of an escape.

"I can't do this," I whispered. While I wasn't lost in the panic that had initially seized me, I still couldn't imagine a way my coronation would end well.

Knight reached around me and hefted me into his arms like a child. "You can, and you will, and I'll be beside you the entire time. You will *not* be alone." He sat on the bed, keeping me tucked in his arms.

"I wouldn't be the queen the people wanted, and I can't be anything other than who I am. I'm not about putting on airs and fancy parties. If it were up to me, I'd say it was time Faery progressed. Hell, if it were up to me, I wouldn't raise the walls back up—at least, not for the Seelie. I would do *everything* differently—have knowledgeable counselors and methods for dispute resolution, accountability, and transparency—things a modern government should have."

Knight's golden eyes gazed at me warmly. "Nothing about Guin's rule was good—what makes you think different would be bad? What makes you think a change isn't exactly what the Seelie people would want?"

"People don't like change, no matter what their race or background. We are creatures of habit. I don't want to have to fight against resistance every time I change something. I battled upstream all my life; it's exhausting and demoralizing. I thought after I got Galath back and killed Guin, I could finally relax and learn to enjoy life. Now, that's been taken away. This feels like just another prison sentence."

"Did you not listen to Lochlan and Rebecca? You have their support, and there will be plenty of others. Yes, there will be opponents and obstacles, but we'll face those together."

I glanced down at my fingers, where they toyed with the sleeve of my gown. "I spent a good deal of the past two hours thinking about the wall between Earth and Faery. For centuries, I was kept out of my home—I can't reconcile reinstating the walls. So much of what Guin accomplished was because of misinformation and repression. I know it means the Fae might be discovered on Earth, but I think it's a necessary risk. The Seelie people should be allowed to thrive and progress naturally, and that means having access to Earth. Rebecca and the others, they'll argue about the walls. They won't understand my desire to leave them down."

"We'll explain your reasons. They may not agree with your stance, and that's their choice. What makes you so perfect for this job is that you are wise enough to listen to your critics and strong enough to make your own decisions. This is your chance to make the Seelie Lands a place where Galath can grow up happy and healthy—a culture to be proud of."

"How are you handling this all so well? I keep waiting for you to run screaming. I know I said my path wasn't going to be easy, but this is far more challenge than I could have predicted."

"If there's one thing I've learned in this life,"—he inhaled deeply—"it's that you never know where each day will lead. I try not to have expectations because fate has a way of ignoring each and every one. Yesterday, I learned I had a son. Today, you became the queen of the Seelie people. Who knows what tomorrow will bring? Some surprises will be better than others. Right now, I have you in my arms, so the rest is irrelevant."

"You would truly do this with me?" It was too much to hope for.

"There are many, many things I would do with you." His eyes lit deviously. "I would stand by your side as a dutiful consort each and every day. So long as you were mine to do with as I pleased every night."

"That's your queen you're speaking to." I narrowed my eyes with a smirk.

"I'm *very* aware." He gave me a devilish smile. "Now, my queen, on your hands and knees." He tossed me on the bed and swatted my ass.

Never in a million years would I have thought a smack on the ass would bring me such relief and pleasure—not physically, but emotionally. It was exactly what I needed to reinforce that not everything would change. The bond between Knight and me had survived a millennium, and there was no doubt in my mind it would continue to thrive.

As long as I had him, I could endure whatever challenges came our way. I wouldn't say he was the only thing that mattered—we had a son and a race of people to guide —but he made the things that mattered that much more special.

He made me want to be a woman worthy of being a queen.

EPILOGUE

MORGAN

One Year Later

I wasn't sure I'd ever get used to seeing Mom working in her garden again. It was surreal. Each time I visited and saw her tending to one of the many beds of flowers and vegetables, I had to fight back tears.

She'd restored the property to its original splendor and made it her home again so that she could be closer to me and Galath in Avalon. We were only an hour's ride away but hadn't had much time to visit in the year since I'd become queen. Being a just and vigilant ruler was a lot more damn time consuming than it seemed, but things were finally calming down. Knight and I were taking advantage of the lull by slipping away to Earth for a long weekend, and I'd decided to stop by the cottage with Galath before we left.

As always, Mom was thrilled to see her grandson. After giving me a welcoming hug, she lifted the growing toddler in her arms and blew raspberries on his neck, making him squeal with giggles.

"I can't believe he's a year old already!" she gushed.

"More than a year!" Technically, he was hundreds of years old, but time spent in a magically induced coma didn't count.

"I know. He's growing so fast. I'm just so glad I'm here to see it."

"Me too, Mamma," I agreed warmly.

Boredom already setting in, Galath wriggled free to toddle after a pixiefly. Mom and I watched him waddle away, smiles on our faces.

"It's so strange to see him here when it feels like just yesterday that I was chasing you around the lake's edge instead." Mom's gaze lifted off into the distance. "I remember everything—all the time between—but it still feels like a strange dream that didn't really happen. I feel like you should still be my sweet little shadow following me around, asking endless questions and getting into trouble behind my back."

I playfully bumped her shoulder. "I don't know what you think you remember, but I *never* got into any trouble."

She met my innocent stare with a raised brow. We both burst into giggles.

"Trouble or not," she said. "Those were some wonderful times."

"Definitely." I nodded. "So where's Merlin?" The eccentric sorcerer had sorted his priorities this time around and now lived full-time with Mom at the cottage.

"I'm here," came his cultured accent from the cottage doorway. "Just thought I'd give you ladies a minute on your own." He grinned and swept into the yard, scooping up Galath, who grinned up at his adopted grandad excitedly. The two had quickly developed a special bond, which both delighted and terrified me.

Merlin turned his attention back to me. "How are things at the palace?"

"Calm, at the moment. We're taking the opportunity to slip away to Earth and see everyone."

It had been a busy year for Faery and the men of the Wild Hunt. I'd been working hard to transition my people to new leadership, and the Hunt had been busy tracking Unseelie who had found their way either onto Earth or Seelie Lands while the walls were down. Despite my initial reluctance to limit Seelie travel, I'd reinstated the magical boundaries the following day after long discussions with Knight. He'd convinced me that it would be best to manage one change at a time. I could always drop the walls later when my new government was securely established, and we were prepared to take on the potential problems that might arise.

"And Knight?" Merlin asked. "How is he doing?"

I couldn't help the smile that formed. "He's better than ever, though Lochlan keeps him busy. His previous boss allowed a more leisurely work schedule."

Merlin chuckled and set Galath back down, Mom instantly taking the boy's hand and leading him off to the vegetable garden.

We watched them wander away, entranced in the natural wonders around them.

"I know you probably think me selfish to have done what I did," Merlin began in a somber tone. "I thought it myself and was riddled with doubts for so long."

I was stunned at his words.

He had never talked about our past and everything that had unfolded between us. Not once. Though the weight of those unsaid words wove thick strands of tension through the air every time we saw one another.

"You see, when I use the gift of sight, there is always an element of interpretation required, especially where time is concerned." His sky blue eyes were weary with remorse. "I had no idea it was going to take so long to get to this," he said on a ragged breath, peering around the revived glen. "And I had no idea about *him*."

We both looked at Galath, tasting newly ripe fruit off the vine. When our eyes met again, there were unshed tears pooling in his lashes—only the second time in my life I'd ever seen the man cave to emotion. I was utterly speechless as he continued.

"I can't say why the magic hides things from me sometimes. It was the same with Mab. I never saw the cruelty she'd succumbed to. I just knew that if I persevered and lay out the cards just so, we'd all eventually arrive here. I saw the happiness we'd all feel and convinced myself it would be worth it. I knew you were angry all those years, but I never imagined the depth of your pain. I am so very sorry, Morgan."

Speechless didn't begin to encompass what I was feeling.

Hell, I didn't even know if there were any words.

My own eyes filled with tears.

His explanation and apology stitched together the last remaining tears marring the surface of my heart. Hesitantly I closed the distance between us and extended tentative hands. Merlin saw my intent and eagerly wrapped me in his welcoming arms.

This was love.

This was forgiveness, and it felt better than I ever could have imagined.

When we finally released one another, we both began to laugh at our tearstained faces.

"Oh, how the mighty have fallen," I teased, relieved to lighten the mood, but instead, Merlin sobered.

"Not at all. *This* is true strength—to admit our errors and grow into better versions of ourselves. From here, we can handle anything."

I smirked. "But let's hope we don't have to. I think we all deserve some time off."

Merlin grinned. "That is the truth."

The three of us spent the next hour together before Galath and I had to head home, or we would be late getting to Belfast. Knight was waiting for us back at the palace when we arrived. From the queen's personal portal at the palace, we crossed over to Earth just in time for the family gathering taking place at the Huntsman.

Rebecca and Ashley had spent months working with contractors to install an outdoor oasis on the roof of the building, and we were celebrating its completion with a cookout. The warm August evening had cooperated with perfect weather, and product of their hard work was truly impressive—an outdoor kitchen with tables beneath lighted pergolas, all surrounded in lush plants that made the city center feel like a slice of Faery.

"You two have outdone yourselves. This is spectacular," I told the ladies, my gaze still busy admiring their work.

Rebecca blushed. "It's been such a pleasure to work on something that wasn't life-threatening," she teased, uncomfortable with praise. I'd gotten to know the young woman better in the past year. I wasn't sure we'd ever be the best of friends, but we'd established a mutual respect. That was sufficient for me.

Ashley, on the other hand, had no problem taking the spotlight.

"I knew from the minute the idea hit me that the rooftop was perfect, but it turned out even better than I could have hoped. My favorite is the hammock over there. It's the perfect place to read, if you ever need to escape the little one." She gave me a knowing look.

Ashley had agreed to work with me as a consultant for the court, so we'd spent more time together than I'd spent with the other ladies. She was still developing her Seer abilities, but I was still learning how to rule, so we bumbled through together. She was transparent in a way I greatly appreciated. There was never any doubt as to Ashley's true feelings on a matter, and I needed that quality in my advisors.

"I'll keep that in mind." I grinned. "Now, where's Cat? I want to see the baby. I can't believe she's already three months old."

"I think she's sitting on a bench on the other side of the roof." Becca pointed beyond where the men had all gathered in the kitchen area centralized in the middle of the rooftop. "Go say hi while we make some tea, then dinner should be ready."

"Perfect." I smiled and followed the cobbled path past overflowing planters and patches of bright green grass over to an area with built-in benched seating lined in colorful cushions.

Cat and Fenodree's daughter was beyond adorable. She had her father's black hair and dark coloring but her mother's vibrant green eyes. It was a striking combination. Little Kyrie was going to have the boys chasing after her in droves.

"Look at how big she's getting!" I gushed, gently touching her soft black hair. "She's hardly a newborn anymore."

Cat gave me a hug with her free arm, the other cradling the baby against her. The two of us had formed an unexpected friendship over motherhood. I wasn't any kind of expert, but Cat had been relieved to have someone to ask for guidance, and I was happy to share what I'd learned.

"I'm just glad she's finally sleeping more!"

We both laughed, and right on cue, little Kyrie startled awake and began to cry. Seconds later, Galath was tugging at my leg to be carried, having escaped from his father's purview.

I lifted him to my hip, his attention entirely consumed with the crying baby. He reached for her, so I stepped closer. The instant he moved into her line of sight, little Kyrie grew calm.

"No cry," Galath said in his tiny toddler voice, laying a gentle hand on her head.

Her perfect bowed lips pulled back into a delighted smile.

My eyes snapped up to Cat's, and we both burst out laughing.

"Oh, no. I'm so not ready for this." I went to set Galath back down, resulting in two crying babies. The second I picked him back up, and the two were within reach again, they both quieted.

Unbelievable.

"Don't tell Fen." Cat's eyes rounded. "He's already beyond overprotective. He'll have an aneurysm."

We laughed so hard, tears filled my eyes.

DINNER WITH EVERYONE was a lovely change of pace from my palace duties. I never imagined I'd be surrounded by such a large group of friends. The only group I ever expected to be the center of was a lynching mob.

But that had all changed.

These weren't just friends. Thanks to Knight, I had a larger family than I could have ever dreamed. He'd changed my life in so many ways, I hardly recognized myself anymore. I was happy. Fulfilled. I spent each day learning to live in the present and growing more content with it.

Seeing as how Knight had long since mastered that state of mind, he was an excellent influence.

Neither of us was willing to live full-time in Faery, so

we'd purchased a penthouse condo in Belfast not far from the Huntsman. Even if I was working, we split our time equally between worlds, as best as we could. And on occasion, we took a weekend such as this one to step away from Court and all my duties.

I needed the breaks to stay sane.

After dinner, we took Galath home to our condo. It was late, so we skipped his bath time routine and put him to bed. Two visits with family and friends in one day had exhausted him.

As for me, I felt more alive than ever. My heart was full of love, and my veins still thrummed with expensive French wine.

"That is a satisfied look if I've ever seen one." Knight joined me at the window overlooking the sparkling city lights, his body pressed gently against my back.

"It's been a great day." I chuckled, remembering Galath's fascination with Kyrie. I relayed what had passed between them and could practically feel Knight's wolfish grin as his arms snaked around me to hold me close.

"That's my boy. Already has the ladies mesmerized."

I huffed. "Whatever. She clearly had him in her thrall. You men are so easy to toy with." I bit my bottom lip to keep from smiling, knowing I was goading him.

"Is that so?" he rumbled next to my ear. "Because when the lights go out in our bedroom, I am quite certain of who is in control. And it's not *you*." He pressed me forward until I had to brace my hands against the glass, then used his leg to force mine apart.

I practically purred, arching to press my backside against his bulging cock.

"Hands stay on the glass." He pulled away enough to bring his hands to the tie of my halter top at the back of my neck. One tug, and the silk blouse would slide away, leaving me completely topless.

"People can see in, Knight." We were on the top floor, but that wasn't saying much, considering it was Belfast. Eight stories up wasn't exactly in the clouds.

In answer, he slowly unfastened the tie, easing the fabric achingly slowly down over my breasts before letting it drop to the floor. "Let them see. Let the world see that every inch of this perfection is mine." His teeth raked over the skin of my neck, causing my nipples to pebble so hard they could have cut the plated glass inches away.

He then slid down my pants until I was totally bare. His hand roved over my body, touching, claiming.

Arousal flooded my core. "Knight, please. I need you."

He fisted his hand in my hair and gently tipped my head back. "Who do you belong to?"

"*You.* Always you." I adored when his alpha wolf came out to play.

"Touch yourself." His words licked down my spine.

I did as he commanded while he stepped back to watch. I could feel his eyes on me, devouring me as he stripped his clothes away. My ministrations felt good, but my fingers could never compare to his touch. I wanted more. I wanted *him*, but I knew from experience that this was Knight's terrain.

I ruled over Faery, but my body belonged to him.

Before I knew what was happening, he yanked my hips back, bending me at an angle, then his mouth was pressed to my core. I cried out at the surge of pleasure.

He used his flattened tongue to rub mesmerizing circles over my clit, periodically teasing my entrance. He then kissed his way to the inside of my thigh, where he bit me, just hard enough to leave a mark. The sting only added to the intense sensation of his possession because I knew what it meant to him. To the wolf still prowling inside him.

Keeping my body bent, he rose, placing reverent kisses along my spine until our bodies were aligned.

"I liked seeing you holding baby Kyrie today," he murmured, his cock sliding warm against my folds. "I missed your entire pregnancy with Galath. I think maybe it's time to try again. I want to see our baby growing big in your belly." As though he could make the thing happen upon command, he surged inside me.

We both moaned loudly.

I couldn't concentrate to even comprehend what he had implied. "Another? Already?" I asked dazedly.

Knight's hand cupped my core, two of his fingers sliding on either side of my clit. "No guarantees ... Morgan," he grunted, losing himself in pleasure. "Life never ... guaranteed."

Who knew that lesson better than the two of us?

Besides, I could never withhold anything from him.

"Okay," I breathed, leaning into his thrusts.

"*Fuck*, Morgan. You don't know what you do to me."

My inner muscles clenched at his praise, drawing a ragged groan from deep in his chest. In response, he pounded into me harder and faster, his fingers keeping pace as a magical tug on my nipples sent a fissure of lightning down to my core that ignited an explosion deep in my belly.

My orgasm swept through me like a riot of wild horses. I couldn't have stopped it if I'd tried.

Earthquakes shook my inner muscles in uncontained euphoria.

Though I was barely coherent, I felt Knight grow impossibly thicker inside me as he threw his head back and roared his release. I squeezed him from inside me, milking him dry and delighting in the way he shuddered at my movements.

We both leaned against the window afterward, the cool glass a welcome relief to my feverish skin.

"Tell me you mean it," murmured Knight close to my ear.

Mean it? I had to think for a second before my addled brain could figure out his meaning.

"A baby?" I asked.

He squeezed my middle in response and used his teeth to nip at my earlobe.

A smile teased the corners of my mouth. "I think Galath would love a little sister."

Knight grunted, but I could feel his grin against my cheek. "I suppose we shall see," he said wryly.

I giggled as Knight turned me around but sobered when I saw the intensity in his eyes. He cupped my cheeks and pulled my face close to his.

"I love you so fucking much."

My heart fluttered, and tears suddenly burned the back of my eyes.

"I love you, too." I lifted onto my toes and pressed my lips to his, sealing our love with a perfect kiss.

Thank you so much for reading *Siege & Seduction*!
I sincerely hope you enjoyed the *Of Myth & Man* saga.
These characters were special enough for me to spend
months rewriting the original stories to ensure the tale
was properly told.

Want to check out more of my books?
The Five Families is my bestselling mafia romance series
revolving around the women of the Genovese family as
each seeks to find love in a dangerous world of lies,
schemes, and betrayal.
Check out book 1, Forever Lies, to learn about Alessia and
the chance elevator encounter that changed her life
forever. She landed on Luca Romano's radar, and now he
isn't about to let her walk away.

Make sure to join my Facebook reader group and keep in
touch!
Jill's Ravenous Readers!

ABOUT THE AUTHOR

Jill Ramsower is a life-long Texan—born in Houston, raised in Austin, and currently residing in West Texas. She attended Baylor University and subsequently Baylor Law School to obtain her BA and JD degrees. She spent the next fourteen years practicing law and raising her three children until one fateful day, she strayed from the well-trod path she had been walking and sat down to write a book. An addict with a pen, she set to writing like a woman possessed and discovered that telling stories is her passion in life.

SOCIAL MEDIA & WEBSITE

Release Day Alerts, Sneak Peak, and Newsletter
To be the first to know about upcoming releases, please join Jill's Newsletter. (No spam or frequent pointless emails.)
Jill's Newsletter

Official Website: www.jillramsower.com
Jill's Facebook Page: www.facebook.com/jillramsowerauthor
Reader Group: Jill's Ravenous Readers
Follow Jill on Instagram: @jillramsowerauthor
Follow Jill on Twitter: @JRamsower

GLOSSARY OF TERMS

Below are a number of the important terms and characters from *Siege & Seduction* and the *Of Myth & Man* series thus far. I have included pronunciations as I would say the word, not pronunciations as the dictionary would offer because I have no idea how that works.

Aos sí—The term used for the Tuatha De Danann before they became known as the Seelie.

Arthur—Powerful Fae General who broke away from Queen Guin and formed the Wild Hunt.

Bantiff trees—Large tree on Seelie Lands with canopies of leaves.

Battle of Tirath—Battle where the Seelie forces were outnumbered and lost many lives during The Great War.

Beltane—The day halfway between the spring equinox and the summer solstice (early May). One of the naturally occurring days when the veil between worlds is the thinnest and the availability of magic is greatest. The Druids celebrated the day with bonfires and used ashes to ensure the protection of their crops and livestock.

Bergresar—Ancient, evil Shadow Fae.

Blood Magic—An ancient, dark magic that requires the use of sacrificial blood. Used too many times, blood magic eventually creates a bloodlust in the user so intense he or she is reduced to a state of mindlessness in the search of blood. This condition is considered a flagrant violation of the laws of nature by most Fae, and thus the use of blood magic is often punishable by death.

Blood Mage—An individual who has lost their soul to the use of blood magic.

Canips—Small flowering shrub on Seelie Lands.

Castle Corbenic—The fabled castle that houses the Cauldron of Dagda. It's also called the Castle of Sleepless Dreams because of the illusions it subjects its visitors to.

Cauldron of Dagda—A Fae relic that can produce a never-ending supply of food and has the power to heal and bring the living back from the dead.

Brownie—Small green-skinned Fae that lives peacefully in homes, often known to clean and sometimes steal items for itself.

Cormac Doyle—Soldier who abandoned his post during a special mission in The Great War against the Unseelie.

Draug (*drog*)—Shadow Fae creature that can dissolve into shadow and is drawn to finding jewels and other treasure.

Dream Walk—The ability to draw another person into a waking dream where the subconsciousness of both individuals can communicate.

Druid (*drew-id*)—Descendants of the people who were taught the use of rune magic by the Fae.

Dryad (dry-ad)—A peaceful Seelie caste who live in and among trees.

Elders—Druid leadership council made up of 11 district members, one of which is elected as the chief elder who presides over council meetings.

Erlking (*earl-king*)—The elected leader of the Wild Hunt.

Faery—A world with latent magic that can be accessed from Earth via portals.

Fae—The inhabitants of Faery, also known as Faeries.

Fenodree (*Fen-oh-dree*)—The Fae man exiled to live in the Shadow Lands because he broke Seelie law by marrying a human woman.

Fisher King—The chosen protector of the Cauldron of Dagda.

Formorians—The enemies of the Tuatha De Danann who challenged them for the right to settle on Earth. The Formorians eventually became the Unseelie.

Gally Trot—(aka Knight) The name given to Merlin's k-nine companion by the Fae.

Glamour—The use of magic to change one's appearance.

Gnome Tree—A tree on Seelie Lands with gnarled bark that can often be found protecting Dryads.

Guinevere—Queen of the Seelie Fae.

Hellfire—Unnatural green fire that burns through anything it encounters. One of the only know beings to wield the substance is the Nuckalavee.

Hell Hound—Unseelie creatures usually found in pairs. They are roughly the size and look of a large Earthen dog but have red glowing eyes and violent temperaments.

Hilde (*hild*)—Fenodree's human wife who was killed by Queen Guin.

Holiander—A sharp-leaved shrub on Seelie Lands.

Kaché—Spider-like creature with poison laden pinchers living on Seelie Lands.

Lambton Worm—Dragon-like aggressive Unseelie Fae who lives primarily in water but can survive on land as well.

Leannan-Sidhe (*Lee-an-an shee*)—Vampire-like Unseelie that uses glamour to lure Fae or human prey. They feed their magic through the draining of their victim's blood.

Lugh—Early Fae warrior who helped save his people from the Formorians.

Mab—Extremely powerful Queen of the Unseelie killed by her twin brother Merlin.

Mananaun—The God of the Sea who adopted the warrior Lugh and helped him on his adventures.

Merlin—Eccentric Fae sorcerer.

Nukalavee—Shadow Fae that is so ancient and malevolent that it is believed even the mention of its name brings bad luck. It is known for its unique ability to create Hell Fire, and can manipulate dreams among its numerous dark powers.

Oberon— (aka Alberich) The leader of the Wild Hunt and foster father to Lochlan.

Okeanos Sea—Ocean in Faery in which the Isle of Man and Castle Corbenic are located.

Phooka (*poo-kah*)—Small Unseelie about the size of a young child usually found near large bodies of water.

Portal—Magical doorway between worlds.

Red Cap—Vicious Unseelie known for cannibalism and wearing caps soaked in the blood of their victims.

Rune—Magical symbol used in spells.

Seelie (*See-lee*)—The Fae who live peaceably under the Seelie Queen's rule; most of the Seelie possess light magic.

Selkie—Seelie Fae who live primarily in bodies of water.

Shadow Fae—The inhabitants of the Shadow Lands. Not technically Fae, but became known as such after their world became joined with Faery.

Shadow Lands—A dark and dangerous place believed to have been joined with Faery in an ancient cataclysm of worlds. The landscape steeped in perpetual darkness appears barren, and its inhabitants are a vicious face of beings who possess dark magic.

Sight—The ability to see through a Fae glamour.

Sluagh—(aka The Unforgiving Dead) A host of malevolent souls of deceased evil Fae.

Spriggan—Lesser Seelie creature that can morph from ten inches in height to ten feet. They are solitary Fae and extremely territorial.

Surry—A soft-bark tree on Seelie Lands.

Sword of Light—(aka Excalibur) A sword crafted by an ancient species able to imbue iron with magic. The sword is also known as "The Answerer" for its ability to force any at its blade to tell the truth.

The Great War—Early in Guinevere's reign, the war between Seelie and Unseelie.

Trace—The ability to transport instantly from one place to another.

Tuatha De Danann—Seelie Fae ancestors who first discovered Earth and migrated to Ireland.

Twilight Realm—A temporal plane between worlds that can only be accessed with a combination of light and shadow magic.

Unseelie (*Un-see-lee*)—The Fae who refused to be governed by the Seelie Queen and are thus forced to live in the Wilds of Faery. They tend to be vicious and solitary creatures.

Valkyrie—The all-female guard of the Seelie Queen.

Water Nymph—Peaceful Seelie Fae that helps maintain balance in the waters of Faery.

Wave Sweeper—The self-sailing boat given to Lugh by his adopted father, Mananaun.

Wild Hunt—The group of Fae men who separated from the Seelie kingdom when the Erlking Arthur had a falling out with the Seelie Queen Guinevere. They are self-governed warriors with no lands of their own and who choose to roam in search of prey to hunt.

Wilds—The uncivilized parts of Faery outside of the Seelie kingdom inhabited by the animalistic Unseelie.

Will-O'-Wisps—Tiny Seelie creatures who live peacefully near Dryads and cast faerie lights.

Wollyhog (*wa-lee-hog*)—Small warthog type creature in the Shadow Lands.

www.ingramcontent.com/pod-product-compliance
Lightning Source LLC
Chambersburg PA
CBHW061052190726
48286CB00006B/1725